JOURNEYMAN WARSMITH

The Blademage Saga

Volume 2

Chris Hollaway

Special thanks to:

My wife and kids for their love and support

Ken, for being the Carlo to my Kevon. and Diane, without whom Rhysabeth-Dane would not exist

The crew at Systems Integration, for the constant prodding

Fans of 'The Blademage Saga' worldwide, and Sverre, because everyone should have an eccentric Norwegian in their corner.

*From many an untold age ago, when the Orclords raged
I sing now of the first Hero, and the battles that he waged
From Keldin's Reach, the Twisted Spires, to the Southern Shore
Rode the mighty Bartok, behind him followed war.*

-From *The Ballad of Bartok Brokenblade*

AUTHOR UNKNOWN

CHAPTER 1

Kevon yelped and jumped back, left hand balled into a fist. The hammer tumbled to the dirt floor with a dull thud. Teeth clenched, the Seeker muttered under his breath. He heard a giggle from somewhere behind him, and the other boy in front of him looked about ready to burst.

The Apprentice Blacksmith took a deep breath. "I'm going for a little walk... Why don't the two of you run and get yourselves a treat and nobody else hears about this?"

Grubby fingers snatched at the offered coppers, and the boys dashed out of the smithy, laughing and calling to each other. Kevon knew that before an hour passed, he would be teased about the incident, but he didn't mind. He pinched his thumb to make sure it wasn't broken, and walked outside.

The midday heat beating down on Kevon was a welcome break from the forge heat that had just been glaring up at him. The boys were already out of sight, on their way to the trading post in the center of the mining camp.

He faced into the slight breeze and closed his eyes. He took a deep breath that didn't smell of burnt iron, and smiled. Moments like these, Kevon could almost be happy. He could almost forget who he really was, what he'd done, what he was running from.

Almost.

Kevon heard a noise behind him, and whirled around to see what it was. He found himself staring at a surprised Marelle. She was taller, darker, and more pleasantly proportioned than he remembered, but was exactly as he'd imagined, it being over two years since they met last. She dropped the broken halves of the horseshoe she'd been carrying, and stepped closer.

"I came to buy a horseshoe," she began, her gaze drifting down to Kevon's bare chest. "I may need a few other things." She leaned in closer, and Kevon's already pounding heart leapt as she locked her deep green eyes onto his. Marelle's lips parted slightly, and Kevon's eyes closed in anticipation.

A crackling of thunder shattered the moment, and the Seeker turned toward the sound, Marelle slipping from the beginnings of his embrace.

The blazing rift in the sky spread like wildfire, painting the blue canvas of the heavens with a deep crimson stroke. Lightning danced between the new sky and the arid land below, the rumbling of its passage rolling over in waves.

"Anton," Marelle said, her voice cracking.

Kevon wondered absently how she knew the name he was using while staying here, his attention focused on the winged behemoth that flapped in the sky before him.

"Anton!" she said again, urgently, her voice distorting more.

He said nothing, gazing at the dragon, and the hooded figure he could barely see in the distance, standing tall in the middle of the broken landscape.

The world shuddered as Kevon felt himself cuffed alongside the head.

"Wha-?" he mumbled, trying to re-open eyes that were unusually heavy-lidded.

"Wake up, Anton!" Nic whined plaintively, shaking Kevon. "It's late! Master Farren is looking for you!"

Kevon sat bolt upright. Even though he'd been apprenticing under Farren Smith for over a year now, the word 'Master" still unsettled him.

He blinked several times and the mousy little junior Apprentice came into focus.

"Are you coming?" Nic squealed, eyes wide.

"Yes, calm down, Nic." Kevon reached down to the foot of the cot and picked up his arm bracers. He squeezed his hands through and slid them to rest snugly on his forearms. The smooth steel strips woven into the inner padding felt cool and comforting against his skin. Kevon slipped the iron ring off his right hand and dropped it into a pouch that lay near where he'd picked up the bracers. He picked through the pile of clothing and found a light tunic that was not too soiled, pulled it on over his head, and stepped into his boots.

"Let's go."

Kevon led Nic through the main part of the barracks where the miners and garrison troops bunked.

"It's Anton and his pet rat!" someone called from the middle of the room, and chuckles roiled briefly. Kevon smiled, and Nic scowled and shook his fist in the direction the voice had come from.

They continued on through the hallway that led to the commissary. Kevon picked up a small, flat loaf of bread and two strips of jerky, holding them up until the record-keeper tallied them. Kevon handed one of the strips to Nic, and headed for the exit.

He walked unhurriedly as he ate his breakfast, finishing up as he reached the well near the north guard post. He hauled up the bucket and dipped ladles of water into the tin cups that Nic pulled off the hanging hooks at the side of the wall.

After the two had finished their drinks, Kevon set off for the smithy at a brisk pace, forcing Nic to run at times to keep up.

The sun was just starting to peek over the horizon, but glancing back to the east, Kevon could already see the wavy lines of distortion as the barrens to sunward began to bake. The junior Apprentice kicked Kevon in the shins.

"Go, already!" Nic yelled, scrunching his face up in an attempt to look intimidating.

Kevon smiled and resumed his faster pace.

They reached the smithy as the sun crept just above the horizon and other people started coming out into the street. Kevon noted that the woodpile was fully stocked, and as they neared the forge, he saw that the three quenching barrels were all filled correctly as well. The other junior Apprentice, Tom, sat on a stool, slumped over into a corner.

"You lout!" Tom jumped up and rushed toward Nic. "I had to fill all-"

Tom stopped, and hesitantly took the half piece of jerky that Nic held out to him. The junior Apprentices wandered toward the back of the smithy, Nic telling Tom about how he almost had to thrash a dozen miners, Tom nodding and gnawing.

Kevon pulled off his tunic and worked the bellows on the small forge to get the heat up to working temperature. Once it glowed brightly enough, he resumed the project he'd been working on the day before, a batch of hoof-picks.

His warrior training served him well in the forge. His practiced manual dexterity and arm strength had been amplified over the last year, and he'd learned the slow, easy rhythm that raised a sweat without forcing him to gasp for air after a few minutes.

The tool quickly took shape, but started cooling before it was quite done. Kevon flipped the strip of iron back into the coals with his tongs and worked the bellows for a minute before retrieving it and resuming his work. He quickly made the last few adjustments, turning the tip and pounding it just so, making the slight hook that gave the tool yet another advantage over a knife when used properly.

Satisfied, Kevon dipped the still-glowing metal into the water barrel, swirling it in slow circles with the long-handled forge tongs. When he withdrew it and found it comfortable to the touch, Kevon scraped it thoroughly on the large whetstone that sat on a bench near the forge. Kevon finished smoothing the bumps off the business end of the tool as well as the stem for the handle. This would ensure there would be less chance of the tool's user scratching themselves accidentally. He tossed the finished product into the nearby pile.

Kevon walked over to the scrap bin and dug carefully through broken sword edges and other sharp objects that were not so readily identifiable. He quickly found a scrap that was about the right size, and returned to work.

He had just tossed the next finished pick into the pile when Master Farren arrived.

"Are you almost done with those?" the Master Smith asked gruffly.

The Apprentice nodded. "All they need are handles. I can have then done-"

"No," Farren interrupted. "I'll have the other Apprentices split the batch, and see who can do the best job of putting handles on those picks." The smith spoke louder than needed to inform Kevon, but his words had their intended effect. Nic and Tom scurried in and began taking turns choosing hooked implements from the pile.

Kevon nodded to Farren, acknowledging the tactic. The boys always did better work when they were competing against each other.

"Besides, neither of them has the strength to work the bellows on the good forge," Master Farren commented.

"Awww..." Tom's outburst nearly drowned out Nic's sigh of disgust. The boys quickly finished sorting the pile and took their respective projects outside.

Kevon smiled, saying nothing as he set about helping Farren prepare the forge for use. When Kevon finally got to working the bellows in earnest, Nic and Tom ventured in with their completed batches of tools for the Master Smith's inspection.

"Excellent work, boys," Farren said after making sure that every leather-wrapped wooden handle was snugly fastened so as not to slip during use. "I'm certain you both will be working the small forge by this time next year."

The Seeker nodded in agreement, in time with the

rhythm of the bellows. He watched as the boys, obviously bothered by the heat of the larger forge, remained in the open-ended building. They roamed separately, well out of the way, each checking to make sure that tools and supplies were all in their proper places.

The Master Smith disappeared into the back of the building and returned quickly with a short steel bar in one hand, and his favorite hammer in the other. The Master Smith tossed the ingot into the glowing coals, leaned the hammer against the large anvil standing to the side of the forge, and walked over to sit beside Kevon.

"How is that helmet coming along?" Farren asked over the soft creaking and whooshing of the hide-covered blowing contraption.

"Not good." Kevon scowled. He paused for a moment. "I don't think it would even fit Waine's lumpy head." He pronounced the Adept Warrior's name like the locals here did, more like 'win' than 'wane'.

"So you did see me," Waine chuckled from just inside the entrance to the building.

"The change in light reflected off the swords hanging on the side wall, a glance from Master Farren," Kevon commented blandly. "And you're not *that* quiet."

"Fair enough," Waine agreed. "I can see you're busy now, but we need to talk later." The Adept turned and left without another word.

Farren was already up, fishing the only slightly glowing ingot from the coals. He placed the block of metal on an anvil on an unused bench, and returned to drive Kevon from his spot at the bellows with a series of elbow pokes.

"Something tells me you'll want to finish your helmet today," the Master Smith said, grimacing.

Under the older smith's direction, Kevon finished the helmet to Farren's satisfaction in just a few hours. Nic and Tom sat on stools stitching the leather padding that was going in the helmet, gossiping like old women.

"That's it, then," Farren said, rapping an anvil lightly with his forge hammer. "You've done plenty of tools, several knives, and now armor." The gruff older man squinted and looked Kevon in the eye. "So now you're a Journeyman."

That last word made Kevon's blood run cold. It was not the first time he'd earned that title, though Waine was the only one here that even suspected.

Kevon was a Journeyman in the Mage's Guild, normally a feat that a Warrior or Blacksmith simply could not accomplish. Handling iron or steel was the touch of death for any accomplished magic-user, so the two worlds stayed well clear of each other.

It was only by accident that Kevon discovered he could survive the touch of steel the day before his mentor, the Magi Holten, had promoted him from Apprentice to Journeyman Mage. It was also by accident that weeks later, Kevon discovered his former Master was not as good a man as he pretended to be.

Kevon turned away from the forge, rubbed his eyes with the back of his forearm, and nodded to the waiting Smith.

Nic handed Kevon the completed helmet. Kevon ruffled the boy's hair, and earned a swift kick in the shin for his efforts.

The Journeyman inspected the headgear for a few moments, nodding appreciatively at the quality of the leatherwork. He handed the finished product to Farren, who handed him a hammer in exchange.

"Use it well," Farren sighed. "Return when you can."

Kevon nodded. He had picked up on the tension in Waine's voice earlier, and evidently Master Farren had, as well. He was not sure where he was headed, but was certain that in a few days' time he would be well away from this place he had called home for the last few seasons. He turned to say goodbye to the boys, but they were somewhere further back in the building. Kevon could hear their muted bickering over the low flames in the forge, and it brought a smile to his face.

"We'll..." Kevon began, choking on a bit of dust. "We'll see each other again."

Farren nodded once, and turned his back to Kevon. The Master Smith rattled around some of his tools until Kevon's footfalls faded into silence. After a minute of contemplation, Farren tossed the bar of sword-steel into the forge and shouted at the back of the building for his Apprentices.

Kevon hadn't been looking too long when he found Waine and Bertus at the armory. The Adept already had a small wooden case tucked snugly under his arm, and was helping their younger friend get the feel for a heavy crossbow.

"What are you going to be hunting now?" Kevon asked, jokingly.

"Orcs," Waine replied. "And Demons." The Adept waited for Kevon's surprised expression before continuing. "And you're coming with us."

CHAPTER 2

The companions were on the road headed west before dawn. The horses seemed excited, eager to press on faster. They quickly settled into the pace they remembered from the last time the group had traveled together. Their riders maintained an uneasy silence.

Lacking shade and running low on water, the party dismounted and walked during the worst heat of the day. After taking the first road north, they finally came to a mostly dried streambed. The sun was dropping lower in the sky, and the horses seemed fine, but they decided to stay there for the night, not knowing how far away the next water would be.

After the horses were cared for and weapons and gear checked, the three travelers sat about on bedrolls propped against saddles in the still stifling heat. Kevon and Waine gnawed on strips of jerky while Bertus munched on a small, somewhat shriveled apple.

Finishing the swig of water he'd just washed his meal down with, Kevon capped the waterskin, and wiped the corner of his mouth. "You never did give any details on where we're going, what exactly we're doing," he commented, looking at Waine.

"Some ears have no business hearing what we know," Waine answered, before glancing over at Bertus. "I think it's time the boy knew what you were about. We'll need that advantage, and you'll need to practice."

"I've seen you practice before," Bertus said, eyes darting between the two Warriors.

"What is this about?" Kevon pressed Waine, ignoring Bertus for the moment. "I need to know before..."

"The roads west of Navlia are no longer safe to travel, especially at night. Only soldiers moving in numbers seem immune to the attacks, and they will not even go into the ruined valley."

"Ruined valley?" Kevon asked, shaking his head. "Where..."

Waine nodded as understanding left Kevon's mouth agape.

"The very same. Everything seemed fine there for a season after we left. Then no word came from anyone in the valley, and none who ventured there returned." Waine took a few deep breaths. "There is one who escaped the valley. I found him, talked to him, but he made more sense when he was stone-drunk than screaming sober. What I did gather in the few moments between the two was what he described as the center of the evil. It's the ruins of the Tower, and I recognized the imps, at least, from his rantings..."

The Journeyman Smith's mind worked furiously. *Why would anyone go back there? Why would they gather vile creatures... and how could they keep them at bay and survive?* Kevon buried his head in his hands, and a thought occurred to him. "Portals? Someone is opening portals there?"

"No one is safe in that place, Magi or otherwise. No one *is* doing this. It must be something already *done*."

"Of course." Kevon raised his head to stare at Waine. "A portal enchantment? I've never seen anything about it in any book, but I suppose it could be done..." He furrowed his brow in concentration. "Is this what Gurlin and Holten were doing?"

"Perhaps they were keeping it in check," Waine offered sullenly.

The Seeker's blood ran cold. In spite of the lingering heat, he shook and shivered as if it were midwinter. Kevon clutched his knees to his chest and rocked back and forth, eyes tightly shut. "They can't..." he stammered. "They tried to... He wanted me to..."

"I'm not saying that they were, that I even think they were," Waine clarified, watching his friend turn inward with growing concern.

Kevon watched in slow motion as he plunged the knife into Gurlin's back. *Was he testing me for something, thinking that I would strike with magic that could be countered if I failed the test?* He groaned and sank deeper into remembrances. He examined the letter from Master Holten briefly before casting it into the fire. *Was I supposed to find the letter, to approach Gurlin under false pretenses?* Some evenings, when the heat of the day was too slow to surrender to the night, he still dreamed of flames, and could hear the screams of the dead Mage Pholos.

Kevon clutched at his chest and felt the necklace beneath his tunic. He remembered his promise to the new leader of the Myrnar, the Sea-folk, to avenge her sister's death. The accusations of Delmer more than a year past. Shame for not acting sooner knotted in his belly.

"No," Kevon said, uncurling and taking a deep breath. "They were evil, I'm sure of it. Holten's letter, Gurlin assigning me to kill Pholos, those might have been tests. The pearl wasn't. I was never meant to find out where it came from."

Neck muscles grown thick from long hours of forge work tightened as Kevon clenched his jaw. "How do we get there?"

Waine flashed Kevon a tight-lipped smile before speaking. "The only ones to get close safely have been military units. We'll have to find one headed there, and go the rest of the way ourselves."

Bertus piped up. "Excuse me, but I thought you said that nobody that wasn't with a large group has been heard from again..."

The Adept nodded. "They weren't us," he announced proudly.

"Waine, there is no one else I'd rather have by my side..."

Bertus began solemnly, "If I were about to be overrun by a pack of crazed scullery maids! What makes you think that the three of us can do something everyone else has failed at? I know you're in better shape than most for the rank you hold in the Guild, but..."

The Warrior shifted his gaze from Bertus to Kevon. "Do you want to tell him... or?"

Fidgeting with his leather armbands, twisting them to feel the comforting steel strips slide across his skin, Kevon sighed deeply. The bands, and the ring that he wore in their stead, kept him safe from his former Master's scrying magic. The constant touch of iron and steel also denied Kevon one of his favorite things in life: the use of magic itself.

"I don't know if I can..." Kevon said softly. "He could find me... use me..."

Images of his friend Pholos's face in the blank, soulless gaze of a Control spell surfaced in Kevon's mind, deepening his reluctance.

"When winter comes, and the hours of darkness grow longer, how far do you think the evil will be able to spread? Where will anyone be safe?" Waine asked harshly. "This needs to end now, and we need to finish what we started."

"If Holten tried to find me, and has failed, he may believe I am dead." Kevon volunteered. "It's just been so long, I don't know if I can even..."

"If you can *what?*" Bertus asked impatiently.

Kevon sighed and looked Bertus in the eye. "If I can still use magic."

"Use?" Bertus asked, bewildered. "What are you...?"

Waine laughed and nodded confirmation when Bertus looked his way.

"That's not possible!" the younger man exclaimed. "It's just not *right!*" Bertus was staring at Kevon, obviously discomforted. The youth maintained his icy gaze for what seemed an eternity, and was just starting to tear up when he quietly spoke again. "Can I see some?"

The same relief Kevon had felt when he'd told Waine about his magic flooded over him. He slipped the armbands off slowly, and despite the overwhelming sense of vulnerability, packed them away in a saddlebag. "It will be a short while before I can even try," he explained as he sat back down.

"Why?" Bertus asked after a few minutes of strained silence. "No, I know why. I'm not angry. That's a dangerous secret to even know." Bertus picked absently at a stalk of snake-grass, flicking the sections in random directions. "But we spoke *every day*. I just…"

"You're right," Kevon agreed. "It is dangerous just knowing. For you, and for me. I just wanted to protect both of us. But you, of all people, deserved to know." Kevon put a hand to his head thoughtfully. "Now it's safer that you do know, so I guess that's why… I'm not going to change *you* into a toad."

Kevon pushed energy into the illusion He'd formed in his mind, and projected a puff of smoke in front of Waine. He threw up a flat image of the Adept's bedroll and saddle with a large toad on the blanket, keeping the image clear of Waine and any metal that would instantly disrupt the spell.

The toad's image croaked once at Kevon's direction before Waine stuck a hobnailed boot through the plane of illusion that concealed him from Bertus. The image wisped away, the symbol dulling immediately in Kevon's mind.

"Just an illusion," Kevon explained to Bertus. "I can't change anyone into anything. Most of the stories about that sort of thing are just stories. You'd be surprised what you can do with a good illusion, though."

"It looked to me like a mirror with a toad sitting in my place," Waine scoffed. "That had to be the worst illusion I've ever seen you do." The Adept squinted at Kevon. "Are you losing your powers?"

"I don't think so," Kevon answered. "It did seem like it took more effort than it did before I stopped using magic. Not as much as before, when I was studying with Holten, but..." he frowned and thought a minute longer. "I'm going to have to be careful about this for a while now," he continued, "At least until I get back in the habit of using both."

The Mage looked back at Waine. "The illusion I used was simpler than most I've done, but only because it was meant for Bertus alone. It would have taken too much power to present that image from all directions. It would have looked odd from any other perspective, I suppose."

Waine nodded, and resumed talking. "If nothing has changed by the time we reach Navlia, we should be able to get within a day's ride of the ruins." He sighed before continuing. "If we were to ride hard and get to the tower by dark, we'd be worn out, and just in time for whatever it is that everyone's so afraid of to wake up."

"So we need to go slower?" Bertus asked.

"Exactly," Waine answered. "We'd only want to travel during the brightest hours, when the danger would be least. Morning and evening we could hide, and Kevon could rest."

"If I'm resting morning and evening, and we're traveling during the day..."

"You'll need to keep whatever's out there away from us at night," Waine said soberly. "I don't know how you're going to manage it, but there's no way we can fight those things in the dark. Even a handful of those little imp-demons would slaughter us in full dark."

The Journeyman sighed. "I don't know either, but we'll have to manage somehow." He reached into a tunic pocket and found the pouch with the iron ring. Kevon twitched as the jolt from the ring's touch hit him harder than he had expected. He looked at Waine, then at Bertus. "We've got a lot of work to do."

CHAPTER 3

Kevon whirled around, blocking the edge of Waine's sword with the two short clubs he brought up to shield his face. The steel bit into the wood, but Kevon's magic did not falter. He remained focused on controlling the movement of his body, no longer bothering to extend the spell to his weapons and risk the interruption.

Allowing himself a quick smirk, he shoved Waine's blade away with his left club, stepped lightly over the sweeping kick directed at his front leg, and raked the edge of his right club against Waine's ribcage. Comforted by the Movement rune glowing brightly in his mind, Kevon blocked three more sword strikes and leapt backward about five yards to gain a moment to look at his weapons. The clubs were notched in quite a few places, and he did not even want to think about the shape Waine's sword was in.

The Adept closed the gap in seconds, chopping fiercely at Kevon, yelling. Kevon blocked hard with his left club, and wrenched the embedded blade from his opponent's hands, casting both weapons aside. He hurled his other club high in the air above Waine's head. Dumping the rest of his magic into the other rune flickering hungrily in his mind, Kevon projected a roaring column of flame that incinerated the thrown weapon before it reached the top of its arc.

The two combatants sat down on nearby rocks, breathing hard.

"Better," Waine gasped. "The combat, and the fire, both better than you were doing before the mines."

The Mage shook his head. "Raw power, maybe." He took a deep breath and held it, exhaling slowly. "It still takes too much effort. I get tired from using magic again, and I didn't before. And handling metal hurts again."

"Another week until we reach Navlia," Waine sniffed. "Do you think you'll be ready then?"

"I am improving," Kevon agreed. "A few more days of practice, I'll be better than ever. But having to ride with a whole Guard unit for three, maybe four weeks... I won't get any more chances before we leave them for the tower."

"Do what you can," Waine said, clapping Kevon on the knee. "Bertus is getting better, too." The Adept Warrior raised his voice and continued speaking. "It'll be interesting to see how he does with a real bow, someday."

The youth looked up from the leatherwork he was mending to glance at his crossbow, then back at the Warriors. "It does fine for now."

Kevon shivered inwardly. The crossbow he'd been shot with was not nearly as sturdy as the one Bertus used, and that bolt had been for hunting small game. The quarrels Bertus used left huge, gaping wounds, and he had been forbidden to use it for hunting after he'd all but torn a rabbit in half with a single shot. Bertus would carry his own weight in combat.

His magic did improve, and Kevon felt more confident than ever when they rode into Navlia. Spellcasting took almost no effort, and the touch of metal only turned his stomach slightly now.

The Seeker gave Bertus money for stabling the horses, and extra for the young man's room at an inn. Then he and Waine walked directly to the Guild, still unsure of who might know them on the street.

The Guildhall was abuzz with excitement. Rewards were now being offered for completed patrols of the westward roads, additional rewards for the carcasses of whatever it was causing the troubles. No one who had returned had yet to see any sign of what caused the others to disappear.

That did not stop some of the more brash Novices and Seekers from speculating, and boasting of their plans to be first to solve the problem.

"They say this new Commander leads from the front," one Novice said flippantly. "All the better," he continued, "He'll get a clear view of my skills from there."

"Turning from green to yellow isn't a skill I'd boast about," a nearby Adept drawled, inspiring chuckles from nearby listeners. "It sure won't impress a man who took down two bull orc by himself when he was up north."

Waine stopped drinking and turned to ask the speaker a question, but at that moment, six uniformed soldiers marched into the Hall's common area. The two rows stepped to each side, and turned to face each other, flanking the hallway they'd just emerged from.

"Attention!" one of the soldiers droned loudly, and those already present in uniform stood quickly.

"Enough of that!" a familiar voice admonished roughly. "Save the theatrics for the nobles. We're all friends here." Carlo walked into the room and shooed his escort off to some empty tables. He nodded curtly at Kevon and Waine before speaking again.

"I need ten men. You two," the Blademaster said, pointing at Kevon and Waine, "and eight others."

Kevon grinned and raised his mug in salute. Heads turned to gawk briefly at the newcomers who had been chosen, then voices rose to compete for the remaining spots.

The Commander waited until all the volunteers had spoken, then quickly pointed out eight. The six other uniformed men moved quickly to provide the new recruits with paperwork and instructions. Carlo spoke loudly, "That is all."

"Two bull orc?" Waine teased as Carlo pulled up a chair at

their table.

"You know how the men like to exaggerate," Carlo answered gruffly. "That's why I didn't tell them about the other two."

"So, four?" Kevon asked, lowering his mug to the table. "Bertus told me about the two..."

The Blademaster nodded. "About a week after we turned back for Eastport, the horses panicked again. I knew that the only way to safety was forward, so we charged on through. They weren't expecting that, and rushed out too late. They chased us for about two hours, and by that time, I had used all of my crossbow bolts to wound the smaller orcs that kept gaining on us."

The Commander paused to accept the mug of ale that a serving maid brought him, drank deeply, and sighed. "I caught up to Bertus and gave him the stallion's reins. Dove into the brush and waited until the bulls ran by. I managed to hamstring the larger one and get clear, but had to face the other one down. It almost... ended badly."

Kevon noticed Carlo's left hand clenching and unclenching as he spoke. The Seeker followed the line of the older man's arm and saw the lighter skin tone mottled up and down the length of the exposed limb. Kevon's hand went unconsciously to his left arm, where two circles of similar discoloration were barely visible.

The older man nodded to confirm Kevon's suspicion. "Sometime during the trip, your healing potion wound up in the boy's bags. He wrapped the arm and made me drink the accursed thing." The Blademaster took a swig of ale, as if to wash away the remembered taste. "Luckily, it helped enough we were able to keep up the pace we'd set. We came out of the forest and rode hard until we met a patrol. We split the patrol in half and switched to fresher horses. Two patrols later, we reached Eastport. They raised the alarm, and took us to the barracks. I was half dead, and couldn't find the boy. No one knew where he was. Next thing I know, he's standing over me with two more of those potions, pouring them down me, and nothing I can do about it." Carlo chuckled. "The squad thought it would be cute to have him be the one to mark me again after my brand healed."

The Seeker's right shoulder twitched involuntarily as he thought of the pain he'd felt when he received his sword-brand. *At least I passed out*, he thought grimly. *I can see now why Warriors don't particularly like the idea of healing potions.*

"How is the runt doing nowadays?" Carlo asked, not managing to hide much of the warmth that crept into his voice.

"He's doing well," Kevon began.

"He'll likely test for Novice when we return from this mission," Waine said cheerfully.

"So he's here, huh?" Carlo asked. "I can arrange for him to stay here at the barracks until we return, and then..."

"He's our third," Waine interjected, "not you." The Adept smiled as the Blademaster glared arrows at him and slowly lowered his mug.

The Blademaster tsk'd softly and glanced at the silver buttons stitched on the breast of his uniform. "And here I thought I was the one who decided matters like this."

"Not this time," Kevon said quietly. "You don't have any idea what is going on over there. You and your men can get us close quickly, but then the three of us will have to go on alone." He sighed and looked up from his mug to stare into Carlo's confused eyes. "It's not that we couldn't use your help, but you're just not ready for..."

"I'm not ready?" Carlo shouted, and all other sound in the room abruptly ended. "You've grown some, I'll grant you that, but you're in no position to tell me that I'm not ready for *anything!*"

"I'm sorry, Carlo," Kevon responded, his hushed voice fairly echoing in the becalmed room. "But that's just how it needs to be."

"I like you, boy," Carlo growled, "That's why you're not in chains right now. But by the *gods*, I will put you in your place!"

Carlo stood and removed his outer uniform tunic. Kevon swiftly but deliberately removed his armbands. Waine slid his chair back and spread his hands in a gesture of noninterference.

"Now hold on," Kevon said evenly. "If I win..."

Bursts of laughter rocked the room. Carlo continued his preparations, moving his healed arm in circles in an apparent attempt to limber it up.

Is he really warming it up, or trying to draw me into a trap? Kevon thought, amusedly. He waited for the laughter to end.

"If I win," Kevon continued slowly, "Will you concede that it is only by the strength of my conviction?"

"What are you babbling about?" Carlo barked, even more annoyed now.

"Will you agree to let me have my way in this matter, and that there is no shame in losing?" Kevon asked, standing and carefully preparing himself, handling his scabbarded sword gingerly until Waine took it from him.

"You're stalling..." Carlo mused, "And I won't have it. Choose your conditions; first blood, or forfeit?"

Kevon glanced at Waine for a moment before turning back to face Carlo. "I doubt anyone here could make you forfeit."

"First blood it is." The Blademaster gestured to the sand-filled arena pit. "After you."

"Who'll lay odds on the Seeker?" Waine asked cheerfully in the hush following the combatants' exchange.

The tense silence that had gripped the room dissolved as the common area quickly began to sound like a market square on a busy day. Waine pulled out his coin pouch and began betting with anyone that gave halfway decent odds. Several minutes later small piles of coin lay on most of the tables, and Waine tipped his empty pouch over and shook it.

The Seeker shot Waine a concerned look, but the Adept just smiled and raised his mug. "Please win?" he pleaded loudly, getting several laughs.

Kevon strolled over to the sword rack and picked up a wooden blade, swinging it experimentally. He exchanged it for another that had a slightly longer handle. He tried a two-handed grip, took a few swings, and then switched back to using one hand. Satisfied, he kicked off his boots, stripped off socks and tunic, and hopped lightly down into the recessed sand pit.

He smiled and tromped around the arena, shuffling to knock off the skin of sand that had adhered to his sweaty feet. He turned to face the center of the square, and raised his sword in a salute to Carlo.

"Are you sure you don't need to use the privy?" the Blademaster asked condescendingly. "Another mug of ale, perhaps?"

"We'll have time for that after," Kevon replied, readying the runes in his mind. "One way or another, this will be over quickly."

Carlo smiled and raised his own sword. The Blademaster stepped forward into position and began advancing on Kevon. The older man seemed to be turned further left than Kevon remembered from previous sparring bouts, and when Kevon caught a glimpse of Carlo's healed arm, the fist was still clenching and unclenching.

Feeling no need to press an advantage that was almost certainly a trick, Kevon ignored the ruse, and stood his ground, prepared as well as he knew how. He stepped out and crouched into a fairly straightforward two-handed stance that was far too open for a normal fight. He hoped it would encourage Carlo to take an easy shot that could be used to unbalance the Blademaster and allow Kevon to secure a quick win.

Kevon blocked the older man's first two strikes without the use of his magic. Even though he was prepared to deal with them, Kevon was still surprised by the two lightning-fast follow-up strikes that were something he'd never seen Carlo do before. He pulsed magic into the formed runes, and focused on his motion, the Movement spell sped his practice sword beyond what he could manage with even his forge-tempered muscles.

Carlo danced nimbly back, nodded, and pressed the attack again. Kevon's swordplay mentor leaned hard into his next series of attacks, trying to knock his opponent's sword away, or just wide enough to open an easy follow-up that would end the match.

The Mage could have parried the strikes one-handed with the same amount of effort and resistance, but it looked better with two hands against a visibly superior combatant. He stepped over the low sweeping kick that Carlo used to try and unbalance him, and while the Blademaster was extended awkwardly from the attack, Kevon shoved hard on his opponent's sword where it was locked with his own.

The Blademaster planted his left foot at an odd angle, almost backwards from the spin the extra shove had given his already rotating body. He swiftly twisted his right foot and slid it out to stabilize his stance.

The shuffling footwork almost distracted Kevon from the sword that had used the momentum from the shove to spin around the Blademaster and redirect unerringly toward Kevon's head.

With a pulse of magic, Kevon brought his blade up and Carlo's sword deflected high. Kevon still had to lean back to prevent the tip of Carlo's weapon from smacking into him, and that was when the older man acted.

The fist that Carlo had been clenching lashed out faster than Kevon thought possible, the older Warrior lunging in and extending into the punch to reach his leaning target.

Kevon dropped backwards to the sandy floor, arching his back to roll and absorb some of the impact, but thrust his foot upward to catch Carlo in the gut. Pulsing more energy into the runes, he gently 'helped' the Blademaster's forward motion by lifting him, and amplifying his unchecked momentum. A quick upward shove of the foot, and Carlo went flying over Kevon to land on his back at the far end of the arena, almost ten feet away.

He rolled back up to his feet, and turned to see Carlo recovering his. The Seeker moved slowly toward the Blademaster, who had taken a more defensive posture, and stood unusually still.

He must be hurting if he's not moving, not wanting to give away any specific weakness, Kevon thought to himself. I just want this to be over with.

Focusing more on his sword than he had been doing the last few weeks, Kevon closed to within striking distance and fed a stream of magic into the runes. He began with a downward chop, and halfway through the motion, shifted left to slam his sword directly into Carlo's, with more than enough force to knock the Blademaster's sword and the arm grasping it a full ninety degrees.

The Blademaster launched another lightning-fast left-handed punch, but Kevon had already stepped left and reversed his wooden sword to graze Carlo's forward-thrust shoulder just below the collarbone, *thwacking* into the extended left arm of his opponent mostly on accident.

The Seeker's meager magical resources gave out and the runes sputtered to darkness in his mind.

Carlo roared, whipping his sword up, turning with force borrowed from the attack Kevon had just landed. Without his magic supporting his movements, Kevon could not respond quickly enough against Carlo's superior reflexes and years of training. The Blademaster's wooden sword moved faster than thought, colliding with the side of Kevon's face, causing his head to whip to the side violently.

The exhausted Mage stumbled and fell awkwardly onto splayed knees, dropping his weapon to catch himself before he pitched forward. He was unsure if the crowd had stopped yelling, or if they had merely been drowned out by the ringing and pounding in his ears. He closed his eyes tightly as the salty blood-taste registered, and his tongue touched the split at the left corner of his mouth. He spat, opened his eyes, and shakily clambered to his feet without picking up the sword.

As he looked up, the first thing Kevon noticed was Carlo's weapon lying in the sand, not far from his own. The Blademaster stood facing the crowd, which had indeed fallen silent. Kevon gasped as Carlo turned to face him. He winced at the pain the movement and sharp intake of air caused, and tried not to wobble as Carlo nodded to him and gestured to the stripe of abraded skin on his right collarbone. Kevon put his hand to his bleeding lip and showed it to the Blademaster and the crowd. "Tie?" he asked timidly.

The Commander grinned and clasped Kevon's extended arm to a mixture of cheers and relieved laughter. "We'll discuss this plan of yours later," the Blademaster said, releasing Kevon's arm and clapping him on the shoulder. "It may not take much more convincing."

Novices scrambled to put swords away and hand the combatants their footgear and other garments. Kevon sat in a chair to pull his boots on, and spotted Waine glaring in his direction as the Adept recovered his own coins to refill his money pouch.

"At least you didn't lose," Kevon offered as he returned to his seat by Waine. "I'd say that's something."

"It certainly is something," Carlo agreed, standing nearby, straightening his uniform. "But how about something else? Come see me tomorrow morning. I have some things to take care of in the office before lunch, things that may interest you. Bring the boy if you can."

Kevon and Waine each shook Carlo's hand before the Blademaster stood completely straight and cleared his throat. The half-dozen men who'd accompanied Carlo into the Guild scrambled to flank the hallway as their Commander strode briskly away.

The Adept sighed loudly. "Not bad for our first day back, I guess..." he began. "You almost win a fight, I almost win a fortune, and we're signed up for the patrol that will take us back to the tower."

"Hey, you," an older Adept called from a table over. "Waine!"

"You already got your money back," Waine answered, not bothering to look at the speaker. "What more do you...?"

The man and the rest of the Warriors sitting at his table all stood at once, and moved to surround Waine. "You need to come with us," the man growled, "And you," the man jabbed a calloused finger in Kevon's direction. "You need to stay right where you are, if you know what's good for your friend."

Runes danced in Kevon's head, ready for use at a moment's notice. Kevon struggled to remain calm; if he used magic here visibly, they were both as good as dead.

Waine stood slowly and allowed himself to be herded across the room and out the front of the building, no one present said a single word.

As Kevon started to stand, a soft touch at his neck gently pressed him back into his seat.

"They're not going to hurt him," a barmaid said, moving to where Kevon could see her. "I heard them talking. Before you offered the tie, they had lost. They agreed Waine deserved something."

"Any idea what?"

She shook her head and smiled. "Is there anything I can get you?"

He shrugged. "I'll wait for Waine for a while, but I need to go see a friend later. Something to eat in about an hour or so?"

The serving maid nodded and disappeared into the kitchen, grabbing empty plates and mugs as she wove through the crowded room. The glance she shot him over her shoulder before he lost sight of her only made him think about Marelle.

The low conversation resumed around Kevon, and individual Warriors came over to introduce themselves and offer their congratulations. When asked if he would like to test for Adept, Kevon politely refused, commenting that he needed to be prepared for the coming mission, not nursing wounds caused by pride.

The hour passed swiftly. Kevon ate the meal the serving maid brought, and waited a little longer. Waine still had not returned. Kevon said his goodbyes and made his way out into the early evening crowds, and headed for Bertus' inn.

The Seeker's young friend was just finishing up his own supper in the inn's common room. Bertus motioned to Kevon as soon as he spotted the Warrior at the entrance to the room, and Kevon walked over to sit down and join him.

He noticed immediately that the young man would not look him in the eye. "Bertus, what's wrong?" he asked, concern lining his voice.

"I'm sorry, Anton," Bertus said, voice cracking as he turned tear-filled eyes to look at Kevon.

The Journeyman Smith leaned forward to grasp Bertus' shoulder. "What's happened?" he whispered, trying not to upset the boy further.

"Do you remember Liah?" Bertus asked, sniffing, pointing to a familiar-looking serving girl.

"I..." Kevon began, trying to remember where he'd seen her.

"She worked with me at the *Maiden*."

"Yes, of course," Kevon answered quickly, remembering the morning that Bertus had bought her freedom from the indentured servitude Kevon had unwittingly freed him from. He peered closely at Liah, then turned back to his friend. "She seems fine..."

"She is..." Bertus nodded slowly. "She's been here for three seasons, and is doing well. It's the news from Eastport that..." Bertus choked on the words and wiped his runny nose on his sleeve.

"News from Eastport?" Kevon sat back, scratching his head. "What could... What news?"

"Before Liah left," Bertus began, "She heard that Rhulcan and Marelle..."

Kevon's heart leapt at the mention of her name, but the sight of tears flowing freely down Bertus' face clenched a knot in the pit of his stomach. "What about them?" Kevon asked, his voice wavering.

"Liah heard they were killed… by bandits… just days after she was freed. Days after we left."

Kevon twisted at his armbands shakily. He was glad he wore them, the Fire symbol in his mind pulsed hungrily, but the red hue that permeated the symbol spiked and ebbed with the pounding of his heart and the blurring of his vision.

"That's all she knows," Bertus continued, "After Carlo and I returned to Eastport, those who were able fled westward, some to Kron, others turning south for the Inner Cities."

Conflicting thoughts and emotions cascaded over Kevon. The joy and wonder of knowing Marelle for even so short a time was immeasurable. Alternative scenarios crowded his mind, vying for attention. *If I'd never left Laston…* he thought grimly, *She'd have finished her planned route with Carlo, and would still be alive.* Kevon clenched his teeth and shut his eyes hard against the tears that fought to the surface. *If I had convinced her… even asked her… to go away with me…*

He opened his eyes, sniffed once, and refocused his anger. Holten is the reason I left the North Valley, the reason I went to Eastport. The traitorous scum is the reason I wouldn't consider staying with Marelle, not until he was dead. He'll pay for her life with his own.

Not only had his former Master sent him to be killed, he'd done something awful to a Myrnar princess, and was now partly responsible for the death of the only woman Kevon had ever loved.

Holten was not the only one responsible. Kevon stood and walked over to where Liah was cleaning a nearby table. He spoke quietly to her for a minute, and passed some coins into her hand. Liah nodded, removed her apron, and hurried out of the inn.

The Seeker returned to the table and sat down across from a puzzled-looking Bertus. "She's going back to Eastport, finding out who killed Rhulcan and Marelle. She'll leave word about how to reach her at the *Maiden*."

The boy frowned, but Kevon spoke again quickly.

"The orcs have been dealt with in the east. She'll be safer there than here, with the darkness spreading to the west."

"You're sure?" Bertus asked, still not convinced.

"If the greater danger lay east, would Carlo be here, heading west?" Kevon asked, and saw the boy's eyes light up. Pushing aside his own grief and rage, Kevon answered Bertus' questions about Carlo and told him briefly of the fight.

"Well, sure," Bertus scoffed, "Because you cheated."

The Seeker glared at the young man for an instant before glancing around the room to make sure no one had heard. "I did what I had to," he said quietly.

Bertus rolled his eyes.

"Regardless," Kevon continued, "Be up and ready early in the morning. We have to meet Carlo at the palace."

CHAPTER 4

Kevon strode purposefully down the nearly empty morning streets alongside Waine, grinning. He jostled his companion in the ribs with his elbow, and whispered out of the corner of his mouth.

"Waine, have I mentioned..."

"Yes, how *nice* my new tunic is," Waine growled back, throwing an elbow in response. "About a dozen times."

"And how," Kevon continued, "it..."

"The mushroom." Waine interrupted. "Half a dozen, at least."

The Seeker chuckled to himself as the two Warriors turned in to the front of the inn where Bertus was staying. They found their young friend finishing up breakfast in the common room.

"I'm almost ready," Bertus told them as they entered the room to stand by his table. "The cook promised me a bowl of Bloodhead soup, though."

Kevon stifled a laugh, and Waine crossed his arms, further enhancing the similarity of his appearance to the mushroom that was considered a frontier delicacy. He knew that the Adept's tunic was two shades darker than the fungus they were comparing it to, and by no means did it have the waxy sheen the mushrooms were famous for. Nevertheless, the combination of the red top and brown trousers was too striking to ignore.

The youth wolfed down the last few bites of his morning meal, sprinkled a few coppers on the table, and stood to leave.

Halfway to the palace, Waine lengthened his stride and

pulled a few steps ahead of his companions. "Mirsa!" he called cheerfully, stopping to draw her attention.

Using the cover his friend had provided, Kevon averted his face, and jabbed Bertus in the side with his elbow. Half a step later, Kevon was in full Novice Warrior swagger, his younger friend scrambling to keep up.

A hundred yards or so later, Kevon slowed, and Bertus caught up, winded.

"Friend of yours?" he asked Kevon, wheezing.

"Hardly," Kevon answered tersely. "She was from the tower."

"Oh..." Bertus' soft response melted into the early morning street murmurs.

The two continued slowly on until Waine rejoined them just short of the palace gates.

"We may have a problem," the Adept said calmly as he stepped in alongside his friends.

The Seeker turned to stare blankly at Waine.

"All right, all right." Waine conceded. "We have a very serious problem. With great dimples?" he offered.

The hair on the back of Kevon's neck stood on end, and he stopped, then shuffled over to the side of the street, out of the flow of the increasing foot traffic. "How bad is it?"

The three huddled together for a few minutes while Waine told the others what he'd learned. Mirsa was now an advisor to the royal family, and had been assigned to this next military patrol to gain a magical perspective on this threat that loomed to the west.

"That's about like having an orc for a nursemaid," Bertus spat, and his companions smiled despite the gravity of the situation.

"There's a good chance she already knows what the problem is," Kevon sighed. "There's an even greater chance she'll recognize me from the tower, and that *cannot* happen."

The Adept shrugged. "You were at the tower for about

two days, and saw her a handful of times. You've grown since then, I don't think there's much chance of her remembering you... It was more than two years ago." he rubbed his chin thoughtfully. "Just to be safe, I'll have to provide a constant distraction..."

Kevon shut his eyes tightly and rubbed his temples for a moment, as Bertus huffed in disbelief. "But..." the young man stammered, "She's... evil!"

The Warrior ruffled Bertus' hair and laughed. "Someday you'll understand." he said cheerfully.

They continued on through the gates, and having been expected, were led through some of the interconnected outer structures to the officers' quarters.

The Commander waved them in as soon as they reached the doorway to his office, dismissing their guide and two other officers he had been speaking with. As the room cleared, the Blademaster closed the door firmly, and returned to his desk.

"Have you decided to tell me what's going on?" Carlo asked, thumbing through a pile of papers on the desk.

The Seeker shook his head slowly. "No, sir."

Carlo dipped a quill in an inkpot and scribbled his signature on one of the pages and set it aside. "How about you two?" he asked, eyeing Waine and Bertus.

Waine laughed out loud, and Bertus hung his head and mumbled a soft 'no'.

"Well, then," the Blademaster continued, "We'll have to figure out how this is going to work." He shoved the pile of papers aside and motioned to the chairs in front of the desk. When his visitors were seated, Carlo spoke once more. "You're already famous around here," Carlo growled, pointing a calloused finger at Kevon. "The detail that was with me last night wanted me to pressure the Guild into promoting you to Adept status immediately. I refused."

The Seeker swallowed uncomfortably. He glared at Waine after his friend snickered quietly.

"They would follow if you led," Carlo raised his voice and spoke over the question Kevon had begun to ask. "It would save me hauling another lieutenant away from the palace. What do you think?"

"Even if we were not going to abandon you halfway through the mission, I don't know that I'd be comfortable giving orders," Kevon admitted.

"Who gets to keep an eye on the Mage?" Waine asked, grinning.

"You've done your research, I see," Carlo chuckled. "She is advisor to the Prince himself, you'll have to behave. There are four, all hand-picked by the Prince. None that I would have chosen, they'll be more trouble than they're worth." The Blademaster thought for a moment. "I have to take them along, but I don't have to deal with them. Mirsa's detail will report to you, Waine, since you seem so interested."

"Four lackeys," Waine commented. "I'm surprised the prince isn't coming himself."

"He wanted to," Carlo replied. "I wouldn't allow it. There's a difference between leading an army to war, and walking into a Mage-spawned apocalypse."

Kevon's eyes dropped for an instant, and Carlo leaned forward.

"So you do know... That's what this is, isn't it?" the Blademaster asked, rising out of his chair.

"Something like it," Kevon answered meekly. "What's more, the Mage that is going to 'investigate' is part of the problem. She was Gurlin's top student, and left just before I assassinated the Wizard."

The Blademaster sat back, fists clenched in frustration. "I chose the way of the blade because I had no stomach for wizardry or politics. Now I'm waist deep in both. And the three of you aren't helping matters! Tell me what is going on!" he barked gruffly.

"Carlo," Bertus spoke quietly in the silence after the Blademaster's outburst. "I was upset when Kevon told me what he'd been keeping from us. But he did tell me, right when I needed to know."

The room was silent for long moments, and Bertus looked back and forth from Kevon to Carlo several times.

"And I think I agree," Bertus continued, "That now is not the best time for you to know." The youth looked into the hard eyes of his hero, and said softly, "You're not ready."

The Commander sat, glaring at the three of them for minutes before his gaze began to soften, as the words of his young friend sunk in. "All right," he conceded. "Tell me what I do need to know, and how you're going to work this, so I can make it official."

Two hours later, the four emerged from Carlo's office. Bertus waved and scurried down the hallway with a set of orders and a pouch full of coin. He would make arrangements for long-term care of their horses before returning to begin his assignment with the support staff that would be traveling with the company.

Kevon and Waine followed their new Commander through a warren of hallways to a storeroom where they found uniforms. After finding two suitable uniforms each, the new recruits lugged their bundled clothing back through several more hallways to the armory.

Delighted to hear of Kevon's blacksmithing experience in the south, the Blademaster had penned orders working Kevon into a squad with the company's only other Warsmith. Carlo also insisted that Kevon not leave without a guard-issue warhammer.

The Smith was somewhat disappointed with the selection of hammers; Warsmiths were uncommon around Navlia. Out of four hammers in the entire armory, only one did not feel like a toy when Kevon hefted it. Having apprenticed to a southern Blacksmith near the iron mines, he was accustomed to heavier weapons. He imagined the hammer was about the same weight as Master Farren's forge hammer, and it did not feel too awkward to swing.

With those matters settled, Kevon and Waine left to return to the Warrior's Guild to stow their personal items in the Guild storeroom.

The Warsmith loaded his things into the sturdy cedar chest that was provided, cautiously aware of anything that could be construed as magic-related. He'd sent all of his magical equipment with Bertus when they'd arrived in Navlia, and did not think anyone would go through his belongings, but he wanted to take no chances.

The Seeker kept only his Guild necklace, the shell necklace he'd gotten from the Myrnar, armbands, ring, and dagger. He changed into the uniform he had brought, folded his clothes, and packed them atop the rest of the items in the chest. He wrote his name on a thin wooden placard, and after closing the chest, slid the piece of wood into the slots that flanked the hasp. He hefted the box from the table to one of the shelves lining the wall, and waited for Waine to finish.

They returned to the palace by lunchtime, and were informally introduced to some of the other members of the company over the midday meal. Carlo was less than free with his conversation, as he was reluctant to call Kevon 'Anton', they ate quickly and moved on to other matters.

The Commander took Waine deeper into the palace and introduced him to Mirsa's retinue. It seemed to amuse the Blademaster that the four young nobles took affront to being placed under Waine's supervision rather than reporting directly to Carlo, or to no one at all.

Kevon was left with Xæver, the company's other Warsmith. The two spent the greater part of the afternoon packing tools and parts of a field-forge into a supply wagon. It was only after all the gear had been stowed and lashed down to Xæver's satisfaction that the Warsmith really began talking with Kevon.

"It's not that hard to learn," Xæver reassured Kevon after

finding out that the Seeker had no experience with a warhammer. "In my experience, though" he continued thoughtfully, "Armorers bear the hammer much more ably than weaponsmiths. You learn the weaknesses of armor from both sides, and it makes it that much easier to break through an opponent's defenses. Against a Warsmith, poorly made armor is worse than none at all."

Xæver walked Kevon through some basic techniques. The heavier weapon used a slightly different approach, not so much concerned with getting through an opponent's active defenses, but striking correctly when it inevitably did. "A sword requires the correct angle of *attack*. A hammer only needs the correct angle of *impact*." Xæver explained.

The Seeker spent several minutes hammering away at a straw-filled suit of armor that hung from several ropes attached to the ceiling. Xæver would call out a target, and Kevon would strike at it a handful of times, until directed elsewhere. The differing lengths of rope caused it to lurch awkwardly at certain places, adding to the difficulty, making precision strikes nearly impossible for Kevon and his new weapon.

Finally, Kevon's mentor instructed him to attack the dummy full-on.

He began with a downward swing to the suit's right clavicle, knocking the target back and to the left. He stepped forward, transferred the momentum of his swing into an upward backhand strike at the bottom of the opponent's right ribcage. The suit jerked violently back further, and to the right before one of the longer ropes reached its end and immediately brought the heavy metal target rushing back. Kevon stepped back and to his left as he continued his follow-through swing to the right. He twisted the hammer's handle as he avoided the suit's return swing, and he completed his spin, burying the curved point deep in the armor's left side from behind it.

The point of the hammer stuck, and the momentum from Kevon's swing almost pulled the weapon from his hand. Kevon stumbled a few steps before arresting the dummy's movement. After yanking several times without freeing the weapon, Kevon stuck his foot on the suit for leverage.

Xæver laughed and took the handle of the hammer from Kevon. He wrenched it quickly up and down, and it slid free easily. "Very good," he commented. "You're a quick study. You'll do fine. You may want to use a shield... Hammers are not nearly as defensive as swords, as you can imagine."

The Seeker sat and rested, listening as Xæver talked about different smithing techniques for field-forges versus established ones, tricks for setting up quickly, as well as more combat pointers. When he'd caught his breath, he stood.

"That'll be all for today," the other Warsmith said. "Get some food in you, get some rest. The first day out is usually the toughest."

CHAPTER 5

Kevon sincerely hoped Xæver was right. The next morning was a nightmare.

Bells clanged, whistles blew, and irritated officers strode to and fro barking orders. The noise began what seemed like only minutes after he closed his eyes to sleep.

The fledgling Warsmith rolled groggily out of his bunk to pull on his uniform. Once up, he and the other members of the company were shepherded through narrow hallways toward the palace courtyard. At one branch, everyone was handed a cooked sausage folded into a griddle-cake, and a mug of cider. Two halls down, mugs were collected and the men were goaded back to a faster pace on their way to the stable yard.

The Seeker kept shifting his belt to try and get the warhammer he'd hung from a loop into a comfortable position. His sword rode easily now on his hip and his dagger was strapped lower on his leg, but the hammer seemed to catch on *everything*.

The stream of soldiers, guardsmen, and the rest of the company erupted from the cramped stone passage near the stable in the courtyard. The four wagons the company would be using were already lined out; Bertus among the hostlers checking harness and tack on the teams ready to pull them.

He recognized the wagon they had loaded with the forge supplies and other heavy equipment at the rear of the column. Two other wagons of similar, if lighter construction appeared to be for food and other such provisions, burlap could be seen poking out from tarpaulins here and there.

The lead wagon was smaller, lighter, and was hitched to

a quartet of elegant looking, pure-white horses that Kevon imagined would be more trouble than they were worth.

The column swept past the wagons to the stable entrance, where horses waited to be saddled. Kevon saddled the horse that was given to him, and before he could even put a foot in the stirrup, it was led away by one of the stablehands.

Then the Destriers were led out. The warhorses were huge, three hands taller, at least, than Carlo's horse. Kevon found himself holding the reins of one of the beasts, staring up into its flaring nostrils, as a large cavalryman began affixing barding to his steed. He held fast throughout the ordeal as the restless charger stamped and snorted, until the armoring was complete.

The cavalryman strode off, leaving Kevon with his unhappy ward until the rest of the larger horses were ready. Finally, before Kevon resorted to trying a Control spell on the increasingly agitated warhorse, another stablehand took the reins and led it outside.

Kevon spent the next half-hour helping two of the cavalrymen into their heavy armor, and assisting them onto their steeds.

"This is mostly for show," Xæver reassured Kevon after the last of more than a dozen of the heavy cavalry rode into flanking positions along the wagon column. "On the road, we'll have less help, but they won't ride in full armor unless they know there's going to be a battle."

The Seeker nodded, relieved. He was sweating as hard as he would have after an hour over a forge. He had no idea how the men could stand the weight of the armor, even when they were riding. He followed Xæver over to their waiting horses, and the two mounted and wheeled into their positions behind their squad leader.

After several minutes of standing still, even the calmer horses began to get restless. Kevon sidestepped his mount back into line and looked to his fellow Warsmith.

"Magus..." Xæver whispered low over at Kevon.

The younger Blacksmith nodded almost imperceptibly. Indeed, Mirsa had yet to appear, as did Waine.

Almost as if on cue, from around the other side of the courtyard, rode Mirsa and her escort. The four hand-selected guards led the way on a matched quartet of chestnut mares. Mirsa followed on a dainty appaloosa, Waine riding closely at her side.

Wizard, not Mage... Kevon thought to himself, noting Mirsa's hoodless black riding cloak and matching beret that jaunted smartly to the side. *She's decided to settle in at the palace, then.* He feigned disinterest and rechecked the fastenings on his saddlebags.

"Look sharp!" Xæver whispered as their squad leader circled around to make sure everyone was ready before returning to his place.

Fanfare sounded, and the first unit's cavalry squad moved out the opening palace gate in a wedge formation, armor and barding clanking as they steadied into a trot. The rest of the company fell in beside the wagons as they hastened to follow Mirsa, her detail, and Waine.

Kevon rode behind Xæver, on the right flank of the rear supply wagon. The second unit's cavalry squad rode in two lines behind that, bringing up the rear.

The people they passed on the streets seemed only mildly interested or annoyed, Kevon observed, except for the children. *Displays like this must be so common that only the young still get excited about it,* he thought, smiling. *One of these cavalrymen riding through Laston would be talked about for years.*

The column stopped for nothing, but it was not moving too swiftly. Still, Kevon was amazed that it took less than two hours before they exited the city gates. Another hour down the road, and a halt was called. Units took turns eating and helping the cavalry units remove and store most of their armor and horses' barding. Kevon had time to wolf down his meal before he found himself in a line passing armor up into a wagon to a waiting Xæver.

Fifteen minutes later, after five minutes of *actual* rest, they helped the cavalry re-mount. They started back down the road, the late morning sun warming their necks as they continued westward.

The miles fell away at an astonishing pace. Carlo led the column as quickly as the wagons could go without threatening to shake themselves apart. All of the horses and riders were well accustomed to rapid travel and the non-military Warriors in the group swiftly, if grudgingly, adapted to their new positions and the strictures they entailed.

The company slept and patrolled by thirds, the youngest third taking the mid-night shift. By the end of the second week, Kevon could have the canopy on the supply wagon stretched and anchored to its support poles before the wagon crews were even started unsaddling horses. He would eat his evening meal while hauling and setting up cots, and no sooner than he would place the last one, he would fall asleep, sprawled out on it.

By the end of the third week, Kevon could feel the tension mounting throughout the company. The countryside was growing wilder. Fields grew untended, some crops rotting within a choking undergrowth of weeds. Farmhouses were found abandoned, with never a clue to point to where the inhabitants had gone, or why.

Carlo directed his troops to resupply at these abandoned buildings as best they could; the supplies they had brought were running low, and there was no longer game to be found. Scavenging parties consisted of two cavalry, two scouts, and five of the mounted infantry or support personnel. There were scarcely more than two dozen of the mounted infantry, and Carlo ran two scavenging parties whenever the opportunity presented itself. Kevon often found himself rummaging through the increasingly slim pickings of the abandoned homes they managed to spot.

The Warsmith became quite skilled at spotting hiding

places where supplies and money might be cached. Different texture in a dirt floor might conceal a buried box, a polished spot on a timber could reveal a hidden cache that more often than not hid valuables, or heirlooms. These alone were left, while supplies and weapons were loaded up and returned to the slowly moving column that the company had settled into.

Four weeks into their journey, the company began finding evidence that homes had not simply been abandoned. Signs of struggles and spatters of dried blood were foremost amongst countless other things Kevon noticed that were not quite right. All of the combatants in the company had rotated out on patrols, had seen firsthand what had been suspected all along. Things were noted and reported back to Carlo, but otherwise not spoken of. The support personnel all took to carrying scavenged weaponry, and all who asked were quickly shown the basics of their use.

The attack still caught them off guard. The horses, picketed nearby, caught wind of the demons, panicking just before the men started screaming.

Kevon had just been awakened for his shift on watch. The moonless night and patchy cloud cover obscured the already dim starlight. That, combined with the prohibition on campfires after dusk, made them effectively blind.

"*Phes-Movra!*" came the cry from the center of camp, and the sky lit up as Mirsa sprayed fire in a wide swath from the entryway of her wagon. The butt of the staff she wielded jostled as two of her guard detail squeezed past her to raise their stout wooden clubs against the horrors that filled the air.

"Fools!" Mirsa shouted, shoving her nearest guardian, sending him sprawling off the wagon. "Stand clear!" The Master Wizard shoved back the sleeves of her nightshirt and began chanting and loosing more bolts of flame from her staff.

Kevon watched the scene with a sense of frozen detachment. His sword was in his hand, but he did not remember drawing it.

Half a dozen torches flared to life around camp, as cool-headed combat veterans worked oil and rags to bring more steady light to the battle. Lit torches were passed to the waiting hands of those too stunned to act.

The Seeker heard a familiar screech behind him. He whirled and slashed, severing the arm and wing of an imp that had been headed straight for him. He ran three steps and stomped on the flailing creature's neck, crunching bones and silencing the awful keening.

The shrieks came from all around him, the dull black creatures soaring on sickly yellow-orange wings just at the edges of the torchlight. Archers loosed bolts and arrows into the darkness, to little effect.

Mirsa's barrage of staff-powered flames slowed, and the Wizard sagged visibly. Even controlling so much stored energy was quickly exhausting her.

Fully half the company now held lit torches, the rest circled warily, weapons at the ready. The screeching quieted, and Kevon could no longer see the fluttering of wings at the edge of his vision.

The Wizard sighed heavily, and steadied herself on the shoulder of one of her escorts. She let the staff clatter to the carriage floor, and slumped even further as the destructive impulses of the Enchanted weapon left her.

The calm lasted only a few moments. One of the torchbearers near Kevon cried out as something struck him in the back, sending him sprawling. The torch he held tumbled into the dirt and sputtered out.

Kevon rushed toward the man, but the pale, hunched figure atop the fallen soldier hissed and slashed at the man's back with a clawed hand before leaping into the night on impossibly long legs.

Two more torchbearers went down.

"Form up around the wagons!" Carlo called above the panicked cries of untried soldiers. "Torches to the center!"

Kevon stepped past the ring of torches and gazed into the night with slowly adjusting eyes. He could see the leapers hanging just out of clear view, taking lurching bounds at unexpected intervals to circle the company.

One of the creatures thumped to the ground two sword-lengths away from Kevon, an imp twitching erratically in its mouth. The leaper eyed Kevon for a second before springing back into the darkness.

What would it be like if they were working together? Kevon wondered as he stepped back, eyeing the sickly yellow patch of spilled blood on the ground.

The company stood watchful for another hour before Carlo came around and let every fourth man rest, a two-hour nap beneath the wagons.

Kevon stayed awake and watchful until the last shift, and the first glow of morning showed in the east. Knowing that the imps, at least, would be seeking shelter from the day was relief enough that Kevon fell right to sleep as soon as he crawled into his bedroll.

CHAPTER 6

Morning brought Kevon's quest into harsh perspective. Over a dozen men had been lost. Four of the Destriers lived, because the men had rushed to save their horses. Two of the others had died of their wounds during the night. Of the four remaining mounts, only two were mostly uninjured. One was limping badly and refused to eat.

Traces of blood and trampled ground were all that remained of those that had been lost. The imps and 'night leapers' as the men were calling them, had either consumed or carried off every scrap.

Carlo made rounds, personally inspecting wounds for signs of infection, ordering several men to take healing potions. After meeting with his division leaders, the Commander pulled Kevon aside.

"Are we close enough?" Carlo asked wearily. "Can you make it the rest of the way on your own?"

"We're about ten days out, on foot, moving during the lightest hours," Kevon answered. "It's closer than we were counting on."

The Blademaster nodded. "I would bring the whole company along, if I thought it would help. These men..." Carlo struggled to find the words. "They would follow wherever I led, to end this madness. But I can't take them deeper into this, not when there is another way. I'm going to have to trust that the three of you can somehow make it through. We'll stay here again tonight, but we're leaving in the morning."

Kevon nodded and turned to leave.

"But," Carlo gripped Kevon's shoulder until the young Warsmith turned back to face him. "Don't think I won't bring back a full battalion to make sure. I still don't like not knowing how you're managing this."

The Seeker forced a smile, and hoped that everything would be set right by the time a force that large could make it back even this far. "Carlo…" Kevon began, "You've trusted me this far, and I suppose I should do the same. People should know what they face if we fail." He reached into his tunic and withdrew a folded letter, sealed with red wax, marked with the signet symbol that Carlo had carved for him over a year ago. "Open this when you reach Navlia, when the troops are settled, and you're sitting at your desk. I think by then, you'll be ready."

Carlo accepted the letter, and stared at the seal for a moment before grunting in amusement. He nodded to Kevon and walked back toward the center of camp, issuing orders as he went.

The kitchen crew started cooking a late breakfast while the rest of the company made preparations. Mirsa scowled in disapproval as she watched extra bedding and casks of oil loaded into her carriage. When all that remained in the arms-wagon was the cavalry's heavy armor and barding, and various other items not worth carrying, breakfast was ready.

There was plenty, and it was *good*. Kevon stopped himself short of overindulging, but the rest of the men ate heartily. Several friends had died the night before, more could die in the coming days. No one would starve.

After breakfast and a brief rest, the hostlers managed to harness two of the Destriers, and haul the heavy arms-wagon into a field, far from the road. They no longer needed it, it would be foolish to try and stretch their defenses around it any longer. The hostlers brought the warhorses back and tied them with the others in between the two remaining wagons.

Carlo ordered the company to resume resting in shifts,

to prepare for another night of battle. Details were formed for care of the injured, burial of the dead, and gathering of fuel for torches and bonfires. Kevon, Waine, and Bertus managed to rest the first shift, and were conveniently assigned to collect firewood just before the cooks started lunch. Bertus secured rations for the three of them, packing his bag as full as he could without drawing undue attention.

Waine flirted once more, unsuccessfully, with Mirsa, before leading his friends off toward the tower. The party stalked down the road until they were sure they were no longer visible from camp before they abandoned all attempts at stealth. Certain the bulk of the danger would come at night, they hurried as fast as they could toward the base of the nearby mountains.

They reached the foothills of the southern wall of the valley as the late afternoon shadows began to deepen. Though several hours of light remained, the lack of direct sunlight was particularly unnerving.

Even though their ultimate goal was down in the valley, the three continued upward, toward the steeper part of the mountain. Soon, they found what they were looking for, a small cave in one of the wrinkles at the base of the mountain.

Kevon peered around the edge of the entrance, spells at the ready. He knew that such an appealing place for them to hide at night could be just as tempting for creatures of the dark to use during the day.

Seeing nothing, Kevon glanced back at Waine, who moved up and eased into the opening, sword bared. Kevon followed, a tongue of magical flame suspended over his upturned palm for light, ready to direct into an attack if needed.

There was nothing to fear. The crack narrowed to nothing less than thirty feet from the entrance, and was completely empty. Bertus collected their packs and set to making things more comfortable while Kevon and Waine hauled rocks to stack in the entrance. After the two Warriors had the entrance mostly blocked, they ate and rested while Bertus carefully placed the last few smaller stones to completely seal them in.

"Easier than I thought it would be," Kevon commented, feeding power into a Light rune, bathing the narrow cave in a soft glow. "We'll see how it works, come full dark."

Bertus edged by Kevon to the back of the cave and wedged himself into his bedroll, making sure his crossbow was within reach. Waine did much the same, staying nearer to the blocked entrance, readying both sword and bow.

The three talked softly for a little while, concerned more about how Carlo and the rest of the company would fare this night than themselves.

Kevon felt his reserves drained below where he felt comfortable, and began dimming the light. The others nodded, and Kevon released the magic, returning the interior of the cave to total darkness.

CHAPTER 7

A thin shaft of morning sunlight speared through the rocky barricade, striking a rough patch of rock and splashing dimly around the cramped space. The muted glow teased Kevon back to wakefulness, and his startled gasp instantly woke the others.

"Oh! Good morning!" Bertus said cheerfully. "Late morning, more like," he amended, yawning. "I think we all needed that rest."

The Warsmith remained silent, thinking. Getting enough rest had been one of the concerns for this leg of the journey from the beginning. Now, dwindling rations and a lack of any game to hunt was another major factor. They could survive on what they carried with them for a week, maybe more. If today was wasted because they had slept too long...

He forced his concerns to the back of his mind. He got up and started taking rocks that Waine handed him, and passed them to Bertus, who stacked them neatly about halfway down the length of the cave.

When the entrance of the cave was open enough that they could pass through without much difficulty, the three climbed over what was left of the rock pile, and out into the morning sun.

It was later than Kevon would have liked, but not by much. The sun hung only a hand's-breadth off the horizon, and was warming away the last of the morning chill.

"We can't depend on shelters like this for the rest of the trip," Kevon sighed. "It would be nice, though."

Bertus shrugged. "Go look for one. I'll stay around here and see if I can dig up something to eat."

The Seeker looked at Waine.

The Adept grinned. "I'll take the far side, I can cover more ground. Scout until noon, then come back?"

Although he did not really want to split up, there was a greater chance of finding another shelter if they did. "All right," Kevon agreed. "Can we eat first?"

After a quick meal, the group said their goodbyes and parted way. Kevon held to the south end of the valley, while Waine struck out northwestward to the other side.

After several minutes, Kevon could no longer see Bertus or the camp behind him, and shortly thereafter he lost track of Waine through the sparse trees and other growth. The only sounds were the soft crunch of dry earth beneath his boots, and the occasional buzz of an insect.

Kevon suddenly felt out of his element. The glimmer of his magical reserves in his mind's eye, and the weight of the guard-issue shortsword at his hip were some comfort, but Kevon was used to the strength of his friendships helping carry him through his trials.

Once again, Kevon began to doubt himself. Granted, he'd accomplished things, but much of that had been luck, or trickery. In fair combat, he'd be no match for Waine or Carlo. He had few traditionally useful magical Arts mastered, and felt that his Blacksmithing apprenticeship had been rushed. The fact that he was able to do all three, as no one else could, still brought a smile to his face.

He kept walking, trying to be extra aware of his surroundings while ignoring the ache in his stomach. The sun burned high in the sky, but he pressed on. He could see the end of one of the foothills, and wanted to get a look at what lay beyond before turning back.

As he got closer, Kevon decided to climb over the ridge, rather than walk around the base. Halfway to his target destination, he stopped to rest and down the last few mouthfuls from his waterskin. Minutes later, Kevon reached the top of the ridge. He continued over far enough that he wouldn't be silhouetted on the ridgeline, and sat down to rest and survey this new section of landscape.

Between the brightness of the midday sun, and the choking dust that mingled with sweat to run into Kevon's eyes, he almost didn't see the cave entrance. It was half-covered behind a waist-high scrub brush, and looked like it could have been an animal den at one time.

The Warsmith hurried as quietly as he could to within a dozen yards of the entrance. He was alone, so he'd have to do this differently. Kevon envisioned the symbol for Light, and powered it up, focusing the energy into a small globe. Concentrating, he willed the sphere into the cave's mouth.

The glowing orb floated a few yards into the tunnel, illuminating the interior nicely. Kevon shifted his focus and directed the globe around the tunnel's bend.

Then the shrieking started.

Four imps flew around the corner to the cave mouth. The rear imp crashed into the rock wall and slumped to the ground. The remaining three screeched and flapped toward the entrance.

He dropped his Light spell and backpedaled while he formed the symbol for Fire in his mind. He felt the warmth of the afternoon sun beating down on him, and fed that into the rune with everything else he had. He shouted triumphantly as the rune blazed bright red, and flames rushed from his outstretched palm, incinerating the first two imp-demons and charring the third's wing and arm, sending it spinning to crash into the brush a few paces from him.

Out of magic, Kevon drew his sword and leaped at the wounded creature, slicing its head neatly from its body. He turned to enter the tunnel to dispatch the last imp, but it had started crawling back into the darkness, chittering. Other voices chattered back, and Kevon was not prepared to face any more of them, at least not by himself. He wiped his sword clean on a piece of cloth, returned it to its sheath, and immediately started back to the east.

The return trip was swifter, Kevon was not as intent on searching for caves as he had been on the way over. He kept replaying the battle over and over in his mind, impressed with how he'd done under pressure. If the cave needed cleaning out tomorrow, the three of them should have no problem handling the situation.

As Kevon got closer to the cave where he'd left Bertus, he noticed a plume of smoke coming from that direction. A sense of urgency welled up, and he began jogging.

Kevon settled into the pace, knowing he could hold it until he arrived back at the cave, but not sure if it would be fast enough. He concentrated on a Movement rune, which sprang to mind easily. He planned his focus, and leaned forward as he began to run. Kevon trickled pulses of magic into the rune as every footstep fell, amplifying the push-off with the spell, easing the physical exertion while doubling his speed. He factored in the distance to his goal, and estimated the physical and magical reserves he would have when he reached it.

Kevon redoubled his pace. His legs were devouring the distance at an alarming rate. After several near-misses with rocky outcroppings and snarls of brush, Kevon reduced his speed to where he felt comfortable that he would not misstep and fall, a delay now would certainly kill them all.

Minutes later, Kevon sped over a hillock that was the last obstacle that obscured his view of the campsite, and the source of the smoke.

Bertus crouched between two fire-filled trenches with makeshift smoking racks that looked as if they barely supported the enormous fish that they held. He heard Kevon coming down the hill, and turned in time to see the relieved Seeker nearly tumble as he ended his spell and shifted sideways to dig his boots into the rough earth and skid to a stop.

"How did you catch those?" Kevon asked, for a moment forgetting the panic of earlier. "I've never seen a fish that big."

"Crossbow." Bertus grimaced. "Snapped one of my bolts killing the second one, but I didn't know how long it would be before there was another chance like this."

The Seeker glanced nervously at the twin plumes of smoke that twined together, snaking up into the afternoon sky. Not only did he hope that there were none of the creatures of darkness that could tolerate light, but he also feared the company they'd left the day before. If Carlo and the others had been unable to travel in the early morning, they might be drawn to the fire, and that could ruin everything.

"Well, that's a relief," Waine called from a short distance away. "Now I don't have to go back and finish dragging that leaper's carcass the rest of the way here."

Kevon turned to watch the Adept's approach. As Waine walked back into camp, Kevon spotted bruises on his friend's face and neck, and could see that Waine was masking a limp. "Rough fight?" he asked the Adept, knowingly.

The Adept nodded, eyes closed. "The cave wouldn't have worked, anyway. The entrance is too big to block off or defend. We'd be better off burying ourselves in the open."

"We might have to do that once we start getting closer to the tower," Kevon agreed, "But the cave I found should work for tomorrow, at least. How many were there?" he asked, overcome with curiosity.

"Three that I saw," Waine answered. "And daylight makes them easier to kill, but just barely. Also," Waine grimaced and drew in a sharp breath. "They kick like horses."

"Those are some nice sized salmon," Waine added as he neared the fires. "It's been a while since I had any, they weren't running the last time we came through here." The Adept Warrior winced as he sat down on a nearby rock. "Bertus, you may have just saved our tails."

The Warsmith told his friends of the encounter he'd had with the imps, as they waited for the fish to finish cooking.

"Well, I'd rather fight imps than leapers," Waine said cheerfully. "And the cave you found should work even better than this one."

The others agreed, and the three sat and waited for dinner in relative silence.

Bertus carved up a third of the smaller salmon as the first long shadows of evening stretched to where they sat.

Kevon ate slowly, despite the severity of his hunger. He was unsure how long their food would last, even though Bertus' catch had more than doubled their provisions. Waine ate slowly also, but it appeared to Kevon that his friend's difficulty was in the swallowing of his food with bruised neck muscles. Bertus finished quickly, and after looking at the fish wistfully, began sectioning the rest of the food for storage.

There was little discussion. Tired, bruised, and almost adequately fed, Kevon and Waine covered up the traces of the cook-fires while Bertus hauled supplies back into the narrow cave. Once finished, all three worked to barricade themselves back into the fissure, and began trying to sleep.

CHAPTER 8

The Adept woke at the first hint of light, and roused the others. They quickly dismantled the makeshift doorway and transferred all of their belongings outside of the cave.

"The fires got dug up," Waine observed. "We'll have to be more careful about that."

Bertus passed out hunks of smoked fish, and repacked his bags as they ate.

Kevon finished eating first and walked over to where Bertus was sitting. He lifted the bags Bertus had just arranged, compared them to his own. Together, they were heavier. Kevon walked over and hefted the pack Waine had been carrying. The Adept's pack was also heavier than Kevon's.

"Bertus," Kevon began, "Would you carry my pack for a while?"

The youth shrugged. "Sure."

The Seeker shouldered Bertus' two bags with one arm, and held Waine's pack in the other. "All right, I'll see you in a while."

The runes from the spell he'd used the day before flared to life in Kevon's mind. He turned and sprinted out of camp, leaving his companions to their own pace. Familiar with the terrain, Kevon picked his path with more surety, avoiding spots that had slowed him before. He reached the last ridge before the cave with magic to spare. He dropped the bags by a shrub just under the ridgeline, and turned around, beginning the sprint back to his friends.

The Mage accelerated to the speed he felt most comfortable sustaining. Falling into the now-familiar rhythm, he smiled and allowed himself to enjoy the experience. He tried varying his technique, using more power in pulses to launch himself over medium-sized tangles of brush instead of going around them. The longer jumps saved Kevon some distance that he would have had to detour around. The lack of control from the increased interval between steps made Kevon nervous, so he returned to his previous pace.

If I get all of our supplies over to the cave, the others won't have to worry about packing them, Kevon thought. They'll get here faster, less worn out. I can wait there after this trip, and have full use of my magic before they arrive.

He rounded a hill and spotted Waine and Bertus a short distance away. He slowed, and sat down, waiting for them to reach him.

"Tired?" Bertus asked as they approached.

Kevon stood and shook his head. "Drained. Without magic, I could keep that pace up for about five seconds." He took his pack back from Bertus, and began walking alongside his friends. "In a few minutes, I'll be rested enough to run this back to drop with the rest of our things," Kevon explained. "You'll only have your weapons to worry about carrying, and by the time you reach the cave, I should be more than ready for a fight."

Kevon kept pace with them until they reached a tree that he had noticed before as about halfway between caves. With his full magic nearly restored, he focused on renewing his Movement spell.

"See you in a while."

The Seeker sprinted off toward their destination once more, elated to be running again. The amount of concentration the spell required began to frustrate Kevon, and he wished he'd been able to bring along his rod of Movement. He sighed, and swallowed a bug. Flustered, he stumbled to a stop. *I'm almost there anyway*, Kevon thought as he tried to clear his throat. *The other things should be just up-*

He dropped to the ground as soon as he spotted the orcs. *They won't see me...I can hide in the brush...* he thought hopefully. Then he saw the cloud of dust his passing had raised billowing over him.

The Mage stood as the orcs noticed the dust cloud.

The smaller scout shrieked and fumbled with a short bow as it backed away. The larger one spat out a mouthful of half-chewed fish and dropped the bag it was holding to pick up the cudgel that lay at its feet.

The scout loosed an arrow that fell harmlessly short, and turned to run.

Kevon sighed. The last thing he needed was this orc running off and bringing more. He concentrated, and expended the rest of his magic into a burst of flame that lanced out and caught the fleeing orc squarely in the back.

The larger orc looked over its shoulder at the squealing scout. It grunted, raised its cudgel, and began advancing toward Kevon.

Stupid. Kevon thought angrily. *I should have held something back for this.* Out of options, he drew his sword and waited for the orc to come closer.

As the orc approached, Kevon realized how much larger this one was than the smaller scouts he'd seen before. He stood only chest-high to the beast, who was only beginning to grow tusks. *Carlo's killed four that were bigger than this?* Kevon wondered as the young bull lunged the last dozen feet, swinging its cudgel high overhead.

Kevon surged forward and to the left, dragging his sword along the orc's ribcage with a solid two-handed grip. He spun away and leaped back, fearing a backswing from the orc's club that was easily twice as long as his sword.

The bull turned, hefting the cudgel again. It bellowed and stepped forward to swipe at Kevon once more.

He held his ground and the club whizzed past him. He

leapt in and swung at the hand that held the club, but missed. A chip spun away, gouged from just above the orc's handhold. Kevon grimaced at the damage he knew was done to the blade's sharpened edge.

The orc grunted and stepped to the right, reversing the club into a backhanded swing.

The Seeker ducked and rolled under the attack, sword slashing upward as he sprang to his feet, feeling the blade cut through the hide armor before glancing off of something more solid. He crouched to avoid the orc's follow-through punch, and sprang into a roll that put him behind the orc once again.

The orc howled with rage, whirling to face Kevon. It charged at him twice, with savage, sweeping attacks that the Seeker barely evaded.

As the orc rushed him for the third time in quick succession, Kevon noticed that it held its left arm tightly to its side. The effort seemed to slow, but not stop, the flow of greenish blood from a gash in the creature's underarm.

He's slowing down, Kevon thought. *I can outlast him.*

After a few more close calls, Kevon wasn't so sure. The running he'd done the last two days was starting to take its toll. His legs burned, and he struggled to keep his breathing under control.

Kevon could feel the fear rising as he grasped at possible options. Even though the orc was wounded, it might still overtake him if he tried to flee to rejoin his friends. He glanced over to the nearby cave entrance, wondering if the opening was too narrow for his large foe.

I can't take the chance, Kevon thought, dodging an overhand strike from the orc and landing a shallow gash to the front of its right leg. *If more imps are sleeping there...*

Kevon danced around another swing of the orc's cudgel, and darted inside for another swipe at his opponent's already wounded leg. His sword cut deep, slicing through muscle and tendon, sticking for a moment in bone. Kevon twisted the blade free and lunged aside to clear the range of the orc's weapon.

Too late... he thought, as the club struck him from behind, sending him sprawling toward the cave mouth. He could hear the orc's pained grunting behind him, but did not waste any effort looking back.

Twenty yards from the cave's entrance, Kevon started shouting as loudly as he could manage. The orc behind him raged in frustration. Kevon veered to the side just before he reached the opening, and instead bounded from a rock formation near the entrance to the lip of stone just above it. He scrambled up the steep hillside, grasping at weeds and rocks to speed his ascent.

Hoping he'd climbed far enough, Kevon turned around and leaned back against the hillside, bracing his feet on the ledge below him. His chest heaved as his lungs demanded more air than he'd been allowing them. Dust and sweat stung Kevon's eyes, obstructing his view.

The ledge Kevon stood on trembled as the orc snarled and slammed its club into the hillside below. Through the clearing dust, Kevon could see he was well out of reach, unless the orc decided to climb up after him. Kevon wiped his eyes and slowed his breathing, continuing to watch the wounded creature.

Blood stained the orc's whole left side below the lacerated arm. The orc kept glancing along the route Kevon had taken to get up the hill, but as the minutes dragged on, its shoulders sagged more; it showed no real interest in following Kevon up the steep embankment. Finally, it grunted and turned to walk away.

Kevon pitched a rock and hit the orc in the head. "Hey!" He called. "Come back here!"

The orc roared as loudly as it had when the battle was just beginning. It took two steps, and flung its club at Kevon. The weapon cartwheeled toward the stunned Seeker, and slammed into the hillside an arm's length above his head. The cudgel tumbled down, hitting Kevon in the shoulder and sword-arm, almost knocking him off the ledge. He shrugged the weapon off, and watched it fall the rest of the way down the hill.

The wounded bull dropped out of Kevon's vision for a moment. It reappeared with its recovered weapon in hand, growling.

Over the throaty rumble of the orc, Kevon heard another sound that made him smile.

The orc backed away as the shrill keening of the imps grew louder. At least five of the tiny demons swarmed out of their sheltering cave and began attacking. The orc waved his club, trying to fend them off, but his reactions were too slow. In seconds, the imps had torn the orc's face to bloody ribbons. Throwing its club down, the orc swatted at its face with both hands. Two of the imps fell, crushed by fists nearly as large as themselves.

The struggle lasted a dozen seconds. The imps that evaded the orc's flailing defenses fell to the midday sun. The orc staggered back, looking at the smoldering piles of ash, wiping weakly at its face. It slumped to the ground, using both arms to keep itself upright. It paid no attention to the blood still gushing freely from its side.

The Seeker began his cautious descent, watching the fallen orc as much as his footing. Before he was even halfway down, the orc moaned and fell backwards.

He hurried the rest of the way, and approached the still form with sword at the ready. The orc's eyes were already glazed over. He poked it in the side with the tip of his sword. Seeing no reaction, Kevon sheathed his sword, and walked up near the ridgeline to sit by the supplies and wait, watchful for more orcs.

It was nearly an hour before Kevon peeked over the ridge and spotted his friends. He stood and waved to them, motioning for them to hurry.

"What happened?" Bertus gasped as he reached Kevon just seconds after Waine. "That looks like orc blood…"

"It is," Waine said, eyes sweeping over the hillside. "How

many were there, and did any get away?"

The Warsmith shook his head. "Two of them, a bull and a scout. The scout was easy..." He pointed to where the smaller orc lay hidden in the brush. "The other..."

"How long ago?" Waine pressed.

"An hour, maybe more." Kevon answered.

Waine sighed. "We need to hide, and soon. I don't know how well the night creatures tolerate the orcs, but they're going to be a danger for at least three more hours."

"Imps don't care for them," Kevon offered, smiling. "And the cave may already be clear. I didn't check it yet."

The Adept drew his sword and hunting knife. "You're ready, right? Since this happened an hour ago?"

Kevon nodded and followed the Adept, preparing a Light spell as he walked.

"Watch our backs," Waine called back to Bertus, but the boy had already loaded his crossbow. The Adept crouched to enter the cave, and Kevon formed his Light spell a few yards ahead, near the bend in the tunnel. Hearing nothing, they pressed forward, and Kevon focused the light further into the passage.

The floor of the passageway, which had slanted uphill to the bend, now turned downward. Waine continued slowly ahead, almost able to stand upright.

The Seeker crept along behind Waine, listing to the left so he could see to direct his Light spell. They made their way around another bend, deeper into the mountainside. About ten yards later, the sphere of Light seemed to stop illuminating the tunnel walls. Kevon intensified his concentration, and the globe brightened, becoming painful to look at.

"Don't!" Waine hissed. "It's a..."

Wingbeats and shrieks punctuated the silence. Waine backed up, and Kevon softened his concentration and drew the floating orb back into the tunnel from the cavern beyond.

The first imp swooped into the tunnel, skimming the

upper right side of the opening, staying as far from the light as it could. Waine batted at the creature with the flat of his blade, then twisted his body to the left to dodge the flurry of wings and claws as he slashed downward at the tumbling imp.

Focusing on the Light spell, Kevon sidestepped and avoided the injured creature. He smiled as he heard the crunch of bones and a triumphant cry from Bertus.

The other two imps charged the tunnel a moment later. One took the same path as the first, high and to the right. The other came in lower, to the left. Waine swung high, his sword-tip glancing off the tunnel wall before biting into the rightmost imp's collarbone.

The imp to the left screeched and flapped, claws out-stretched toward Waine, who was trying to turn sideways in the center of the passage to avoid both creatures. The downbeat of the imp's wing passed through the Light sphere, scattering the rune in Kevon's mind.

Flames flared to life from the contact, throwing night-marish sweeping shadows along the length of the tunnel as the burning imp tumbled past Waine. The miniature demon crashed into Kevon's left shoulder even as the Mage turned and leaned to avoid it.

He refocused his will into another Light rune, emitting a stream of light from his outstretched palm to play over the thrashing creature.

Waine quickly dispatched the imp he'd struck with his sword, getting enough light from the blazing pyre the other one had become. "Kevon," he coughed, raising his arm to shield his eyes from the acrid fumes. "Enough!"

The Mage released the spell, and the companions looked over the scene by the dying flames of the charred imp. Waine edged out into the cavern and stood upright. "Is that all of them?"

The Seeker crept out of the tunnel and resumed his Light spell, shining his cone of light all around the large room. Several fissures extended outward, but nothing large enough to hide an imp or a leaper. Debris littered the floor, evidence of several previous inhabitants. What animal droppings there were seemed old; Kevon could not smell anything over the smoky tang of the burnt imp. "That's all." Kevon announced. "If you two will wait outside, I'll clean this place up."

The others exited, conversing quietly.

Kevon waited alone in the darkness until he could no longer hear his friends talking. He stilled his mind and envisioned the symbol for Wind. Picturing the Enhancement rune alongside it, he began infusing them both with power.

The Wind rune accepted the magic, haltingly at first. The air around Kevon began circling, picking up speed. Two revolutions and it whispered. Two more and it whistled. By the sixth cycle, the wind screamed and tore at his clothes. With the last of his will, Kevon directed the wind down the tunnel, along with all it carried.

His ears popped as the pressure in the underground chamber dropped. Sand and dirt from crevices above pattered down on him. Air rushed back in from the tunnel, and as the dust settled, Kevon took another breath.

Glimmers of light from above and the patch of sunlight from the bend in the tunnel allowed Kevon to make his way outside. He stepped out into the midday sun and stood up straight, stretching. Mounds of imp-flesh burned where they had been ejected from the cave. One, lodged under a bush, smoked heavily. Bertus took turns at trying to kick the carcass free and kicking sand at the flames that jumped up into the low fronds of the brush.

The Seeker looked around and spotted Waine up the hillside above the cave mouth, scanning the countryside. He left the Adept to his watching, and moved to help Bertus, who was starting to go through the supplies. The orcs had torn through half of the fish, which had to be discarded. The rest of the provisions were untouched, and none of the gear required more than minor repairs.

Waine met Kevon and Bertus back at the tunnel entrance when they reached it with their packs. "How will we secure this?" he asked. "There are no rocks nearby as there were yesterday." He paused to spit on the fallen orc's corpse. "Even if there were, they'd not be proof against orcs."

"I'll think of something," Kevon answered. His legs felt weak, and the orc baking in the afternoon sun turned his stomach. "I just need to rest, first."

The Warsmith walked into the cave, managing not to stagger until he was around the first bend in the tunnel and out of sight of his companions. He stumbled into the cavern and felt his way along the wall into a corner. He checked for sharp rocks and uncomfortable protrusions. Finding none, he settled into a fairly comfortable seated position before falling asleep.

Waine prodded at the corpse of the fallen bull orc. "The deep wounds are clean-cut," he explained to Bertus. "Kevon's sword. The tears on the face are shallow, nothing that could kill. This..." Waine kicked the arm up to expose the deep cut underneath. "...is what killed it." He thought a moment longer. "The imps attacked in panic. They don't normally prey on orcs, they can't kill them outright. That's why the orcs are still around, and people are not."

"We expected the night beasts," Bertus said, looking at the dead orc. "Now this? How are we supposed to make it...?"

"It's two days travel on horseback from here," Waine cut in. "With luck, we'll cross it in less than seven." He looked at Bertus for a minute. "Can we make it seven days?"

Bertus glanced over at the sack of provisions. "Three, four days at the most," he answered. "If I could get back to the stream..."

"No." Waine countered. "Stay with Kevon. Move everything inside. I'll be back soon." The Adept unslung his bow and checked his quiver. He winked at Bertus and stalked down toward the bottom of the valley.

Bertus roused Kevon when the first shadows of evening stretched across the cave mouth. "It's an hour until nightfall," he said, handing Kevon a piece of fish and a waterskin. "No sign of orcs, but no sign of Waine, either."

The Warsmith lowered the waterskin. "Where did he go?"

"Hunting, I think," Bertus answered, fidgeting. "I wanted to go to the stream for more fish, but he made me wait here. He should have been back already."

Kevon and Bertus left the near-dark of the cavern to sit outside and watch for Waine.

The later the hour grew, the more the knot in Kevon's stomach twisted. He could only imagine how Bertus must feel, the boy's concern had been growing for hours longer than his own.

The high scarlet clouds that streaked the sky above faded toward grey, and the first stars began twinkling. This was the nearest they had come to being exposed at full dark since the attack on the company, and the dropping temperature made Kevon shudder.

"We'd better get inside," Kevon said, finally. "We're not safe out here."

"But, Waine..." Bertus stammered.

"Can you think of anyone better suited to handle these conditions alone?" Kevon snapped, surprising himself. "He's out there, taking care of himself. He expects us to take care of ourselves. We can't risk it. Get inside."

The youth peered out into the gloom for a few moments longer. "You're right," he sniffed.

Kevon followed Bertus into the cave. Once they had gone a few feet inside, he turned and sat, facing out the entrance.

Kevon spread his hands apart to press his palms against the smooth stone walls. After a few deep breaths, he formed an Earth rune in his mind's eye, and touched it with power.

The rune glowed a deeper, richer brown than Kevon had ever seen while using it before. Acting slowly and deliberately with the elemental rune he was least familiar with, he sharpened his focus, and began bending the magic to his will. Kevon pushed his awareness into the ground beneath and around him, trying to determine its composition. He could tell immediately that he was surrounded by granite, apart from scattered imperfections in the makeup of the mountain. He felt deeper, where the stone groaned from heat rising from below. He spread his awareness wider through the earth, the magic deepening the further he opened to it. The soil whispered to him where the grasses' roots tugged from the breeze, ached at the freezing cold of the river further down in the valley.

The thunder of footsteps shocked him back to himself, wrenching the spell and the rune apart.

"What is it?" Bertus asked, and Kevon realized he'd gasped aloud.

"I..." Kevon began, "Felt footsteps. A lot of them." He re-energized the rune, and reached down with his mind, coaxing a column of stone from the mountain's roots below into rising. The earth rumbled, and a nearly smooth cylinder of rock shook its way upward, stopping only when it touched the ceiling.

He reluctantly pushed the power away, and his hands dropped to his sides. The spell had not drained Kevon as much as he thought it would, but the control required to focus the extra power flowing in from the mountain had nearly broken him. Exhausted, he recalled a time not so long ago, and not too far from here.

"Fire is easier to use when it's hot, Water when it's raining. It's rarely useful."

Kevon's friend, the Mage Pholos, had been right. He wondered if it would have been more difficult deeper in the mountain. He was in no hurry to find out.

The Seeker looked at the sides of the tunnel entrance, and after a brief inspection, decided the raised stone pillar would prevent even small imps from getting into their new sanctuary. He got to his feet and walked back toward the cavern, feeling the top and sides of the passage as he went, instead of trusting the feeble glimmer from the blocked entrance. He waited until he reached the large chamber before calling up his Light spell. When he powered the spell, the sphere shone dully, and rapidly consuming energy Kevon was already low on.

"Make yourself comfortable," Kevon suggested, as the light grew dimmer before vanishing completely.

CHAPTER 9

The Warsmith woke hours before dawn, too anxious to return to sleep. He called a dim sphere of light into being, and crept closer to the blocked off tunnel entrance. Nearing the magically raised pillar, he sat, turning sideways to brace his feet against one side of the passageway, propping his back against the other. After a few minutes of wriggling, he closed his eyes and tried to rest until dawn.

Twice, brief bouts of scratching on the stone snapped Kevon back to full alertness, but each time, the noise lasted only a few seconds before ending in a flurry of wingbeats.

At the first sign of light, Kevon went back to the cavern to wake Bertus.

"Is Waine?" Bertus gasped, startling awake.

"No." Kevon answered. "It's morning." He lit a torch with his Art, and handed it to his friend. "It's time to leave."

The Seeker went back down the tunnel, leaving Bertus to gather their belongings. Just short of the obstructed entrance, Kevon sat and reached out to touch the walls as he had the night before. Focusing intently, he trickled power into an Earth rune, and spread out his senses to the valley outside. He sensed no immediate danger, as he had before. Relieved, he shifted his attention back to the tunnel, and forced the stone pillar back down until it was flush with the floor of the cave.

He struggled to cut the power from the rune without losing control of the magic. Even as the spell concluded, the rune still tugged at the corner of his mind, as if it were insisting to be used. Kevon stood and hurried out of the cave, breathing deeply of the fresh morning air.

The scene outside was eerie. The spots where the orcs had fallen were trampled flat and picked clean. Kevon saw not a bit of blood or bone, but found a few fragments of torn cloth and leather.

Bertus walked up alongside Kevon and set the bags down on the ground. "They're eating *everything*..." he whispered. "Do you think...?"

"Waine's fine," Kevon said firmly, as much for himself as for Bertus. "We need to move, quickly. We don't know where the..." Kevon trailed off as he thought for a moment. "I need to check something." He walked back into the cave, and knelt just inside the entrance, a palm spread on the smooth stone floor.

The Mage pushed his will into an Earth rune, then instead of feeding it any more magic, concentrated on guiding the sympathetic energies that were collapsing in toward him from the surrounding mountain. He spread out his senses as he had done earlier, but widened them exponentially. Time stretched, and Kevon *became* the valley. He felt the sharp sting of the stream cutting its way down to the ocean. He felt the itch of a band of orcs miles distant, and fought back the cascade of power that tried to push its way into him to shrug them off. He felt a sickening, festering, *something* buried deep to the west, the portal at Gurlin's tower. Something large stirred, but before Kevon could sense any more detail, he felt a different spell probing at him. Kevon cried out, shoving at the influx of power from the mountain with all his might. The connection severed, he fumbled at the pouch around his neck, and touched the iron ring within, discharging the rest of his magic, leaving him feeling both vulnerable and safe.

The memory of the valley lingered even though the connection had been severed. He could guess what path the orcs would take, based on their heading and the surrounding terrain. If not for the night creatures, Kevon thought they could reach

Gurlin's tower in two days, if they headed straight for it instead of skirting around the valley for hiding places. He stared toward the north, where he thought the other magic had come from.

"*Mirsa.*" Kevon growled. "There's no one else. She's headed for the ruins."

"The Mage from…" Bertus began, "How do…"

"Someone close felt me using magic, and started looking for me." Kevon answered, rising and walking to where Bertus stood with their belongings. He waved his hand at his friend, showing the ring. "This should keep her from finding us directly, but we need to move. Now. We can't let her catch us here." He strapped on his swordbelt and knife, then hefted the bag of supplies that he was going to carry.

"Here," Bertus said, digging two small pieces of fish out of one of his sacks and handing one to Kevon. Bertus slung his crossbow's carrying strap over his head and a shoulder and shifted it a few times before picking up his bags and taking a bite of his fish. "Which way?" he asked between bites.

The Seeker pointed toward the northwest. "That way. And we're not going to rely on finding caves, we're going straight for it."

Bertus nodded and started off in the direction Kevon had indicated, without pause for concern or question. Kevon smiled and followed.

After a while, Kevon stepped around Bertus and began leading through the obstacles in the terrain. His memory of the valley was not as sharp as it had been earlier in the morning, but he could recall details fairly easily as they walked. Kevon had already chosen the point at which they would cross the stream, and shortly thereafter, they would be able to follow the road the rest of the way.

The Seeker walked, half-alert, but confident they would not have any trouble, at least today. The soft plodding of footsteps twined with the whisper of burlap across the tops of the tall grasses. The rhythmic noises would have lulled Kevon toward sleep had he not been so concerned with the task at hand, and the whereabouts of Waine.

A new sound grew, the rushing of water as they neared the stream. The path Kevon took led down to the water where it widened and slowed; there were places where the gravelly bottom was less than a foot deep.

Mildly annoyed with the prospect of getting wet, Kevon infused the Water and Control runes he'd been readying with power, and stepped down.

The water parted upstream and flowed around Kevon and Bertus, creating an eye-shaped space where the rock-strewn streambed was merely damp. The phenomenon traveled with them, the water gurgling loudly as it splashed back together downstream.

Near the center, where the water deepened, the spell became easier to maintain. Kevon felt a flicker of awareness expanding, much as he had the first night he'd used Earth magic in the cave. Opening himself up to it, he could taste the differences in the types of earth the water ran through. Upstream, he tasted fish, and with a flick of power, formed a geyser that spurted a large salmon in a glittering arc over the far bank to land in the high grass. Bertus's laugh so close to his ear shook Kevon's concentration, and water splashed his boots.

The Mage refocused and resumed his walk across the stream. They climbed out on the far bank, and Bertus laughed again.

"Maybe you should go get the fish," Kevon snapped.

The boy started over to where the salmon still flopped wildly. "Maybe you should take your ring off if you want to use magic," he called over his shoulder.

Kevon glanced down to where the ring shone dully on his right hand. "I..." he said, weakly. He was still unable to speak when Bertus returned with the subdued fish. He tried to fathom why this time had been different, but could not think of anything. "Why now?" he wondered aloud.

"Well," Bertus began as he crouched near the stream to clean the fish. "You did forget you were even wearing it."

"Could it be that simple?" Kevon formed a Fire rune, and summoned a flame into his upturned palm. "No," he commented. "That's not it."

Bertus continued cutting. "Now that you know you can do it, there might not be any problem with it anymore."

He considered Bertus's words. Could the simple act of conquering one's fear of metal, and having faith in the magic be all it took? The possibility excited and scared Kevon. If it were true, it made him vastly more powerful, and a bigger threat to Warriors and Magi alike. Being able to handle a sword like he used a practice blade…

The Seeker reached to the sword at his side, and felt the magic jolt out of him at the first touch. He sighed. "It's just the ring," he grumbled.

Bertus nodded, and finished filleting the salmon. "I guess that means I'll have to start the fire, then."

Kevon ignored the jibe and collected some dry branches from under a nearby tree. Before he returned, Bertus had already cleared the area of grass and dug a shallow pit.

Soon the fish was sizzling over a nearly smokeless fire, supported by slender green branches that Kevon had helped Bertus arrange over the pit. The method was much faster than Bertus had used on the previous catch, and was intended for immediate consumption, rather than long term storage.

Kevon wandered up toward the road, which he knew was less than a quarter mile distant. He topped a small hillock and scanned the valley. He was not surprised when he saw only trees and grass, given the impression from his spell earlier. Curious, Kevon knelt and spread his palm on a patch of bare stone. He focused, and an Earth rune sprang easily to mind. He directed his senses downward, but only got a vague sense of the immediate area before his magic was depleted.

Kevon had felt only the slightest influx of magic from

his contact with the stone. He worried that his plan might not work, that he had brought Bertus with him to die once night fell.

I just touched the sword... He thought, nearly laughing as a sense of relief washed over him. *I'll be able to do more once I've recovered.*

Kevon returned to the firepit just as Bertus was finishing the cooking. Bertus pulled the fish off the flames to cool, and Kevon pushed dirt back in on the pit, choking the fire out with a minimum amount of smoke.

"If we follow the road for another three hours," Kevon said, rinsing his hands in the stream, "We'll be halfway from the cave to the ruins. "That will give us plenty of daylight for me to prepare our shelter."

"I was starting to wonder about that," Bertus admitted. "No caves around here."

Kevon smiled. There were three caves within easy walking distance, he knew exactly where from his survey this morning. However, he was in no mood to fight for them. "Something that Waine said a few days ago... that we'd be better off burying ourselves in the open," He stopped short as Bertus sighed and rubbed at his eyes.

"I think I can do a little better than that. Once I get down a little deeper, I'll try to make an underground cave that they couldn't get into." Kevon patted Bertus on the shoulder, and added, "Waine's probably already waiting for us at the ruins. Wondering what's taking us so long, and getting sick of orc-jerky."

"And wearing leaper-hide trousers," Bertus added, smiling.

"Right." Kevon chuckled. "So we've got some catching up to do." Spirits only slightly lifted, Kevon hefted his share of the supplies and resumed the march northwestward, bearing more west than before. This path would intersect the road later on than their previous heading, but would find them considerably further when they stopped.

"There," Kevon said, some three hours later, wiping his brow and pausing to drink from a waterskin. He pointed up the road to the few standing remnants of the Tower that could be seen from a distance. Two sections stood opposing each other, looking ominously like horns peeking over the crest of the hill ahead.

"So that's where all of these things are coming from?" Bertus asked.

"I certainly hope so," Kevon answered, drawing a sideways glance from his young friend. "If it's not there, or if it isn't just a Portal to the Dark Realm, we did all of this for nothing," he explained. "It's strange to think that I'm hoping this turns out to be the worst possible thing I can think of, because it may be the only thing we can deal with."

They walked a while longer, until Kevon spoke again.

"This should be far enough," he said, gazing at the broken tower in the distance. "If we start early tomorrow, we should reach the ruins not much after midday. I suppose that's the best time to deal with such things."

The Seeker set down his share of the supplies and walked down to the stream to refill his waterskins. Bertus followed with fish, berries, and some bread that Kevon hadn't known they still had.

They ate silently, watching the sun slide closer to the mountains that lay beyond the ruins.

At last, Kevon sighed. "Are you ready?" he asked Bertus.

Bertus turned and relieved himself on a bush, then washed his hands and face in the stream. "I am now," He headed back up to the road where they'd left their belongings.

Kevon returned to the road a few minutes later, but crossed without stopping to pick anything up. He formed an Earth rune, and wandered around a small area until he felt a mental tug from below. Kevon bent down and scooped away handfuls of dirt until he exposed the bare rock below. He cleared an area about three feet in diameter before stopping to rest.

"What now?" Bertus asked uncertainly from behind Kevon.

"I'm not sure how well this will work," Kevon admitted. "Just wait, and watch. You'll know as soon as I do."

Kevon crouched in the center of the cleared slab, hands pressing against the still cool stone. The Earth rune formed easily, and Kevon could feel the latent magic lurking below, trickling slowly upward toward his spell. He willed the stone downward.

With a low grinding noise, the cleared area began sinking slowly, freed from the rock surrounding it. As Kevon descended further into the stone cylinder, he could feel the Earth magic pressing in on him. Twenty feet below the surface, he stopped, and shifted focus. Stone and earth rippled, protesting, forming a staircase that led away from Kevon, back up to the surface near Bertus. The larger opening to the sky and remaining daylight seemed to ease the crush of Earth magic, and Kevon severed the rune from the inflowing power.

"You can come down now," he called up to Bertus, "Or you can wait a few minutes."

Bertus started down the rough stone steps as Kevon began the next phase of his spell that pressed the cylindrical walls outward. The earth groaned from the strain, and Bertus hurried back up the trembling staircase. "I'll wait!" He shouted back down to Kevon.

Lost in the Earth magic, Kevon heard nothing but the cries of the stones as he turned their magic against them, squeezing them into places they didn't belong. The smooth walls surrounding Kevon crumpled outward, groaning in protest. Kevon gripped the cascading power tighter, and the walls and floor rippled and smoothed. Already the area he'd carved out was larger than the inside of his mother's house. Kevon gasped and *pushed* mentally, as hard as he would have to cast a spell when he was an Apprentice. This time, however, he was pushing against power that flowed into him against his will. Kevon tried again, and this time, severed the influx of magic. The Earth rune faded, but would not dissolve completely from his mind.

"Is it over?" Bertus called, poking his head over the edge to peer down the stairwell at Kevon.

"I've done as much as I can, until you get down here."

Bertus took two trips to bring their belongings down to the bottom of the chamber. Carrying bags in one hand, he trailed his other along the wall, more for comfort than support. "So now you're going to…"

The Mage didn't even let Bertus finish before he grasped the Earth magic again, and the walls and ceiling flowed and shifted to close the gap above them. The rumbling of the sculpted earth above them subsided, but still the magic pressed in on Kevon. Uncomfortable with the total darkness of the sealed chamber, he directed small pulses of power to open thin shafts to the surface, letting in air and a small amount of light.

The magic continued to weigh on Kevon, the pressure on his mind clouding his senses, threatening to use itself through him.

Thinking only of a way to make it stop, Kevon reached for his sword hilt.

The Seeker's magical resources, nearly full because of the borrowed power he'd used, drained into the blade. The pressure from the surrounding magic trying to squeeze into him recoiled. His sword arm burned for an instant before the backlash of Earth power knocked him unconscious.

Kevon woke in a cold sweat, wrapped in a blanket, head propped up on one of the supply bags. His right arm tingled as if half asleep, and ached sharply when he tried to move it. His head throbbed, waves of pain washed over him with every pulse beat. Kevon groaned, and the room brightened. A face swam into his blurred vision, and resolved as he forced himself to focus.

Mirsa smirked. "Good," she chuckled. "You're awake."

CHAPTER 10

K evon startled into a sitting position, gathering the Earth magic that surrounded him, readying it to strike out at Mirsa.

"Well, now," Waine said, stepping into view. "He *is* alive."

The Journeyman gritted his teeth and fought to stifle the magic raging through him.

Mirsa's smirk softened into a smile, rather than the concern Kevon expected, considering the Earth power he'd nearly unleashed on her.

"What's she..." Kevon stammered, wresting the Earth magic back to its silent waiting in his mind's eye. "How?" he asked, sighing.

"I wanted to handle this on my own," Mirsa began, "But the Prince simply wouldn't allow it." Her lips curled into a more familiar sneer. "As if he could have stopped me."

The Adept reached over and lay his hand on the curve of Mirsa's shoulder by her neck, and rubbed gently. Her eyes narrowed and the smile returned.

"Well," she continued, "I could have traveled like this, in safety the entire way, if not for the military escort. I couldn't abandon them, either, knowing what I did about the Portal. When you three left, and the company turned back, I took my leave of them.

"And followed us?" Kevon asked.

Mirsa shook her head. "I assumed you were dead," she answered. "Had I thought otherwise, the steel you bore would have made finding you nearly impossible."

Kevon scratched his head with his left hand. "But you found Waine, right?"

Mirsa and Waine both laughed, and exchanged glances.

"The day you last saw me, I went looking for food. I found orcs." Waine moved closer, eyes dancing in the Mage-light as he eased into the storytelling. "Two scouts raised the alarm. I missed spotting them in the high grass, but killed them both before they could bend their bows. Three bulls burst from a nearby copse, followed by two more scouts. I wounded two of the bulls, slowing them so that I could circle wide and draw them off to the northeast. I ran, stopping only to fire an arrow at the nearest orc when I could afford the delay."

Waine paused and accepted a stone mug from Mirsa, and drank deeply. "I felled the last scout with only two arrows left. The two smaller bulls had slowed considerably, but the larger one was steadily gaining ground. Between its hide and armor, I'd been unable to damage it."

"I ran until the other orcs were no longer visible in the distance, then turned to wait for the bull. I fired an arrow as it charged into range, but it struck the thick leather on the beast's chest, only to be slapped aside as a nuisance. Then, I nocked my last arrow, and waited."

Bertus was wholly entranced by Waine's story, straining silently forward, eager to hear more. Kevon's mind listened to only fragments of the tale, focusing instead on the way Waine and Mirsa were behaving toward each other, and trying to guess the events that had unfolded leading up to the present situation.

"I waited until I knew I couldn't miss," Waine continued. "The arrow sank up to the fletching in the bull's neck, but it didn't miss a step. I cast aside my bow and drew my sword, hoping for a sign of weakness in the next few steps before it reached me. I saw none. It charged at me, swinging a club the size of Bertus like it was a willow switch. I ducked the attack and sprang in close, to try and hamstring it. I slashed out as we passed each other, striking at an exposed part of its leg." Waine sighed. "It was like chopping at a walnut tree. The blade stuck. The next step the bull took wrenched the blade free, but not before yanking me far enough with it to lose my footing, and fall flat on my back. I recovered before the orc turned, and that's when I saw the arrow had done more than it appeared to at first. Blood oozed out from around the buried shaft, and the orc coughed once before charging at me again. I slid around to the side as it attacked, and once I was clear of the weapon, I started running again, knowing the orc couldn't last too much longer with that wound. It chased me another quarter mile before stopping. It turned to look for the other two bulls before squaring off against me again. I spotted one of the other bulls approaching in the distance. I knew I could outlast the big one, if he was by himself. But now he was waiting for help, and that made him far more dangerous. I knew then that I had to..."

"Waine..." Mirsa whispered.

"Then I killed all three orcs, and wound up sleeping under their piled corpses because I was too tired to do anything else," Waine summarized with a glare of mild annoyance.

"I came upon the remains the next morning, and followed in the direction the tracks indicated," Mirsa added. "He wasn't going very fast... It was easy to catch up with him."

"I told her most of what we knew, and she confirmed our suspicions, and more." Waine continued. "Then I got cleaned up, and we needed to escape the midday heat, so we spent a few hours... talking."

Mirsa grimaced, jabbing at Waine with an elbow. She focused on Kevon. "One of the things we eventually discussed was *you*. Waine seems convinced of your virtue, but in light of all that has happened, I have doubts about many... myself included."

"What do you need to know?" Kevon asked.

"Tell me everything, beginning with Holten."

Kevon told Mirsa of his apprenticeship in Laston, how he

had progressed, how Holten had trained him. He recounted the incident in the woods, where the then nameless Warrior had been killed by the bear, and how he himself had been spared. When the tale reached the revelation that Kevon's Master had betrayed him, sending him to his death, Mirsa's demeanor softened. Her eyes darted about the room from time to time, as though she sought answers in the far corners.

Mirsa's gaze locked on Kevon when he told of meeting Pholos 'ap Tarska along with Waine on their first journey to Gurlin's tower. She sat quietly, rarely even blinking, as the story drew inevitably toward Gurlin's assassination at Kevon's hand, and the subsequent destruction of her former classmates.

The Warsmith continued, detailing their travel afterward, through Navlia, West and East Thaddington, and finally south to the mines on the frontier.

The Master Mage's eyes were glassy, and she seemed to not hear what Kevon said, but he kept talking, unsure of how she would react when he stopped.

He spoke of Waine's visit to the smithy, and the beginning of their trek north. When Kevon told of the news he'd received of the deaths of Marelle and Rhulcan, Mirsa gasped softly, and seemed to return to herself.

Tears welled up in her eyes, and she clasped Waine's hand. "Such a power should only be entrusted to one like him."

The Adept nodded, and brushed a tear from Mirsa's eye.

Mirsa sniffed. "There is so much you need to know before we attack the ruins tomorrow. I thought that I was..." She breathed deeply for a few moments before resuming. "The source of my pride, what made me feel so self-important, the secret good we were all doing... Was all a lie. Pholos and the brothers, they knew nothing of our 'duty'. Only Shofud and I, though he may have known the whole truth."

"About the portal?" Kevon asked.

"The portal is only half of the problem," Mirsa whispered. "The Orclord is the other."

"Orclord?" Bertus asked, eyes widening in fear. "They're just legends, aren't they? How could there be one…"

"The caverns beneath the tower are vast, and had been partially created with Earth magic." Mirsa answered. "The portal lies across a great chamber where most magic will not work. The only thing that held the creatures of darkness back was a magical barrier at the edge of the chamber, a shield of Enchantment woven with Light and Wind. We Keepers…" Mirsa paused as though the word left a bad taste in her mouth. "We were charged with renewing the enchantment regularly, to keep all of the creatures, especially the Orclord, at bay." Mirsa sighed. "It must have been Gurlin's intent to unleash it at some point, and if we can't contain or destroy it, not even death will have stopped him."

No one spoke for a time.

"I'm sorry about your classmates," Kevon offered. "If there had been any other way…"

"I did not care enough for them when they were alive," Mirsa whispered. "I'm not sure if I should mourn them more, or less, because of that. I… Don't…"

Waine took Mirsa by the shoulder and pulled her to him. She wept softly into his chest. After a moment, he spoke.

"Enough talk for today. This is a dismal end to an onerous quest, and I for one could use some rest. We can plan in the morning." Waine led Mirsa to the far end of the underground chamber, and without sound, the walls flowed inward from the sides and divided the halves completely.

Bertus exhaled deeply. "Glad that's over," he said, grinning. His eyes widened as he continued. "When she tore into this place, she was ready to kill you. Seeing you holding your sword didn't help much either. She and Waine argued for almost a half hour, like old married folk. Then, I had to drag you the whole time we walked. This floor is not easy on the feet. I see now why she didn't take the whole company underground with her. I trust magic more than most, but the last few days have been trying."

Kevon frowned. He tried to recall how many times he'd almost been killed in the last few weeks, but events had blurred together in his mind. He knew the road ahead held no less danger, but he found he was eager to face it so that he could move beyond it. *Just like last time, two years ago,* he thought. *We're all that's left of those that were there when the tower fell, come back to finish the job.* Kevon looked at Bertus, thinking how alike he and Pholos were, excepting magical aptitude. He fervently hoped Bertus would fare better.

"We'd better get some rest, too." Kevon said, rearranging his things.

The boy grinned in the direction of the wall that had closed between them and the others, but nodded and settled in for the night.

◆ ◆ ◆

"Excuse me," Kevon said, peering at the eye behind the barely opened door. "I was wondering if you know..."

"I don't know anything." came the gruff answer, and the door started to close.

"But they told me..."

"They told you wrong!" the man growled louder, slamming the door.

Kevon pounded on the door in frustration. He'd come so far, following any clue he and the others could find. Five Guildhalls, countless taverns, and half a season later, he'd been led here. "They said he might have been your son," Kevon groaned in exasperation.

The door creaked back open, and the eye returned, studying Kevon more intently this time.

"What did you say?" the man asked Kevon after a short silence.

"Your son," Kevon answered. "I've come halfway across

the Realm searching for anyone who knows about the bearer of this sword." He drew the weapon from its scabbard and rested it on his left arm, presenting it for inspection.

The man inside had to open the door further to get a good look, as Kevon had intended. Strands of unkempt hair hung across half the man's face, partially concealing his scraggly facial hair.

Despite the man's haggard appearance, Kevon recognized the resemblance immediately. The fallen Warrior's face was etched forever in his mind. Nearly a year ago, Kevon had stood over the Novice Warrior and watched him die, unable to do anything for his terrible wounds.

"How did he die, then?" the man asked sullenly.

"He was killed by a bear," Kevon replied. "I managed to frighten it away, and spoke with him before..."

The Warrior's father nodded, and gestured for Kevon to enter. Kevon sheathed the sword and followed the man inside.

The room was sparsely furnished, even more so than Kevon was used to since he'd joined the Warrior's Guild. A table and two roughly-hewn chairs sat near the center of the small chamber, offset toward the fireplace. A single plate with knife and fork sat, still needing to be cleared from the last meal. Other than that, the room's only other contents were a suit of hardened leather armor and a scabbarded sword, piled haphazardly in the corner, thick with dust.

The man grunted and pushed the plate to the side of the table and sat down. "How far did he get?" he asked. "Where did you find him?"

"In the North Valley, near Laston."

The man sat forward, and for the first time Kevon could see, appeared interested. "And how did you come to be there?" he asked, almost urgently.

"It is... rather, was... my home. I grew up there."

"He must have been close..." the man whispered, eyes darting back and forth, as if remembering things long forgotten.

"You! You lived there for years before...had anyone suspicious arrived in the year you met my son?"

Kevon's jaw tensed. "A Wizard," he began, "The only new-comer I can remember. Holten Magus."

"I don't know the name," the man said, pushing back from the table and rising to his feet. "Wait here a moment." He stepped into the other room for a minute, and returned with a rolled parchment. The Warrior's father held the scroll out to Kevon. "Is this him?"

The hair on the back of Kevon's neck stood on end. Had the Warrior been seeking Kevon's former Master? It would explain the Wizard's sudden departure, his odd behavior when he learned of the Warrior's death.

Kevon carefully unrolled the parchment, studying it for a minute before sighing.

"What do *you* want with him?"

CHAPTER 11

Kevon woke drenched in sweat, despite the chill air of the underground chamber. Besides his dream of the meeting with Delmer, father of the slain Warrior Melwin, other memories and twisted visions had crowded his sleep. Rosy remembrances of his time with Marelle had given way to nightmarish scenes of burning caravans circled over by carrion birds. Lectures and lessons with Holten spun about, winding up on high walls above a raging battlefield, blinking back crimson light from a rift in the sky.

He sat upright, taking a deep breath. The movement stirred dust motes that swirled in two shafts of light, brightening the darkness by a shade. He stood and moved into one of the beams, feeling its miniscule warmth play on his skin before forming a Light rune to illuminate the room.

The image in his mind resonated with three other Light runes that poked at the edge of his awareness. Curious, he fed them power, and three orbs burst into dazzling radiance.

He released the spell, but the three glowing globes shone on after the power stopped.

Bertus stirred, sprawled across the stairway on the far side of the chamber.

"Good morning," Kevon offered, smiling.

Bertus nodded, eyes still mostly closed. He yawned and stumbled to the washbasin that seemed to grow out of the floor and wall behind it.

The Seeker followed Bertus, and examined the basin as his friend washed up. Water sluiced in from an opening in the wall, down a gentle slope bordered by low sidewalls. The water filled the inner ring of a double basin, before spilling into the outer basin through a notch near the top of the rim separating the two. Water overflowing into the outer basin flowed around both sides to disappear in the back, underneath the ramp that fed the water in the first place. Kevon whistled appreciatively.

The youth nodded. "She said she's done this quite a few times. It didn't look like it was any effort at all."

Kevon remembered the apparent ease with which Mirsa had closed off the other end of the chamber, without even a sound. When Bertus finished, he washed up, then drank a few handfuls of water scooped from the inlet above the basin. He leaned over it and formed Earth and Water runes to examine the construct more closely. He swept his senses about, and traced the inflow of water through a sandy channel that cut directly over from the river nearby. He followed the outgoing water as it drained straight down into an underground lake.

Behind them, even though he could not hear it, he sensed the dividing wall flowing apart. He felt footsteps entering the near side of the chamber before he heard the voices. Kevon pushed the runes aside in his mind and turned to greet Waine and Mirsa.

"Good morning," Kevon offered, nodding to Waine.

"Sun's up, we're still breathing," Waine agreed.

"For now," Mirsa added darkly. "The path to the Tower and the surrounding valley is clear, as far as I can discern. The Tower itself, I cannot say for sure." Mirsa frowned, continuing. "It appears that the corruption has spread. The Elements are of no use below ground, any closer to the Tower. I can feel the weakening even here. We will not be able to create shelters as we have been."

"Will that change any of our other plans, then?" queried Bertus. "With your magical abilities reduced, I mean."

Mirsa's haughty glare returned briefly before melting into understanding. "I suppose these two would understand as much as any uninitiated, traveling with you," she said, glancing toward Kevon. "I don't know," she confessed, looking uncharacteristically unsettled. "I haven't felt this useless since I was a Novice."

"That's why we're here," Bertus said, handing her a strip of cured fish. "You're an amazing addition to our little band, but no one expects you to carry us through our mission." Bertus finished doling out provisions, and the companions ate quietly.

"There's obviously a way in, if creatures are getting out," Mirsa said, finally. "It's just a matter of finding the passage and navigating it safely." She frowned. "Without elemental magic, it might prove difficult."

Bertus chuckled. "Difficult, perhaps. With these two..." he pointed to Waine and Kevon, "Interesting would be a better word."

The Wizard nodded. "I've been wrapped up in the Arts for so long, I feel unable to judge what can be accomplished without them." She ruffled Bertus' hair. "Wisdom springs unexpectedly."

Bertus and the Warriors collected their gear, and Mirsa opened up the stairway to the surface. Waine and Kevon led the way out, and Mirsa brought up the rear, closing their temporary sanctuary behind her.

The midmorning sun climbed steadily, following the four as they neared the ruins of the tower. A mile or so from their destination, Mirsa slowed, and after a few more steps, stopped completely.

"The corruption worsens here," she announced, closing her eyes. "It's not as complete as it was beneath the Tower, so I may still be of some use before we reach the Barrier."

They resumed their trek toward the shattered tower, and before long, Kevon could feel the effects that Mirsa had spoken of. It was as if a part of his magic, and with it, part of his spirit, had been drained away. Each step required more willpower to take than the last, each heartbeat in his chest felt a little more hollow. He glanced at Mirsa, who continued on, expressionless, perhaps a shade paler than normal. Kevon clenched his jaw and trudged ahead, heartened that their journey was reaching its conclusion, but as weary as he'd ever been.

A fly buzzed around Kevon's face, and he swatted at it before realizing it was the first one he'd seen in over a week. Another fly circled the group, and flew back in the direction of the tower. The wind shifted, and Kevon suddenly smelled something that made him forget about the wrongness in his head.

Waine and Bertus groaned in disgust, Mirsa dropped to her knees and vomited. Kevon followed Waine's lead and tore a strip of cloth from his tunic to fasten around his head to cover his nose.

"What is that?" Kevon asked after a few mouthfuls of air.

"Death," Waine answered, helping Mirsa to her feet. "Old death."

The four pressed on, and at a quarter-mile distant from the tower, entered the marsh. The road dipped into a brackish pond, and Waine guided them around the edge, boots squishing loudly in the mud.

They quickly abandoned the fragments of road, navigating back to them was more time-consuming than the few yards of clear travel was worth. Instead, their winding path took them across most of the drier high spots, as well as slogging through some of the shallower bogs. Only once did Waine make them turn around and retrace their steps because the way ahead was too deep to cross.

The flies seemed to grow thicker with each passing yard. Kevon was unsure if they were converging on the party, or if they just swarmed thicker nearer the tower. Twice, he had to spit out flies he'd inadvertently inhaled, and he finally resorted to breathing through his nose again, doubly thankful now for the masking cloth.

At last, they reached the drawbridge. It seemed the only part of the entire structure untouched by the foulness that surrounded the tower. Broken timbers and refuse clogged the moat, which seemed to be the source of the marsh.

Waine advanced cautiously, sword drawn. Bertus followed with his crossbow readied, edging to the side to get a better view of what lie ahead. Mirsa stumbled forward, and Kevon resisted the urge to steady her, wary of the iron in his ring and the steel at his hip.

The Mage fell to her knees, nearly pitching off the side of the bridge, face inches from the fetid water. She gasped, and scrambled backward, eyes wide with horror.

Kevon looked closer at the twisted twigs that protruded from the littered moat, and spotted a fingernail hanging from the end of one. Realization flooded over Kevon as he swept his gaze across the landscape with newly opened eyes. The mossy rock he'd nearly stepped on before reaching the drawbridge had a shriveled edge of an ear exposed.

Kevon's eyes darted about. Now every crooked branch was a knee or elbow, every splintered plank a sun-bleached bone. Disgusted, he turned back to the bridge, and Mirsa's trembling form.

"It's going to be all right," Kevon assured her, extending his left hand to help, keeping his left hip pivoted away to distance the Mage from the sword.

Mirsa smiled weakly as she retook her feet. She turned to the entrance that Waine and Bertus had already passed through. "I'm sure that…"

"Kevon!" called Bertus. The young man's cry was punctuated by the muted twang of his crossbow firing.

The Seeker stepped around Mirsa and advanced, keeping himself between her and the threshold to the ruins. He stalked forward, the runes for Light, Movement, and Illusion forming in his mind while his hand hovered inches from his sword-hilt. He passed through the broken arch and saw Bertus crouched behind a boulder, reloading his bow.

The Adept stood nearby, scanning the jumbled terrain.

"Get down!" Bertus hissed, peering over the rock. "They're..."

"Not going to hit us, at this range anyway?" Waine asked. "That's what you were going to say, I assume."

Two small orcs leaped from behind a standing slab of wall embedded in the middle of the courtyard. They screeched and fired their bows wildly before jumping back behind their cover. One arrow glanced off a rock twenty yards ahead of the party, the other landed ten yards farther back.

Waine sighed. "Take your time, we have range and position on them," he explained as the orcs jumped out for another shot. "Unless..."

A young bull orc stepped into view around the slab, flinching back as Bertus' bolt toppled one of the scouts.

"Unless *that*." Waine groaned. "I didn't really want to..."

Kevon paid no attention to the Adept's complaints, as he dropped the Illusion and Light runes to focus on aiding the Movement rune he felt Mirsa beginning to use. He felt the power build, then release suddenly as the slab toppled over on the orcs that hid behind it.

Nearly a dozen orcs scrambled out into the open, less than eager to share the fate of their brethren. Kevon gaped as a female orc herded five children away from the party, leaving three scouts, one young male, and the largest Bull Kevon had yet seen.

Kevon felt the magic build again. "Mirsa, no!" he barked. "Keep watch behind us."

The Mage's spell ebbed as Kevon poured power into his own, hurling three medium-sized boulders at the old Bull before his reserves gave out.

"I'll take the other one, then," Waine snickered, flourished his sword, and stalked over toward his target. Bertus felled one of the scouts with a crossbow bolt and started reloading.

The Warsmith grasped the hilt of his sword. Mirsa's sharp

intake of breath made him smile, and as he drew the blade, he turned to nod at her before advancing toward the Bull.

Waine reached his adversary first. The beast howled in rage and brandished a rusted longsword. "Are you sure you don't want to use that club there instead?" Waine taunted, pointing at the nearby weapon with the tip of his blade.

The orc ignored Waine's suggestion and charged, slashing wildly. The Adept parried one of the swings and whirled past, almost successful in his attempt at hamstringing his foe.

What the orc lacked in finesse, it made up for in strength and natural speed. It turned to face Waine, sword transferred to its left hand, already slashing. Waine rolled under the attack and leaned in close as he regained his feet, trying to disembowel the orc. He ducked the orc's right cross, kicking at the already bloodied right leg to leap away.

The orc grunted and flung the sword at Waine, and the flat glanced off the Adept's ribs, slowing his recovery. Seeing its opportunity, the unarmed orc charged at Waine. Two steps away from tackling the Warrior, the orc hesitated, back arching. The brief pause gave Waine the moment he needed to finish the disemboweling stroke and leaped to the side.

The beast crumpled to the ground where Waine had been, a feathered bolt shaft buried in its back.

"Help Kevon!" Bertus shouted, scampering around the corner of a boulder to shield himself from the remaining scout, who was well within bowshot range by now.

Bertus readied the crossbow again, arms shaking from exhaustion as much as fear. He peeked over the boulder to look for the scout. Seeing nothing, he stepped out to get a better look.

The orc fired its last arrow from ten yards away, striking Bertus in the left side below his ribcage. The youth's reflexively triggered shot caromed off the boulder he had been using for cover. The bolt wobbled in midair and stuck into the ground halfway to the orc.

The small scout shrieked gleefully, cast aside its bow, and

drew a long, cruel looking knife as it leapt forward to finish its prey.

Bertus clutched at the shaft of the arrow with his left hand, and fumbled for his knife with his right. He backpedaled to buy a few seconds more to prepare, but it looked like it was not going to matter.

The orc leapt atop the boulder that had sheltered Bertus, and sprang high into the air.

Bertus drew his knife free of its sheath, and took two more pained steps back to avoid being landed on.

The scout landed, and lunged forward.

It fell, flat on its face, legs tangled in a tree branch that Bertus could not remember stepping over.

Bertus fell forward, pinning the orc's arms down with his knees. He plunged his knife into the creature's back and twisted until the struggling stopped. He pulled the knife free and wiped the blade on the orc's tattered leather as he rolled gingerly off into a seated position.

The youth grunted in pain and frustration as he heard the sounds of continuing battle behind him. He sheathed his knife and had just begun checking his wound when Mirsa reached him.

"It's deep," she mused. "Too deep to pull out." The Mage knelt and eased Bertus onto his back before turning him to the side, tracing her finger along the protruding arrowhead. "This will hurt,"

With a swift motion, she pushed the arrow through and broke off the end before drawing the stone tip and the rest of the shaft out of the exit wound. Mirsa placed Bertus's hands over the bleeding wounds before standing and looking toward the last orc still alive in the courtyard.

Kevon and Waine had the bull on the defensive, but the pace of the conflict was starting to slow. The Warriors circled and darted several more times before they separated themselves enough for Mirsa to unleash the spell she'd been preparing.

The arrow-shaft Mirsa held sped from her hands to strike the bull squarely between the shoulder blades. The orc bellowed and reached back to try and pull out the arrow that pained him so. It clawed at the spot the arrow had entered, but the broken shaft was buried completely.

Kevon and Waine reacted the moment the orc's guard was down, slipping inside its reach, and cutting swiftly at the brute's neck.

The orc lunged forward, flailing ineffectively. The Warriors stepped aside as it fell. It gurgled, twitched, and was still.

The Warriors hurried over to where Mirsa knelt by Bertus.

"Bind his wound, quickly!" the Mage commanded, tearing a strip of cloth from her robe, and handing it to Waine. She grabbed at Kevon's shoulder. "Come with me!" she snapped.

Kevon followed Mirsa deeper into the broken tower, alert for danger, but crawling over broken walls and rotting timbers where his sword would be less than useless, had he even time to draw it. Mirsa muttered to herself, climbing over obstacles seemingly at random, until they arrived at a mound Kevon could not distinguish from several others around it.

"What're you..."

"Wait!" Mirsa scolded, closing her eyes.

Kevon formed an Aid rune in his mind and offered what little power he'd regained in the short time since the fight. He felt the energy drain away over the next few seconds, and Mirsa gasped.

"Here!" she cried, rushing to the rubble and straining to lift a timber that jutted out of the pile.

Kevon took hold of the beam and nudged the Mage aside so that he would have room to lift properly. His muscles were weary from the encounter and the climbing, but the wood groaned and creaked upwards, levering aside a slab of stone. The rubble shifted, and several smaller chunks tumbled into the opening where the slab had been. Kevon heard a hollow *crack*.

Mirsa gasped and rushed to the opening, thrusting her hands in, oblivious of Kevon still straining to keep the slab from sliding back into place. She carefully withdrew a cracked bowl, half full of liquid.

Spent, Kevon dropped the beam and sat down. "All that for a bowl of..." Kevon got a closer look, and then understood. The bowl was too rounded, a few of the jagged edges curved back over the top. It was, instead, half of a potion bottle. *A healing potion.*

Kevon climbed to a safe spot, and Mirsa handed him the broken bottle. She climbed around him and down, and he handed the delicate vessel back. The two repeated this process carefully until they reached open ground, only once spilling a few drops of the precious liquid.

Kevon hurried across the last few yards with the remains of the potion. Bertus coughed and his breath rasped softly in his windpipe. Flecks of blood-tinged foam hung at the corners of the youth's mouth.

"Drink," Kevon directed his friend, holding the broken vessel to Bertus' lips. Bertus choked down half the liquid between coughing fits, then as the potion started to take effect, swallowed the rest.

A few minutes later, when Bertus' breathing had eased somewhat, Mirsa spoke.

"We need to hurry," the Mage said, pressing the back of her hand to Bertus' forehead. "He's not feverish yet, and we don't want to leave him out here in the open." Mirsa stood and looked around. "The entrance to the passage should be right over there," she gestured. "It has to be open, as many orcs and other creatures as we have seen. Maybe there is someplace nearer the passage he can rest safely."

Kevon and Waine helped Bertus to his feet, and supported him as he limped after Mirsa.

The entrance was not difficult to find. It was a shallow

pit with a rounded stairwell leading down into darkness. Kevon and Waine helped Bertus over to a mound of rubble where the injured youth could lean back against a slab of stone and watch the stairway, yet still stay partly concealed. Waine loaded Bertus' crossbow and handed it to him.

"Keep quiet, stay alert," Waine ordered softly. "This shouldn't take long."

Bertus smiled and nodded, grin giving way to grimace as he shifted to try and get more comfortable. "Good luck."

Waine led the way down to the stairway through the refuse-strewn pit. He took one more sweeping glance around the wreckage of the tower, drew his sword, and started downward.

The Master Mage followed. She called two small globes of Light into being, directed one in front of Waine, and one between herself and Kevon.

The Warsmith lingered, watching Bertus until the others were nearly out of sight. He made his way down, following with his sword sheathed. He navigated by the dim light from above and ahead. He refrained from using magic, even to aid Mirsa's spell that danced at the edge of his awareness.

The first hundred yards down the stairwell was difficult to navigate. The passageway, untended and exposed to the elements, had collected mud and debris between steps. The result was a steep, mucky slope that threatened to pull the boots off the adventurers' feet. The few places the steps angled out from the mud seemed more treacherous than not. The party moved as silently as they could manage, though Kevon thought he could hear soft exclamations of disgust coming from Mirsa ahead.

Further on, the stairs were not mired as heavily. Kevon scraped clumps of mud from his boots against one of the steps, wanting nothing to disturb his footing.

Ahead of Waine, an orb in a torch-like sconce began glowing, and Mirsa ended her spells as they neared the new light source. Every twenty paces, a small pulse of magic to another orb lit the way down the twisted passage, and faded as they passed far enough beyond the magical torches.

At last, the stairs ended and the path straightened into a hallway that extended far ahead into the darkness. Kevon followed Waine and Mirsa down the passage, passing three orb-lights that Mirsa did not activate. Instead, they forged ahead in the dim light of the last lit orb they had passed.

"Almost there," Mirsa whispered, as they closed ranks in the deepening gloom. "The tunnel opens up just ahead, and the barrier is perhaps five paces beyond."

Kevon could feel the barrier in his mind, an extremely weak pulsing of Light and Movement. "Shouldn't we be able to see it?" he whispered ahead to Mirsa.

"It must be further than I remember," she answered in hushed tones. "I don't..." Mirsa stumbled over a rock and tumbled, crying out.

Kevon stepped forward to help the Mage, and felt the breeze and heard the hollow rasping as something crowded the hall ahead.

Waine screamed, something Kevon had never heard the Adept do before. The cry seemed to lurch down the passage, as the rasping noise intensified and receded. Waine's voice fell suddenly silent. A thunderous bellow shook the hall around Kevon.

"No..." Mirsa whispered as the rumbling subsided. "NOOOO!"

Lights along the passageway flared to painful brilliance as the Mage pushed away from Kevon to charge ahead. Waine was nowhere to be seen.

Kevon recovered and sprinted after her. Mirsa's headlong rush was faster than Kevon had expected. He compensated with magic, focusing a Movement rune to speed himself ahead.

Kevon reached the entrance to the cavern mere steps behind Mirsa. She screamed in rage, and magical torches flanking the end of the passage flashed to their fullest illumination.

The huge figure standing before them raised its left hand

to shield its eyes, Waine's limp form clutched in its right. The Orclord took a step back and shook its head before unceremoniously biting Waine in half.

"Waine!" Mirsa cried, runes flickering through her mind so furiously that Kevon could feel them. "Back!" the Master Mage shouted, directing a Movement rune at the huge orc.

Kevon wheezed as his magic flowed into the spell, unoffered.

The Orclord rocked backwards from the force, stepping back to keep its balance.

Mirsa moved forward to where a ribbon of softly shimmering light wavered up out of the floor. She knelt, grasping at it, and focused. The scarcely-visible fragment blossomed upward, spreading to cover the whole end of the cavern. Mirsa slumped to the floor, sobbing.

The light from the orb-torches dimmed back to a reasonable level. The orc lowered the arm that had been shielding its eyes from the glare, and saw the restored barrier.

"Will that hold it?" Kevon asked shakily, still numb from the events of the previous moments.

Mirsa curled in on herself, rocking back and forth, oblivious.

The orc crouched and leapt at the shimmering veil.

CHAPTER 12

"**W**ake up!" Mirsa snapped, shaking Kevon back to awareness. "You've got to help me!"

The ground shuddered and chips of rock pelted them from above. The Orclord rained thunderous fists into the dimming barrier. Rings of distorted light spread like waves in a pond from each impact before diffusing into the dull glow of the magical shield.

"The barrier won't hold, I don't have the strength," Mirsa sobbed, trembling.

"What do I need to do?"

Mirsa took Kevon's hand and pressed it up against the arcane shield, and the runes sprang into his mind.

Kevon closed his eyes to focus, and let his magic flow into the runes until they glowed painfully in his mind. He broke contact with the magical construct, and opened his eyes.

The barrier outshone the torches behind Kevon, illuminating the entire cavern. "How long will this last?" he asked.

Mirsa shrugged. "Half a season? We used to renew it weekly to this strength. At least the creatures of darkness should subside for a time."

"Why don't we stop them permanently?" Kevon asked, gesturing at the carved stone archway at the far end of the cavern.

Mirsa shook her head. "Master Gurlin tried for years..." She stopped. "No, he didn't. But..." the Mage sighed, exasperated. "Elemental magic is useless here. If the portal were closer, we might be able to damage it with a Movement-hurled stone. If we had more Magi, we could focus the light from the orb-torches to try and overwhelm the Dark enchantment. Aside from that…"

The Orclord lowered its face to their level, tusks as thick as Kevon's waist scraping and sparking against the barrier. It stuffed the remnants of Waine's corpse into its mouth and chewed loudly, laughing every few moments.

Mirsa retched.

Kevon helped her up and into the mouth of the passage-way, further away from the taunting behemoth. He crouched by her, and studied the situation.

The orc paced along the barrier twice, then retreated to the shadowy back end of the cavern. It sat down near the portal's alcove, leaned back against the wall, and appeared to doze.

Minutes later, three leapers bounded through the portal. The Orclord's hand shot out and snagged two of them. He wolfed them down before standing to follow the third one over to the barrier, cornering it for an easy capture. The orc stared at Kevon and Mirsa as it chewed its latest prize.

Kevon's breath caught as inspiration struck. "I know how we're going to kill it." he announced, rising to his feet. "Not just yet, though. Will you be all right here while I check on Bertus?" he asked Mirsa.

She nodded and leaned back against the wall, gazing blankly at the Orclord, who paced the barrier once again.

Kevon strode down the hallway toward the stairs, keeping the way ahead lit with effortless application of Light runes to the orb torches. He ascended the stairs with ease, falling into the familiar gait that had carried him around the North Valley his entire life.

That could have been me, leading the way down that tunnel, Kevon thought suddenly. The shock and realization that his friend was really *gone* caused him to misstep in the muck near the top of the stairs. His ankle wrenched in his stuck boot, and he twisted and fell against the wall. He breathed deeply, and squeezed his eyes shut to fight back the tears that threatened to surface.

After a few moments, Kevon calmed himself and regained his footing, treading carefully until he was sure his ankle was not damaged. Daylight brightened the stairwell ahead, and he squinted as he emerged into the full force of mid-afternoon.

Bertus sat where they had left him, and lowered his crossbow as he recognized Kevon. Color had returned to the youth's face, and he breathed easily.

"How bad is it down there?" Bertus called as Kevon approached.

The Seeker's insides twisted as he searched for the right words to tell Bertus about the loss of Waine. "You're feeling better, then?" he asked, eyes lowered.

"It's Waine, isn't it?" Bertus said, rather than questioning. "You would be upset if something happened to Mirsa, but you would have spoken up."

Kevon nodded, lifting his gaze to rest upon the brave front Bertus was maintaining.

"Is Mirsa all right?" Bertus asked.

"She's not injured," Kevon began, "But I don't know that she's all right."

The youth took a deep breath, wincing only slightly as his lungs filled to capacity. He stood and hobbled around in a small circle before sitting back down. "The healing has slowed," he commented, "But it hasn't stopped. With a little more rest I should be able to travel well enough to get us clear of this place before dark." After a moment, he added, "Will you?"

The Warsmith clapped Bertus on the shoulder. "We won't be long." He turned and began his descent back to the cavern, and Mirsa.

◆ ◆ ◆

The Master Mage was much as Kevon had left her, leaning back against the wall, knees clasped tightly to her chest, face buried in her robes. She ignored the Orclord as it pounded on the barrier and howled, but startled at Kevon's hand on her shoulder.

"I'm sorry," Kevon began. "Are you somewhat rested, at least?"

Mirsa turned red-rimmed eyes toward Kevon, and nodded once before climbing to her feet.

He took Mirsa's hand and led her to the barrier by the orc's feet. He smiled as he released her, and crouched, leaning into the magical shield. "Waine would have loved this," he chuckled. "Be ready, but stay very still."

She gave Kevon a puzzled look, but imitated his stance, and stilled her own movements.

The Seeker stayed frozen in place for several moments, analyzing the possible reactions the Orclord might have to his next move. Mirsa's Aid rune glimmered in his mind's eye, and after a deep breath, he began.

The entire back wall of the cavern slid back a dozen feet, or appeared to, covered by an extensive illusion. Mirsa startled as illusions of herself and Kevon melted through the barrier and darted between the Orclord's legs.

The orc turned and swept a huge hand down to sweep up the apparitions, which danced nimbly aside, splitting up to divide its attention.

Kevon dropped the illusion he'd thrown over himself and Mirsa as soon as the orc's back was turned, and focused on maintaining the fleeing figures and the false cavern wall. Runes of Illusion and Enhancement formed alongside Mirsa's Aid rune, and Kevon drew more deeply on the Master Mage's deeper reserves through the newly stabilized glyphs.

The phantom figures leaped and rolled, crisscrossing to and fro, just out of reach of the increasingly frustrated Orclord. Kevon poured more magic into the spell, and the illusions jeered at every missed grab, every dodged stomp, and in moments the pursuing orc was seething with rage.

The illusions raced toward the relative safety of the alcove containing the Dark portal, but just before it, the Mirsa-Illusion tripped on a stone and fell, hard. The Kevon-Illusion rushed to her side, and strained to lift her, to pull her to their destination, no more than a dozen feet away...

The Orclord roared with glee as he aimed a crushing blow to snuff out the pitiful humans before they could escape. His fist crashed into the stone arch that framed the Dark portal, concealed just behind Kevon's illusion.

A backlash of broken magic thundered through Kevon, akin to the sudden surges he'd felt when killing Gurlin, and when the armory in the ruins above had exploded, but more powerful than both of them combined. His vision blurred, and the runes in his mind shattered, ending his spell abruptly.

The portal, visible now that the concealing illusion was gone, pulsed slowly. Kevon could feel the gateway drawing on the residual energy from the broken enchantment. Power intended to keep the rift open indefinitely saturated the area, and even unfocused, fed back into the darkness. The light seemed to dim with every beat of Kevon's heart, and the boundaries of the portal expanded visibly each time the muted light returned.

The Orclord retreated to the barrier, leaving the shattered fragments of the broken arch to be devoured by the expanding darkness.

Waves of terror and despair washed over Kevon, and he dropped to his knees, his mind reeling at the depravity of the Dark rune. He clutched at his stomach and dropped to his hands, gagging.

The void grew to fill half the chamber, and the light of the barrier began to dim. The Orclord resumed pounding on the magical shield, more desperately than before. Kevon managed to pull Mirsa's limp form a few feet toward the exit tunnel before the fear overwhelmed him. He draped an arm protectively over the unconscious Mage, and collapsed beside her.

Kevon turned his head to watch the expanding darkness, a last gesture of defiance. The gloom deepened, sharpened, and he could sense a focused malevolence, as if they were being watched from inside the portal.

The orc halted his attack on the fading barrier, and turned to watch the darkness.

The expanding portal slowed, and appeared to stop. The crushing feeling of despair shifted, leaving Kevon able to sit up and think clearly. Angry sounding whispers issued from the darkness, and the Orclord began taking halting steps toward the sound.

The magical shield brightened as the Dark magic permeating the area began to wane. The black portal began to contract, and the whispering became louder, more urgent. The orc lengthened its strides, reaching out for the subsiding gateway.

The darkness elongated, stretching to meet the giant orc as an immense clawed hand. The Orclord howled and leapt back. The darkness snaked back into the portal, but bulged again in the semblance of a twisted face. The eyes, emptier than even the portal itself, swept around and locked on Kevon and Mirsa.

The whispering shrilled in Kevon's ears, nameless runes assailed his mind in tempo with the quavering of the barrier. The Dark rune found its way into Kevon's center of attention, solidified, and began leeching magic out of him. The whispers faded to occasional soft hisses as the portal swelled again.

Kevon could see the Orclord cowering out of the corner of his eye, huddled against the Light barrier. His attention was mostly divided between the Dark magic that was invading his mind, and the figure that he sensed, more often than glimpsed, in the dark gateway he was now fueling.

A foot, indistinguishable from the darkness except for the bluish-black sheen of polished chitin, stomped out of the portal, cracking the cavern floor where it impacted. Most of a leg, and the arm that had attempted to breach the gate earlier appeared, marking the creature as more than twice the size of the Orclord.

Knowing that such a being crossing into the world would be far worse than anything they had yet experienced, Kevon reached for his sword-hilt and nullified his magic. The sudden outrush of what remained of his reserves was more than his strained mind could bear.

The nightmarish limbs drew back inside the collapsing portal. The warped face pressed forward again, neck and shoulders squeezing outward into the world, screeching wordless curses that twisted reality. The collapsing portal constricted until the being was forced to retreat. Still, from just inside the heart of the void, eyes black as Death watched Kevon's unconscious form until the gateway closed completely.

"Kevon," Mirsa said, gently shaking his shoulder. "It's over. You did it. We need to get moving."

The Warrior rolled to his side and propped himself up to a sitting position. His head spun, and his vision blurred even in the light of the fully renewed barrier. A muffled snarling came from the other end of the cavern, and as Kevon's sight cleared, he could see the sprawled form of the Orclord near the broken fragments of gateway at the rear of the chamber. The beast snored, obviously less disturbed than Kevon or Mirsa about recent events.

He stood, still watching the sleeping orc. "So, that's it? We just leave it here to starve?"

The Mage nodded. "I may have to return once or twice to refresh the shield, so that nothing wanders in, but, yes."

"I thought it would take something more... *heroic*... to defeat an Orclord," Kevon mused.

Mirsa gazed at Kevon with empty eyes. "Heroes die," she responded, and turned to walk down the hallway.

The Seeker watched the sleeping orc for a minute longer, then followed Mirsa up to the surface. He emerged from the stairwell first, to find Bertus pacing. The youth was obviously in better condition than when Kevon had seen him last.

"Well?" Bertus asked expectantly as he met Kevon and Mirsa at the edge of the depression surrounding the stairwell. "It's finished, then? I felt *something* happen a while ago."

"The portal is destroyed," Kevon answered. "The Or-clord... is trapped, cut off. It will starve before long."

"I'd rather it were dead," Bertus said, knuckles whitening on the grip of his crossbow.

"I know." Kevon grimaced. He had spent the walk up the passage thinking of ways to slay the beast, without the use of elemental magic, through the barrier. Nothing had come to mind. "We need to get clear of this place so that we can set up a place to rest," he continued, starting toward the broken tower's entrance. "The sun is still high enough..."

The Warsmith's foot caught on some debris from the rubble pile he'd walked by, and he stumbled, hopping twice to catch his balance. He turned to curse at the protruding fragment of bookshelf, and stopped to stare at it.

Memories of the battle following Gurlin's death here years before rushed in on Kevon. He could see the broken wall and shelves being torn from the weakened structure of the inner tower. He fought the urge to duck as the fragment whirled across the courtyard, guided by his friend, the Mage Pholos.

The twins got it started, Kevon thought, grimacing. Pholos just diverted it. And, he had a focal rod...

"We'll return to Navlia," Kevon said suddenly. "Then we come back to finish this."

The three made their way through the bog lands surrounding the ruins, taking a more direct route in the interest of time, wading more, and staying watchful while they remained within the area of corrupted magic.

While the sun still hung safely above the mountains to

the west, Mirsa called a halt.

"We've come far enough, I can't feel any lessening of magic here." Without waiting for comment from her companions, the Master Wizard stepped down the stone stairs that sunk into the road before her.

CHAPTER 13

Kevon, Mirsa, and Bertus reached Navlia as the first snow of the season sputtered fitfully from a small patch of dark clouds overhead. Darkness was falling, but the three were eager to sleep in beds for the first time in nearly a season.

The Seeker's appreciation of Mirsa's magical abilities had only grown with time. The Master Wizard had done all of the preparations for shelters on the return trip, ranging from elaborate to stark depending on her mood. The two times they had encountered orcs, Mirsa had forced stairwells down, for escape, Kevon had thought at first. But moments later, with sufficient latent Earth magic gathered, Mirsa had drawn the beasts down into the ground, entombing them without a struggle. She still remained aloof, her greatest outward concern was for Bertus's nearly fully-healed wound.

Guards at the western gate spotted the trio from a sizeable distance, and sent out a wagon to retrieve them as soon as they recognized Mirsa's black robes.

"We're expected, I trust?" Mirsa quipped as the wagon, flanked by riders, turned sharply in front of them.

"Mirsa Magus!" A herald cried from horseback, coughing as the dust of their swift approach washed over him. "Prince Alacrit requests an audience with you immediately!"

Mirsa continued walking until she was a few paces from the herald's mount. "My friends and I," she began, "Will bathe, change, and meet the Prince for a late supper."

The herald's eyes widened, but Mirsa's narrowed, and he

spun his horse around, lashed it with the reins, and galloped back toward the city gates. Attendants helped the three adventurers into the wagon, and followed the herald at a more reasonable pace. Torches flared to life on the city walls as darkness settled in. Archers and Mages were visible on the parapets, clustered together, watchful of the deepening night.

"The attacks have spread this far?" Bertus asked over the rumbling of the wagon. No one answered.

The city gates remained open wide until the wagon passed through, but began closing as soon as the escorted conveyance was clear. The wagon and surrounding riders sped up, the only traffic on the eerily empty streets.

The gates to the Palace lay open, the herald that had greeted them waited fretfully in the torchlight, neck craning to scan the sky. As they approached, he wheeled his mount around and led them through the outer courtyard, under raised portcullises and other layers of castle defenses.

The wagon circled as wide as it could in the innermost courtyard before the Palace, and stopped near the entrance. Servants spilled out of the palace gates, and jostled to help Mirsa down.

"Attend to these two, then bring them to me." Mirsa ordered before marching into the palace, with several servants rushing after.

Kevon and Bertus helped themselves down from the vehicle, glad to be on solid ground after the wild ride over the cobbled streets. The royal attendants led them inside, up curling marble staircases to the guest quarters, where baths were drawn and waiting. They washed quickly, ignoring the cries of their travel-weary bodies to linger longer in the nearly scalding tubs.

Dressed in borrowed finery, they were shepherded down the hallways, deeper into the building, until they reached Mirsa's quarters. The head attendant rapped knuckles on the silver-trimmed oaken door, and whispered to the servant who cracked open the door a moment later.

"Bring them in!" Mirsa snapped, already annoyed at the overprotective fawning of the servants. "If they were going to try anything, it would have been weeks ago, on the road, not here, surrounded by soldiers."

The door opened and they were ushered into a large room lined with bookcases, filled with tables and sculptures, except for one corner near the fireplace, where a small bed, chair, and low table stacked with books huddled cozily together.

"Relax for a moment," Mirsa called from the adjacent room. "I'll be done shortly."

Kevon scanned the bookshelves for interesting looking titles, noting that all of the books involving magic were confined to the shelf nearest Mirsa's bed. Histories, almanacs, and exhaustive reports on all manner of subjects took up the bulk of the other shelves. Kevon plucked one at random, and opened it.

The Griffin, once thought to be a myth, is now considered by some scholars to be a real, albeit extinct, creature. Kevon frowned and continued reading. Bones found in caves on the Spire Islands to the south of Kærtis are the primary evidence for this. Bones that appear to be from either large eagles or lions, but too large for either, have been found among other broken bones that would seem to be the creature's prey.

Kevon closed the book and returned it to the shelf as Mirsa entered the room, and his breath caught as he saw her. She wore a simply cut dress of deep, shimmering violet, her Mage's rank evident only in the mid-length black cape that hung off her shoulders. Her hair was a complex mixture of braids, ringlets, and unbound straight lengths that exposed most of her neckline.

Suddenly aware that both he and Bertus were staring, Kevon cleared his throat. "Shall we go?"

Mirsa nodded and swept past them. "We should have any resources we require by the end of dinner," she commented demurely.

The Seeker followed, conflicted by his appreciation of Mirsa's attire, and thoughts of Marelle and Waine.

The Mage's retinue swarmed around and ushered them down to a large dining chamber, where Carlo and three other men sat at a long table laden with food. Mirsa walked over and sat across from Carlo, at the right hand of the man who could only be Alacrit 'ip Kært. Kevon and Bertus were seated next to Carlo, across from two wizened older men, one who Kevon recognized as a royal advisor.

"Briltor Magus," Mirsa whispered, clasping the hand of the remaining stranger. "It has been years. You must tell me what you have been about."

Carlo blanched at the Wizard's name, but shifted his attention to Kevon. "Where is Waine?" he asked. "I'd think he wouldn't miss this for..."

Kevon shook his head. "He fell, at the heart of the blight. He and Mirsa helped us get there, and what we accomplished should stem the attacks."

"The creatures have ranged this far, at least." The Prince spoke for the first time. "Their incursions have been swift, and savage, but to hear the returned members of Carlo's company, nothing like what they experienced on the road."

Mirsa turned and addressed Alacrit. "The wisest course of action would be to send groups to seek out nests during the day. The source of the invasion has been stanched, but they may still breed here. The other matter still remains to be..."

"Need we spread alarm with this?" Kevon interrupted. "You said that it could be dealt with..."

"I shall have the Commander gather intelligence and send out patrols." The Prince announced, nodding toward Carlo. "As to alarming news from the west, what could be so grievous? We already cower indoors at night, and are more watchful during the day than we ever were in wartime."

"Perhaps it is best if this were handled quietly," Mirsa agreed, glaring toward Kevon. "We ask only a day or two to rest and prepare, then we shall take our leave."

"… And?" Alacrit asked, bewildered. "What troops will you require? What supplies? Surely…"

"I require nothing but my Art, and the company of my two friends," Mirsa replied, placing her hand over the prince's. "Together, we stopped the flow of demons into Kærtis. I trust them as no others."

"If I might suggest," Kevon interrupted, "Perhaps it would be best if we had more military experience with us. There may be a need for an extra sword," he said, looking at Carlo.

"Commander, if you would assign a detail to…"

"Many pardons, my Prince," Carlo interjected, "But I will not risk any more men on this foolishness. I'll see these three back to whatever light-forsaken task they wish, and will have answers for you when we return."

"And who will direct our forces here?" the Prince asked, his gaze drifting back to Mirsa.

"Blademaster Marco arrived this past week, and has been staying at the Guild," Carlo answered. "He came looking for adventure. He's capable enough, and spoiling for a fight. Marco would enjoy organizing patrols and hunting parties, not as much as leading them, but I daresay he'll be doing that too."

The Blademaster cleared his throat. "Besides, I think I'm *ready* for this mission, *ready* for some real answers."

Bertus fidgeted, looking away, but Kevon nodded in agreement.

"We would welcome the Blademaster, it's more than we could have hoped for," Kevon agreed. "Thank you, your highness, Commander."

"Nonsense," Alacrit countered. "It appears that we should be thanking you."

Kevon lowered his gaze. "There are others who have given far more to this cause than I…"

The Prince raised his goblet. "Here's to them that have given their all, in service to the Realm, and to Men. Please, no more business. Feast, celebrate, enjoy the rewards that honorable service affords."

I'm not sure how cleaning up a mess I helped make counts as 'honorable service', Kevon thought as he speared a slice of roasted pheasant to put on his plate. *But I am hungry.* The low conversation and bustle of the hovering servants reminded him of the last time he'd feasted with Carlo, before he'd met Waine. Kevon's world had only begun becoming complicated then, he'd had only a vague notion of the evil that lurked ahead. Unlike that night so long ago, there was no singing, and Kevon drank sparingly, wanting nothing to dull the proper mourning he finally allowed himself for Waine, and to some extent, for Marelle and Rhulcan.

Mirsa chatted with Briltor Magus, the younger Master seemed to enjoy being considered an equal to her former mentor. Not wanting to appear too interested in the conversation between the Wizards, Kevon turned to Carlo.

"How did the Company fare after we left?" he asked the Blademaster

"We lost two more men the following night," Carlo answered, "And a third died of his wounds a week later. It seemed that we outran them, then the attacks started in the city five days ago." Carlo's eyes narrowed. "How did you three make it through?"

"Underground. It…" Kevon chuckled at Carlo's puzzled look. "You'll see. It'll be easier that way."

Kevon focused on his food for a while as Bertus chatted over him to Carlo. He could tell from the Commander's attitude that he had not read the letter that he'd been given before they parted. *I wonder what made him change his mind.*

"A Blademaster, a Master Wizard, and you two…" The Prince said, looking at Kevon and Bertus. "How do you two fit into this?"

The talk around the table murmured to a halt.

Kevon cleared his throat. "Bertus is an excellent cook…

And me?" He struggled for words. "Things… just happen to me. I deal with them."

"Ahh… Like the hero Adnoros, from the fables…" Prince Alacrit mused.

Kevon shook his head, frowning. "I'm not familiar with it."

"An average man, he brought together the mighty and the wise to accomplish great deeds." the Prince pronounced, raising his goblet to Kevon. "May you fare… better than he."

Kevon raised his cup and drank. "This Adnoros sounds interesting. What befell him?"

"Having neither great strength, nor dealings in the ways of the wise, he only managed to garner their cooperation in times of extreme need…" Alacrit said, eyes twinkling. "At all other times, they conspired against each other, and against him. His death marked the beginning of the Wars of Man."

With the other races subdued, Men turned on each other, Kevon thought. *They may turn on me before I have the chance to make things right.* "I shall do my best to gather my own strength, and listen closely to the counsel of all, to avoid such a fate."

"Spoken like royalty," the Prince murmured. "I look forward to your return."

Taking one last draught of his wine, the Prince pushed back his chair and stood. "Stay, eat, be refreshed. I must retire, but will see you off as you leave." With that, he turned and strode away, deeper into the palace, guards appearing in the hallway to escort him away.

Bertus elbowed Kevon in the ribs. "*Average…*" he whispered, grinning.

Kevon shot Bertus a chilling glance, and the youth turned his attention back to his plate. He ate his fill, and pushed his plate away. Bertus finished minutes later.

"If you will excuse us," Carlo said, standing and addressing the Magi and the other remaining Advisor.

Mirsa nodded, and resumed her chat with Briltor Magus.

The Blademaster led Kevon and Bertus down through the labyrinthine stairs and halls to the barracks, and showed them to a room where their belongings were already waiting. "If we can make arrangements quick enough, we'll leave morning after tomorrow," he commented as he started to leave.

"The letter..." Kevon asked, sticking his foot out to stop the closing door.

"The last man to read one of your letters... ended badly." The Blademaster shrugged. "I threw it in the fire."

CHAPTER 14

Kevon woke later than usual, and lingered in bed until his conscience overrode his weary bones. The borrowed clothing from the previous night was nowhere to be seen, and a uniform much like the one Carlo was wearing lay folded on the table. Kevon dressed, taking his time to make sure the uniform was presentable, before he opened the door.

"Good morning, Sir," a young cadet greeted Kevon, saluting sharply. "If you will follow me, the ceremony at the Guild will begin shortly."

Unsure of what the guardsman meant, but sure it was something Carlo had planned, Kevon nodded and fell into step without question. They marched down the narrow hallways and out to the stables, where two saddled horses waited. Moments later, they were outside the palace compound, slowing their mounts to a canter to compensate for the bustle of the midmorning streets.

After a brief ride, the two dismounted in front of the Warrior's Guild, and handed the horses over to waiting grooms. The young guardsmen rapped on the door, and he and Kevon were ushered inside.

The common room was filled, nearly every seat was taken, and groups stood in the open spaces, talking quietly. As raucous as Kevon had seen this bunch, the lack of noise was more unsettling than the unusual number gathered. The guardsman Kevon followed headed toward the back corner of the room, where a small stage rose no more than a foot above the rest of the floor.

Through the crowd, Kevon spotted Carlo as they neared the stage. Carlo saw him a few seconds later, grabbed a nearby subordinate by the shoulder, pointed first at Kevon, and then toward a nearby hallway. A hush seemed to spread throughout the already subdued room, and Carlo cleared his voice to speak.

"We are here today to honor a brother," the Blademaster began, pausing for murmurs of assent. "A welcome addition to any Guildhall he happened to find himself in, not one for ceremony or fuss, but always eager to share his ale, or yours, over a story or two."

"Waine, like several others recently, gave his life in the attempt to stop the tide of evil that washes over our land from the west." Carlo paused, until Kevon reached the front of the crowd. "I have it on good authority that he came closest to succeeding in that attempt. The demons have been cut off, their numbers dwindle. Marco will organize and no doubt lead hunts to destroy those still living, while I return to make sure the threat is no more."

Murmurs ran through the gathered Warriors, and Carlo nodded, raising his hands to them.

"I know you want to know more. As do I. I'll have the answers when I return. For now…"

The Warrior Carlo had directed out of the room returned with a large wooden chest, and placed it on the platform in front of Carlo.

"I turn this gathering over to the last Guildsman to see Waine, to dispense with his belongings. Kevon?" Carlo stepped away, and sat down in a chair near the back wall.

The occupants of the room shifted to focus their attention on Kevon. The Seeker stepped up onto the raised stage and circled around the wooden box. He stood, staring at it for a moment before speaking.

"Waine was…" Kevon began, scratching his head. "Arrogant. Reckless. Many things that were important to others were a joke to him."

The murmurs that had quieted moments ago, returned, darker.

"But when it really mattered, he was there." Kevon continued, speaking over the mob. "There was no one I would rather have at my side if the fate of Ærth was at stake. *He was there.* He made a difference. I'll miss him as much as anyone."

"I've been fortunate enough to not attend one of these before," Kevon added, "So I'm at a loss for what to do."

"Open the box!" came a shout from somewhere in the middle of the room.

Kevon nodded and slid the nameplate free to undo the catches behind it. He took a deep breath and lifted the lid.

The sword that lay from corner to corner across the top of the rest of the contents caught and held Kevon's attention. He lifted it out, the touch of the cool steel evoking memories of times he practiced against it. He pulled the blade halfway clear of its sheath. "I know I'll never forget Waine, but carrying this would surely help me remember more clearly."

"It's your right," rumbled Carlo from behind Kevon.

Kevon set the sword aside for himself, and the skinning knife he saved for Bertus. The top few articles of clothing that lay beneath them he assigned to others in the crowd who called out when they were raised into view.

Closing the box on the remainder of Waine's belongings, Kevon announced he was placing the garments, coins, and assorted supplies into the care of the Guild quartermaster, who could determine their best use. He picked up the sword and knife, nodded to Carlo, and threaded his way through the crowd to the exit.

Before he could open the door to the street outside, Kevon felt a hand on his shoulder. He turned to see Carlo standing behind him.

"Finish getting ready, and bring the boy back here for supper," the Blademaster suggested, smiling. "He's got an appointment to keep, as I recall."

Kevon nodded, remembering the plan to have Bertus test for Novice when they returned from the west.

"If I knew more about your training, I would consider having you test for Adept," Carlo added.

Kevon shook his head. "I could pass the Trial, but I would not have earned it, not really."

Carlo frowned, but let the statement lie. "Time enough for that after we leave tomorrow. Bring the boy." The Blade-master turned and made his way back to the gathering.

Kevon stood outside waiting for his borrowed horse, squinting in the glare of noontime. He considered going back inside to eat something, but decided against it. There was still much to be done, and he needed time away from the Guild after the ceremony.

After the short ride back to the palace compound, Kevon hurried to his quarters from the stable. He arranged his belongings so that they could be easily packed when he returned, leaving space for the items he should have picked up from the Guild while he was there earlier.

When he finished, Kevon headed for the kitchen, keeping a lookout for Bertus on the way. He spotted his friend coming up the passageway from the vicinity of Mirsa's quarters.

"Someone's been anxious to see you..." Kevon commented as his young friend caught up and matched strides with him.

"It's not like that... really," Bertus protested, wide-eyed and blushing. "I was just..."

"I meant Carlo," Kevon chuckled. "He wants to have your Trial this afternoon."

"Oh. Right." Bertus settled into a more confident walking rhythm, and Kevon could almost feel the boy's training taking back over.

Kevon smiled. Today's match in the crowded Guildhall would be a far cry from the stone-lined sand pits they had practiced in by Mage-light in the refuges Mirsa had crafted. The nightly sessions had been one of the few outlets for the boy's shock and outrage at Waine's death, and as he'd begun to control those powerful emotions, his skill became markedly more impressive. Bertus had never been able to land a strike due to Kevon's magically assisted defense, but Kevon felt sorry for the Novice that would have to face his friend in the hours to come.

The two stopped in the kitchen and ate and talked with the servants for a few minutes. Palatial leftovers, it seemed, were better than most fancy inn food. Once their hunger was satisfied, they returned to their respective quarters to prepare for the afternoon festivities.

The Warsmith paced around the room, more nervous for Bertus than he had been before his own trial for Seeker. His own Novice Trial had been completely unexpected, so it felt only natural to fret for Bertus, in spite of the boy's obvious talent.

Minutes later, the same cadet that had escorted Kevon to the Guildhall earlier arrived at the door to his chamber, accompanied by Bertus and Mirsa. "Your full contingent is waiting at the stables, and the Commander is ready for the Trial to begin."

Kevon and his friends followed the cadet through the narrow hallways, Mirsa positioning herself between the others so that passersby bearing arms could be deflected away from her.

"Magi do not usually attend these Guild functions," Kevon teased as they reached the stables and the horses were brought around. "Some might consider it taboo?"

"I would not normally accept an invitation to such a barbaric rite," Mirsa responded haughtily, "But the survivors of the patrol seem to have been impressed by my performance, and practically insisted. Warrior - Mage relations are strained enough as it is, not purposefully offending them seemed to be the proper course of action."

Kevon nodded in agreement. Mutual respect between the Guilds was grudging at the best of times, this small act could smooth the ruffled feathers of some of the Guild purists that had voiced concern about the party's return to the tower.

Two of the four guards in the escort Kevon recognized as Mirsa's personal attendants from the company that they'd ventured west with. He recalled that one of the other four had died during the first attack, defending her.

Within moments they were mounted and making best possible speed down the crowded afternoon streets that led to the Warrior's Guild. Two riders ahead of Mirsa shouting and jostling pedestrians off to the side of the procession, two more flanking her, and Kevon and Bertus following as the crowd milled back together behind them.

The riders reached the Guild entrance and formed into a half-circle around the doorway, shielding the Wizard as she dismounted. Grooms led away their horses, and the group crowded around Mirsa protectively as she entered the building.

As they emerged from the narrow hallway into the common area, Mirsa's protectors spread out so that she could see, and be seen. All eyes in the room were fixed on her. Though not as provocatively attired or coiffed as she had been for dinner with Prince Alacrit, she had dressed more for the company she was with than she would have normally. The short black cape draped over her shoulders covered little more than her tightly laced bodice, and the straps winding up her legs from her leather sandals nearly to the bottom of her mid-length black skirt seemed to mark her more as barmaid than Magi.

"Milady," a Blademaster said, stepping forward from a knot of Warriors nearest them, "You honor us with your presence." He extended his palms in a gesture that showed he neither bore, nor wore any metal.

She smiled and extended her hand. "Ordinarily I might not, but your brother Waine was a close friend, as are Kevon and Bertus."

The Blademaster took her hand and kissed it, a gesture far more courtly than normally expected here. "We have a table up front reserved for you and your party, if you would follow me?"

"Thank you," Mirsa answered, "And please, join us."

The Blademaster bowed and turned, leading them through the room, as other Warriors inched away but stared at Mirsa and her following as they passed by.

"I would not normally condone violence of this nature," Mirsa remarked as they neared the empty table, loud enough for half the room to hear. "But Bertus could always use a little more sense knocked into him."

Warriors nearby roared with laughter at the taunt, and the room settled to its usual muted level of rowdiness, the palpable apprehension defused by her well-timed remark. Bertus was introduced to the Novice he would be facing, and the two of them moved over to the far side of the sand-covered arena to prepare.

"A mite different than the intrigues of Palace life?" the Blademaster asked Mirsa, doing his best to hold her attention.

"Where blood is shed within these walls, favor is gained or lost in much the same way," Mirsa answered. "The attacks are more subtle, but we are not as different as many believe."

The room quieted and attention turned from Mirsa and the readying combatants to Carlo as he entered from a side hallway.

"Starting without me, Ralen?" the Commander asked, taking a seat between the other Blademaster and Kevon.

"Never, Sir," Ralen answered, clapping Carlo on the shoulder and smiling. "They haven't even warmed up yet. Get the Commander a drink!" He yelled over his shoulder. "Besides, it's always a while before a new recruit gets an opening on one of our Novices. You might want to nap and come back later."

"I seem to recall a recruit that passed Trial against a Seeker in Eastport, and the very same recruit later defeated a Blademaster, as a Seeker, in ritual combat," Carlo remarked.

"A fluke," Ralen scoffed. "Nothing to do with what we have here."

"Unless our recruit was trained by that Seeker?" Carlo asked, pointing to Kevon.

"Well, I..." Ralen stammered.

"Hush," Carlo chided. "They're ready to begin."

Bertus swung his wooden blade in wobbly arcs around his body, limbering up. Laughter bubbled up from the crowd, and a determined look crept onto his face, his swings tightened a little before he stopped and began stretching out.

The Novice that he was challenging hopped lightly from one foot to another, flourishing his practice sword between calls to friends in the audience. Wagers were being made back toward the center of the room, but Kevon sat, watching, and waiting.

Bertus looked, wide-eyed, to the table where his friends sat, and the jeering and catcalls started anew. Ralen shot a smug look at Carlo, who sat stone-faced, watching only the two in the ring.

"Let the Trial begin!" Blademaster Ralen shouted over the chaos that surrounded them, and the noise dropped to murmurs and whispers.

The combatants turned to face each other, swords raised. Bertus stood almost correctly in a defensive stance that Kevon knew his friend was experienced enough in to get right. The Seeker smiled, but remained silent.

The Novice circled around to Bertus' left, trying to force Bertus to either overcompensate, or allow the Novice to slip further around the perceived weakness in the boy's guard.

Bertus turned in response, quick, jerky steps that shored up his stance in one moment, but left an opening the next. His breathing was erratic, uncontrolled, something Kevon knew was an act. Bertus had faced orcs and held his composure better than this.

The Novice, sure of Bertus's weakness, tensed a moment before attacking.

Bertus, used to parrying Kevon's quicker strikes, shifted his grip and batted his opponent's sword up with a swift underhand swing. A stutter-step for distraction, and the boy's front leg slammed into the Novice's gut. Bertus's sword flashed down and back up as he spun, his follow-through slashing over the doubled-over Novice to hammer into his opponent's practice sword and send it clattering out of the arena into a nearby weapon stand.

Bertus retreated and stood, stance corrected, three sword lengths away from the groaning Novice. He lowered his practice sword and glanced aside to the tables where Mirsa and the Blademasters sat. The Novice dropped to his knees, clutching his stomach. Carlo shook his head and grunted.

"All welcome Novice Bertus!" Ralen shouted, breaking the strained silence.

Bertus smiled and cast aside his wooden sword, wading through the sand pit toward the center of the room, rolling up his tunic sleeve as he went. Celebrating onlookers surged toward him. The new Novice half-yelped, half-laughed as Carlo burned the sword-brand onto his arm.

"Enjoy your evening," Carlo rumbled, slapping Bertus on the back. "We leave the city at first light."

CHAPTER 15

The dull throbbing behind Kevon's eyes reminded him why he did not usually drink so heavily. As he woke, he instantly regretted not returning to the palace with Carlo and Mirsa. The pounding on his chamber door beat a violent counterpoint to the dark melody in his already aching head.

The Seeker staggered to the door, eyes opened only enough to keep from blundering into the sharp-cornered table near it.

"Get moving, lad!" Carlo thundered as Kevon opened the door a crack. "Any one of these soldiers would kill for the chance to go on this mission. I've already got a fresh Novice and a sorceress to deal with, I don't need a bleary-eyed laggard!"

"One moment?" Kevon asked as he shut the door. He splashed water on his face, and washed up quickly. He shrugged into his outer tunic, strapped on his weapons, and hefted the rest of the gear that was already in saddlebags on and under the table. Kevon opened the door wide and stifled a yawn. "Let's go."

The Novice was waiting at the stables, good-naturedly barking orders at the grooms, who were finished readying their three mounts. Kevon noted the way Bertus wore his sword and Waine's knife, exactly the way the fallen Adept had. The Seeker bit his lip, saying nothing.

"The witch is meeting us at the gate," Carlo said, tightening a strap on his saddle before climbing up. "Let's not make her wait, shall we?"

The Warsmith nodded, pushing down the apprehension

that welled up inside him. Carlo's attitude toward magic users had never been a positive one, but as of late had grown even more bitter. He was not sure how well the Blademaster would take the news of Kevon's secret. "Right," he agreed, and finished securing his packs.

Bertus and Carlo were already urging their steeds out into the courtyard before Kevon's foot found the stirrup. Kevon swore under his breath and flicked the ends of his reins. The stallion surged forward, eager to rejoin the others.

Mirsa was already waiting at the palace gate, upon a black stallion that was nearly a match for Carlo's warhorse. She looked like a child astride the larger horse, a marked difference from the daintier mares she had brought upon the last outing. Prince Alacrit and a half-dozen guards waited beside her, the monarch greeted each of them in turn, and wished them well before he was escorted back into the palace.

The Blademaster led the way out of the palace compound, followed by Kevon and Bertus. Mirsa fell in behind them, as they cantered through the empty morning streets. After a brief stop at the western gates to relay a few final orders to Marco and the others assuming command in his stead, the Blademaster led the group out of the city at a gallop.

By midday, they had ridden through farmland that had begun to be tended again, and beyond into lands that nature was determined to reclaim for its own. Carlo called a halt, and Bertus tended to the horses as Kevon rationed out food.

"I trust we are far enough from unworthy ears," Carlo began, "That you can tell me just what in the blazes we are doing out here."

"That, we are." Kevon replied. "We're going to slay an Orclord."

Carlo's face whitened. "Waine..."

"Yes," Kevon answered. "We were unprepared. Knowing now what we face, it should be much simpler."

"*Simpler!*" Carlo yelled, throwing his hands up in the air.

"What's simple about killing an Orclord? Have you ever heard the stories? Are you daft?"

"We would have killed it last time, but for a lack of the proper tools," Kevon responded, lowering his voice, trying to control the conversation. "We now have those tools, and we will not fail."

"I'm not that much better than Waine with a blade, not when a beast like that is part of the bargain," Carlo grumbled. "You'd better have something else you're depending on, boy."

"We do..." Bertus chimed in, walking back over from the horses to collect his lunch.

"*We do...*" Kevon agreed, glaring at Bertus, "But we'll save that talk for this evening. We still have much farther to go today, and Carlo may want to sleep on this news rather than ride."

Bertus nodded, then smiled at Carlo's scowl.

The Commander stomped over by the horses and finished his rations as the others sat and talked.

"Do you think Carlo will accept your explanation?" Mirsa asked, forehead lined with concern. "Especially considering how long you've kept it from him?"

The Warsmith stared toward where Carlo sat sharpening his sword. "He'll have to... We can't afford to lose anyone on this trip. He's helped me through so much..."

"So the betrayal, to him, would seem deeper?" Mirsa whispered.

"The thought had occurred to me," Kevon admitted. "But you two, and Waine, were accepting enough. I can only hope..."

"We haven't lived a lifetime in opposition to the idea," Mirsa remarked. "He has."

Kevon finished the last few bites of his suddenly tasteless lunch, dusted the crumbs from his cloak, and stood up. "*I can only hope,*" he repeated, more for himself than the others. He shouldered the saddlebags with the provisions and trudged back over to the horses to affix them back to his saddle.

Carlo mounted up and was back on the road before Kevon was done tightening up his straps, or the others were even finished eating.

The Seeker sighed and made sure the reins and rigging for Mirsa's stallion was secure, and helped her up into the saddle while Bertus checked his own gear. The two Warriors stepped up into their own saddles, and set out after the Blademaster.

Dusk came swiftly, hastened by a line of dark clouds scudding across the western horizon.

Kevon, Mirsa, and Bertus came upon Carlo waiting in the road, as he had done several times during the afternoon.

"Well, your Wizardness... are you going to do something about a shelter for the night?" Carlo grunted at Mirsa.

"No," Kevon shot back. "She's not." The Seeker swung down from his horse, and handed his reins to Bertus. "*I am.*"

Without waiting for Carlo's response, Kevon stepped off the road, and knelt down to place his palm on a patch of cool, rocky ground. Kevon expended a short burst of magic to force his awareness downward, and gathered in the sympathetic energy as he drew in a mental picture of the ground below. The power built, and Kevon focused it into molding a ramp down and away from the roadway, wide enough for two horses to walk side by side. The walkway led down about twenty feet, and ended in a circular chamber. "The horses will need blinders," Kevon commented, standing. "Mirsa can finish the job, she's better at the fine details..."

"Kevon!" Bertus cried, snapping the Mage's attention back to the group.

Carlo's sword-thrust swept past Kevon as the Seeker sidestepped at the last second.

"Stop!" Kevon shouted, focusing a Movement rune to aid his leap backward to clear the Blademaster's sword-range. "You wanted to know..."

"I almost killed you when I thought you were a thief," Carlo snarled, pausing only momentarily. "Worse, you're a

Mage." The Commander's face contorted with rage as he rushed after Kevon, several more times, each time falling short as his quarry leapt away with unnatural speed.

"Stop!" Kevon repeated, leaping over the opening in the earth he'd made moments earlier, trying to separate himself from his attacker. "We don't have to do this!"

"Stay still for a bit, we needn't worry about it," Carlo retorted, circling around toward the road, then turning to dash back to his horse, and his crossbow.

"Carlo!" Bertus called, leveling his own loaded weapon at the Blademaster. "Don't."

"I would also advise against it," Mirsa added, letting a glimmer of fire light above the tip of her readied staff.

"If you want to chase him around, that's fine," Bertus said, grinning. "We'd prefer you left the sword, but that's up to you."

"You've all known?"

"I nearly killed him myself," Mirsa commented, "I would have, if not for Waine."

"Waine knew?" Carlo scoffed. "That one couldn't keep a secret to save his life."

"He was the first to know," Kevon said, sitting halfway along the side of the ramp opening, dangling his legs off the edge. "Right after we parted ways in the forest south of Eastport. If not for his acceptance of my situation, and his help in my training, I would have had no chance of defeating Gurlin."

"Before the expedition west," Carlo muttered, and sheathed his sword. "All three of you told me I wasn't ready to know what was going on." The Blademaster shook his head. "*He did know.*"

"He pushed me to become better at everything I was capable of," Kevon said, no longer looking at Carlo, but gazing off into the distance. "He knew I would need to be at my best."

"Make no mistake," Carlo warned, "This is not right, it is an abomination. If things were different, if what we faced was in truth as simple as you claim it is, I would make you choose between the sword and the book. I will accept this heresy for now, but I do not like it."

The Blademaster turned to his stallion and began affixing blinders to the harness. "What are you waiting for? Finish the accursed shelter!" he barked at Mirsa.

Kevon watched as Mirsa put away her staff, dismounted, and moved past Carlo, down the ramp. He stood and returned to the road to help Bertus with the rest of the horses, but could feel the magic working as Mirsa sculpted rooms and wrestled water sources into place to feed fountains.

Bertus led his horse alongside Mirsa's down the ramp into the darkness as soon as the blinders were in place. Kevon moved to his steed, and worked while Carlo waited.

"After you," Carlo gestured in an exaggerated fashion.

Kevon shrugged. "I didn't know how close to the entrance you wanted to be when Mirsa closes it back up."

Carlo's eyes narrowed, but he held his ground, following only when Kevon was halfway down the entrance ramp.

Kevon led his stallion to a stall molded from subterranean granite. He tied the reins to a stone post near a small grain-filled depression near the front of the enclosure, where a trough of fresh water gurgled quietly by before sluicing back down into the earth.

"A bit more elaborate than we're used to," Kevon commented, peering around the corner, down a hallway to the other chamber Mirsa had fashioned. "Of course, last trip, we didn't have the luxury of horses."

Carlo grunted, his gaze more one of appraisal than appreciation. The Blademaster finished getting his stallion settled in, and joined Kevon at the beginning of the passage where Bertus and Mirsa had disappeared. "So, is she going to...?"

He followed Carlo's gaze back to the entrance, where the space above the ramp was closing noiselessly.

"Oh." Carlo said, his tone betraying more concern than he would normally allow. "What happens to us if something happens to you? How would we get out?"

Kevon shrugged, and started down the stone passageway.

They emerged into a partial reconstruction of the common room area of the Warrior's Guildhall in Navlia. Several stone tables and chairs sat near a sand-filled pit. Glowing orbs ensconced around the room threw eerie shadows as Kevon and Carlo moved about.

"Someone's just showing off!" Kevon called into the other darkened hallway that led from the room. He ran his fingers over the surface of one of the tables, the patterns in the rock twisted to look like wood.

"I thought familiar surroundings would... help things," Mirsa said, emerging from the passageway. "The rooms are ready, and Bertus is preparing supper in the kitchen."

Carlo pulled a chair out and set about cleaning his sword. Kevon took a seat across the table and began to do the same.

"Boy," Carlo rumbled, "Perhaps you'd best..."

"No." Kevon answered quietly. "I am still the Warrior you helped train, helped inspire. You made me most of what I am today. I ran earlier because I knew you were acting out of surprise. I won't avoid you just because I'm also a Mage." Kevon sighed. "You didn't try to kill me when you found out I'd taken up Blacksmithing. And in all fairness, I was a Mage before I even met you."

Carlo harrumphed, and continued the inspection of his weapon.

The Seeker's gaze drifted past Carlo to the table where Mirsa sat, covering her mouth to hide the beginnings of a smile. The mannerism reminded him momentarily of Marelle, and his guts twisted in knots.

"There's another matter we haven't discussed," Kevon began.

"What the blazes is it now?" Carlo growled, nostrils flaring.

Kevon hesitated, his throat tightening as he searched for

the right words. "When we returned to Navlia, Waine, Bertus, and I, before the expedition west... We heard news... From East-port."

The Blademaster's gaze swept over his sword, and he resheathed it without further inspection. "Rhulcan, and Mar-elle?"

The Warsmith nodded, and kept silent.

"Bertus told me," Carlo explained, "Before we left. I didn't want to mention it until you were ready."

"I should know more when I return to Eastport." Kevon closed his eyes and shook his head. "I don't know what I'm going to do when I get there."

Carlo said nothing, and Kevon missed the conflicted looks as the Blademaster wrestled with the fact that his student was going against one of the major tenets of the Warrior's Guild, but still needed his guidance. He stood and moved to the sand pit, and began his nightly sword practice. Kevon watched, but did not move to join the older man. Mirsa switched seats to sit next to Kevon and get a better view of Carlo's workout.

The Blademaster's brow glistened with sweat by the time Bertus entered with four stone bowls filled with steaming hot stew.

"Mirsa," the boy whispered, "That fire..."

"Already out," the Mage replied softly, the effort Kevon hadn't noticed before draining from her face.

She Concealed it, Kevon thought, peering at her. She didn't want me knowing, so that I wouldn't try and help, and upset Carlo more. It made it twice as hard on her, instead.

"*Thanks,*" Kevon mouthed to Mirsa while Bertus wrangled another of the heavy stone chairs over to the table, and Carlo wiped down his blade again before putting it away.

The corners of Mirsa's mouth turned up in a quick smile that only Kevon saw. "How did the cauldron work?" she asked Bertus. "Would it be better any thinner?"

Bertus shook his head. "Any thinner would burn the food

under that much heat. Also... You might want to stay closer, there were a few times the fire burned larger and hotter than I'm sure you intended."

Mirsa's eyes widened. "Distractions," she agreed. "I will be more careful."

The Blademaster sat and inspected the stone spoon for a moment before digging into the bowl of stew. "What, no ale?" he asked Bertus.

Bertus chuckled, and started on his own meal.

When all four of them had finished and pushed their plates to the middle of the table, Mirsa stood, covering a yawn. She blinked a few times, and opening her eyes wider, held her hand out over the table, fingers spread, as she began working more Earth magic.

Kevon smiled, appreciating the dramatic, though wholly unnecessary gesture that served only to alert Carlo and Bertus of the impending magic.

The edges of the stone table folded upward like a Nightflower at dawn, enveloping the used stone dishes. The table legs slid inward, twining into a stem that pulled down into the floor, taking the now-closed stone bud down into the cavern floor after it.

"I suggest we retire," the Mage said, turning to the hallway that led deeper into the artificial cavern. "This is just the beginning of this journey, and we've no time to waste. Travel when we can, rest when we cannot. The wards we renewed should contain the Orclord until we arrive, but there is nothing to be gained by dallying."

"And what better place to rest than a tomb?" Carlo asked, rising and collecting his belongings.

Mirsa stood and led the way out of the room, past the small kitchen, to an intersection that opened into two sleeping quarters. She gestured, and lit candles in the room to the right, waved the other, and orb torches flared to life in the room to the left.

Carlo snorted and turned, entering the room to the right, depositing his gear on one of the raised stone slabs that was about the size of a bed.

Kevon began to follow the Blademaster, but stopped when Mirsa spoke.

"Kevon," the Mage said quietly, looking over to the other room, then back to the Warrior.

"I'll be fine here," Kevon answered, and turned to continue into the candlelit chamber.

The earth all around them hummed, and dust motes swirled in the flickering light.

"You will not," Mirsa responded, raising her voice. Kevon could feel her wrestling the Earth magic back under control.

"Listen to the witch, boy," Carlo taunted. "She's afraid for you."

"I am afraid for us all," Mirsa hissed at the Commander. "Your actions earlier could have ruined our chance at destroying the Orclord, and I will not have it. I value your sword, and your experience, but *his* life is far more important to our cause than yours. If separating the two of you increases the chances of us undoing the wrong I helped perpetuate..."

Kevon could see the magic in his mind, moving currents of earth far below them, he could feel the ground shuddering from the stress.

"Now *GO!*" she shouted, flinging an arm to point at the other room, where the orbs shone almost painfully bright.

Kevon nodded, and walked into the room, casting a glance over his shoulder at a smirking Carlo.

Appeased, Mirsa focused the sympathetic magic coursing through her, sealing the entrance to the room as she followed Kevon inside.

CHAPTER 16

"Two days now, three at the outside," Kevon remarked, calling forth the energy that surrounded him to reopen the passage to the surface. The ceiling above flowed apart with a bare minimum of sound, marking a vast improvement of his skill over the past few weeks.

The horses, now no longer blindered at night, showed no surprise at the now common event, but instead an eagerness to get back on the road.

Kevon led the way out, scanning the landscape through puffs of frozen breath. Before opening the shelter, he had tapped into the latent Earth power to sense the surrounding miles, as was his morning ritual. He had felt nothing that could be a threat to them, but as near as they were to the tower and the corrupted area of magic, he was particularly watchful throughout the day. As he turned his gaze toward their destination, a thin column of smoke glinted in the morning sun.

"There," Kevon pointed, "What is there?"

Mirsa led her stallion up alongside Kevon's, and peered toward the west. "Marson and Tamika's farmstead. Their daughter worked in the tower kitchen. Could that be chimney smoke?'

"Too dark, and the column's too thick," Carlo commented, leading his warhorse around the others. "If there were no breeze, and it was overcast, I would say there was a chance it was not the farmhouse burning. As it is..." Carlo shrugged.

"We dare not risk ourselves to find out," Mirsa sighed. "Not when we're this close..."

"Agreed," Carlo grumbled, cinching his horse's saddle tighter. "We should make straight for that tower, as fast as we can. Make a shelter as close as we dare, and hope it's within walking distance. I've no intention of leaving any of us behind to watch the horses while the others tromp around in the dark."

Kevon nodded. He hadn't thought about it, but their mounts would only be a liability once they reached the tower. "We'll need to leave before dawn, when the dark beasts are already seeking shelter from the sun." He handed his reins to Bertus, and walked partway back down the ramp that led back to their shelter. He relaxed, and took in the Earth magic that pressed in around him.

Kevon drew shafts of soil and stone up into the chambers of the shelter, filling most of the space, so that they would not cause sinkholes later. Air displaced by the drawn earth breezed past him, smelling of dust and horses. At last, the ramp shifted, levering Kevon up to ground level, and settling evenly with the surrounding area.

Kevon took the reins from Bertus and climbed into his saddle. "Let's see if we can reach the edge of the corruption before nightfall."

The miles fell away as the four pushed their steeds along the track that skirted the stream they had followed, more or less, since they entered this section of the valley. A brief stop to water and graze the horses, and Carlo goaded the others back onto the road, before they had finished eating their midday rations.

"Wait!" Mirsa called, urging her stallion forward to overtake Carlo, who led the column. "I can feel the elemental magic weakening," she gasped, as she reined her mount in to match speed with the Blademaster's slowing steed. "The tower is a few hours distant, overland. We should be close enough to attempt..." she trailed off.

"Are you sure we can't get closer?" Carlo asked, squinting at the sun that still rode a hand's-breadth above the mountains to the west.

"Not if we are to attempt what I plan," Mirsa replied, stepping down from her horse and handing her reins to Bertus. "I'll need help, for this," she added, looking up at Kevon.

The Warrior-Mage dismounted, taking care to avoid the touch of steel. He dropped his reins and his horse snuffled at the grasses on the side of the track toward the stream. "I can feel the lessening of the magic here, too. It's not so much that it should really interfere with..."

Mirsa knelt and connected with the Earth magic beneath them, and the usual ramp burrowed down into the ground before them. The Master Mage walked slowly down the ramp, fingers trailing the smooth stone wall that she'd shaped moments before.

Kevon formed an Aid rune, coupled it with an Earth rune, and began steadying the frayed edges of Mirsa's concentration. He felt the rooms opening up, as normal, waterways wrestled into service, encased in stone tubs and basins. He remained above, less pressured by the influx of magic from below, but still linked to the working through Mirsa, lending support as she needed.

Assuming that the Master Mage was finished, Kevon prepared to release the runes in his mind. Just as he began to relax his concentration, the Earth rune in his mind's eye sprang into stony solidity. The grassy expanse before him sank down, rolling out into the distance like a mammoth ocean swell. Where patches of the runes had shown rough edges before, Kevon felt his mind raked by sharp spikes of obsidian. Crying out, he refocused, pouring magic frantically into the spell to stabilize it.

Slabs of stone groaned as they slid from the sides of the newly formed valley, to cover it over. Kevon fought with the magic a few moments longer, then shifted his focus to drawing the leaking energy from Mirsa, filling his own Earth rune, pulling columns up from below for the massive stone sheets to rest upon. As the movement stretched further out into the distance approaching the mountains to the North, Kevon required more magic to keep up with Mirsa's manipulation of the landscape. He drew it more swiftly from the imperfections in her spell, rather than pull it straight from the Aid rune that linked them, afraid of the toll it would inflict on her. When the work was nearly complete, Kevon labored to turn to Carlo.

"Go... get... her..." Kevon commanded between strained breaths. He could feel Mirsa frantically channeling the inflowing energy into strengthening the pillars he had raised, but it would not last. He siphoned magic from her as fast as he dared, but without anything to do with it, the power saturated his very being. Afraid of releasing too much at once, and endangering those around him, he held it in, until it felt as if his bones were stone, his flesh earth, and dust swirled through his veins.

Just when he thought he would burst from the raw power, or turn to stone because of it, Kevon felt an emptiness, a void that encircled him, that he thought might take the power that infused him. Almost faster than thought, the Journeyman Mage focused the runaway Earth magic into the void.

His senses began to return to him as the excess magic drained away, and Kevon realized that the void encircling him, the receptacle for the unreasonable amounts of magic, was the simple iron ring he wore on his finger.

The Blademaster hastened up the ramp, carrying an almost unconscious Mirsa like a rag doll.

Kevon waited until Carlo was clear of the entrance, and the shaken Mage's connection to the earth was nearly severed before siphoning all of Mirsa's available magic and dumping it into the waiting void.

The Master Mage gasped softly and slipped into unconsciousness.

Carlo frowned. "Too much for her?"

The Warsmith stared dumbly at Carlo for a few moments

before realizing that he and Bertus had seen nothing more than an impressive display of magic and a small show of concern for Mirsa. "Quite," the exasperated Mage sighed. "We all almost died."

The Commander scowled, depositing Mirsa on the ground considerably less gently than he was able. "Mages."

Kevon approached the jumbled pile of sleeping Mage, and arranged her more comfortably, watching her limp form for signs of distress. After a few minutes of quiet observation, he helped Bertus load Mirsa onto her stallion, and together they descended into the shelter.

Walling himself off from the Earth power that surrounded him, Kevon crafted an Earth rune and closed the entrance, relying on only his own magical reserves.

Kevon hauled Mirsa down from her horse and slung her over his shoulder to carry into the living quarters of the cavern, while Bertus turned the horses loose in the vast, grassy chamber to the north. The Mage walked through the dimly lit hall to the main chamber, where Carlo sat, sharpening his sword. He called forth a glowing orb, turned down another hallway, and deposited Mirsa carefully on a stone pallet already piled with blankets.

After arranging his unconscious companion to his satisfaction, and watching her breathe for long enough to ease his mind, Kevon returned to the main room to sit across the table from Carlo.

"Thank you for seeing to the room," Kevon commented

"Well, we need her, right?" Carlo responded, scowling. "*I* don't have to like her to know that." The Blademaster cracked a smile. "Besides, *you...*"

"The stables are amazing!" Bertus blurted, rushing in. "Or pastures, or whatever. I think I even heard a stream running in there."

The other two warriors stared blankly at their young friend.

"Oh. How's Mirsa?" he asked.

"Resting comfortably," Kevon answered. "We'll see how she's doing in the morning, we can stay here for an extra day or two if we need, until we're all ready for this."

"No chance the three of us could handle it?" Carlo asked, sheathing his sword.

Kevon frowned. "Even if we could, I'm not comfortable leaving Mirsa here, where she would need to use Earth magic again to leave." He turned the iron ring around on his finger. "The lessened elemental magic seems to require more control, and I have an... advantage that she does not."

"We're stronger together," Bertus affirmed. "We always have been."

"So we are," Carlo agreed. "So we are."

CHAPTER 17

The Journeyman Mage gritted his teeth and expended a substantial amount of magic to force open the exit to the sanctuary where they had spent the last three days. Glad to see even pinpoints of light, as long as they did not come through magically bored shafts, Kevon stared a moment at the yet-dark sky until Bertus shoved him from behind.

"We're hurrying today, remember?" the youth chided.

The days previous had been anything but hurried. Kevon had spent hours wandering the sunken pasture, using Earth magic to open slender tunnels to the surface at different angles, so that any daylight above would brighten at least some area of the buried field. Using only his own magic, while keeping the unstable forces surrounding him at bay, had drained him, so he napped frequently, staying near Mirsa's bed when not walking among the horses. At times he wondered if that was how he had been watched over when he'd had his own extended magically induced sleep.

Bertus might have, Mirsa still hated me. And Waine would never have let himself be seen that worried...

Memories of the young Adept Warrior swirled, tracing a path from their meeting at Kevon's Novice trial in Eastport, back and forth across the Realm, and down the road that lie just ahead, to where Waine's killer still drew breath. *Not for long*, he promised himself, taking another look at the sky before continuing up the narrow walkway to the surface.

He stood near the top of the exit, waiting as Bertus, Carlo, and Mirsa followed into the chilly pre-dawn gloom. After they were all clear, Kevon forced the passageway closed with a combination of Earth, Movement, and Enhancing runes. While not as quiet or artful as a singular Earth rune under better conditions would have been, it was effective, and less taxing than opening the passage had been.

"Now, we're sure of the direction?" Kevon asked.

"Even in the dark, I know the valley," answered Mirsa. "Four hours brisk walk, *that* way," she said, guiding Kevon's hand in the direction she meant.

"Carlo," Kevon began, "If you were set on the proper heading, could you maintain it without seeing even the stars?"

"Boy, do you mean to ask me if I can march in a straight line?" Carlo complained. "If the Prince's advisor wasn't so fond of you..." he harrumphed. "Of course I can."

Kevon shook his head, the gesture lost in the night. "I've been thinking of something, something that might keep us safe in the darkness, from imps and orcs. I'd like to try it."

"More magic," Carlo muttered. "All right," the Blademaster signaled after a few moments under Mirsa's guidance. "Let's go."

Kevon began his spell, reaching for the darkness, and letting the twisted rune form in his mind. When the Dark rune was fully formed, Kevon envisioned a rune of Light, drawing what little help he could from the approaching dawn. After both runes were joined and stabilized, Kevon gave the mental shove that forced the energy into the world to do his bidding.

A dome of not quite perfect darkness surrounded them. Kevon shifted his focus, and split his concentration enough to call a small globe of light to brighten the interior of the dark shield. He could see the looks of confusion on Carlo and Bertus's faces, and feel Mirsa probing his work with her Art.

"Dark enough to ward off orcs," Mirsa commented, "But light enough to frighten Imps. Impressive."

"And not the easiest to maintain," Kevon griped, rubbing his hands together and drawing his cloak tighter around his shoulders. "Are you going to move?"

They advanced, following Carlo's steady gait.

The Dark rune was not as vile as Kevon remembered it, and Kevon wondered if it was practice, or the fact that the magic was not being used to open a portal to the Dark realm. Nevertheless, after about a dozen minutes, he would gesture, and Mirsa would weave her own energy into the spell, letting Kevon extricate his will from the veil, and regain his composure.

After about an hour, the forces Kevon drew upon for his spell felt evenly balanced. As tired as he was from maintaining control over the two opposing runes, the wearied Mage was loath to maintain the magic any longer.

"Dropping the shield," Kevon cautioned, moments before he let the runes slip from his mind.

The valley snapped into crisp detail, a welcome change from the flat grayness that had surrounded them for what seemed like hours.

The half-light of dawn breaking over the twisted vale to the east betrayed no enemies for as far as any of the company could see. And in the distance, shrouded in the still swirling mists of the morning, the tips of the remains of the tower hid to the west, showing their stony horns for an instant before vanishing again.

The company slowed enough to take full stock of their surroundings before pressing ahead. Their pace quickened, now that their destination was somewhat visible in the distance.

Before long, the foursome reached what had been the edge of the marshes on the previous trip. Instead, a wide expanse of brittle, sun-bleached refuse clustered around the occasional small, dank puddle.

An hour of crunchy footfalls later, the sun was well above the horizon, and had burned most of the fog from the ruins of the tower, which had grown sharper and more menacing in the distance.

"Another hour," Carlo commented, breaking the quasi-silence as he skirted around another miniature bog. "Any other preparations we may have forgotten?"

Kevon glanced down at the cinched hood that covered his sword-hilt, keeping him from accidentally draining away all his magic at this extremely important stage of the expedition. "We take it slow and sure," he answered. "It's not going anywhere." The Mage pushed his awareness outward, feeling the numbing loss of the elemental spectrum of magic, probing at it experimentally with his mind. He pictured a Wind rune, but it twisted about, fading and frazzling, and would not take form no matter how he tried.

He sensed Mirsa forming Enhancement and Aid runes, and then the flickering chaos that his Wind rune had been moments ago. He focused again, and the sigil flared to blurry brilliance as power flowed from both Magi to stabilize it. Wind whipped around the party as the spell, given no particular direction, sputtered and went dark.

Carlo turned to glare at the Mages as they stared at each other.

"Did you just!?" Mirsa asked, wide-eyed.

"I think we can!" Kevon almost shouted. "If we have great enough need for it, we could push through whatever it is that's blocking our magic. We just needed to try harder, to work together."

"A lot of bluster for such a little breeze," Carlo chuckled. "I'd rather we pushed ahead. I'm anxious to see this Orclord of yours."

The Warsmith nodded, and struck out again for the tower, the others following as he took the lead from Carlo.

The party returned to the road as soon as their path crossed it, the general condition of the path was marred only by the occasional washed-out section.

The sun was an hour or more from its apex by the time the four reached the foot of the broken tower, the still-pristine drawbridge that lay across the moat, now only half-full of debris and fetid water.

Carlo approached, weapon drawn, as they neared the crumbled walls, the only obstacles large enough to conceal enemies they had approached during their trek. Kevon readied Light and Movement runes, and felt Mirsa do the same. Bertus fitted a bolt into his crossbow, and without words, they advanced into the ruins.

Little had changed in the time since Kevon and the others had left. More refuse had accumulated, and the unchecked growth of weeds and grasses framed overgrown paths through the rubble. None of the tracks that Kevon could make out from his position behind Carlo looked fresh enough for much concern. It appeared the tower had been largely abandoned.

"Which way?" Carlo asked, eyes sweeping the compound, neck craning at every rustling of the wind

The Seeker pointed down a branching path toward the center of the tower, and the group followed the Blademaster through the brush to the head of the sunken stairwell.

The entrance to the stone staircase had been narrowed by at least half, caked mud and detritus filled the depression that had surrounded the opening, and mounded over it. Some of the formation appeared to have been pushed out from below, as if creatures seeking shelter had needed to force their way back out to the surface.

The Blademaster shot Kevon a look of disgust, and sheathed his sword. The Warrior drew his dagger, clenched it in his teeth, and climbed into the tunnel, bracing himself with all four limbs.

Kevon focused energy into his Light rune, and gave the spell a mental shove, forcing a sphere of light into reality. He began following Carlo down the awkward descent, and sent the sphere whizzing past his mentor, to light the way ahead. Mirsa followed, guiding a light of her own, and Bertus followed, more slowly, crossbow still at the ready.

After a short distance, the passage opened up appreciably, but the stairwell was thick with muck and refuse until the very bottom. From there, the sludge turned to soup, the long hallway was knee-deep in foul-smelling water.

"Something's not right..." Mirsa said, stepping tentatively into the lukewarm slurry. "This shouldn't be..."

The Mage shifted her Light spell from the free-floating orb before her to the ensconced crystalline orbs lining the hallway. As the light before her went out, the entire length of the passage burst into brilliant clarity.

"No surprises here, are there?" Carlo half-asked, sloshing forward without waiting for an answer.

Mirsa concentrated for a moment. "The barrier is still in place..." She frowned, and shook her head. "I don't know what could have happened."

Carlo picked up his pace, and the others scrambled to keep up, the loud splashing of their passage reverberating down the hall precluding further conversation. The Commander emerged into the main chamber, and approached the muted glow of the magical shield.

"Well, looks like he's drowned, or gone," Carlo concluded, squinting to look through the veil of light.

Mirsa shifted her focus from the orbs in the hallway to the ones on the front edge of the chamber, throwing more illumination into the flooded room. Along the right wall, two-thirds of the way to the back of the chamber, strange shadows fell.

"Part of the side wall..." Kevon began.

"Is missing." Mirsa breathed, barely audible over the gentle sloshing. "The Orclord has escaped the cavern, and I cannot sense where this underground stream or tunnels lead. It may have perished, escaped to the surface, or could still be lurking nearby."

"Should we check the break in the wall?" Bertus asked. "It may be close enough to see, or get an idea of what may have happened to it,"

Mirsa nodded. "We should check while we're here, but be cautious. I don't remember how the floor slopes in there, it may be deeper, and there may be strong currents."

The Mage put her hand on the barrier, and the crystalline orbs behind her shone brighter as the magical shield dissolved.

Kevon's ears popped as the last scrap of light flickered out before them. A shallow wave from the higher water in the main part of the chamber slapped against his knees, but the breeze that now whistled in from behind them freshened somewhat, bringing only a hint of the foul water that now mixed with the slowly rising currents.

"Carefully," Mirsa cautioned again, siphoning Light energy from the spheres to call forth a free-floating globe of her own to direct toward the broken wall.

The four waded slowly toward the gaping fracture, in a staggered line to maintain the best possible view of the area in question. As Carlo neared the opening, he stopped, and motioned for the others to do the same.

"The currents are getting worse," the Blademaster rasped a loud whisper over the gurgling of the surrounding waters. "We should turn back."

"No!" Mirsa shouted, surging past the others, buoyed by a hastily crafted Movement rune. The Master Mage grasped an outcropping of broken rock where the new tunnel opened. Holding herself aloft with one hand, she screamed in frustration, sending spears of coherent light lancing down the passage into darkness.

The orbs behind dimmed in pulses, until they darkened completely. One of the crystal structures shattered, releasing the pent-up focal enchantment, the aura of Light magic a glimmering haze that relit the nearest two intact orbs.

"Mirsa!" Bertus cried out as the exhausted sorceress slipped into the dusky churn.

Kevon cleared his mind and focused on his own rune of Movement. He avoided the dull, shadowy Water rune that lurked at the fringes of his mind's eye, knowing that what little magic he had left would be wasted if his concentration wavered in that direction. Instead, he used three points of force to lift Mirsa to the surface, keeping her low enough to limit the magic he needed to expend, but high enough to remain clear of the currents below.

The Mage's limp form skimmed through the gloom, against the outgoing current, until she was close enough for Carlo to grasp by the nape of her cloak

Kevon refocused his magic to relight the nearest orbs.

"She's not breathing!" Carlo called, lifting Mirsa's unconscious form at an awkward angle to keep her well clear of his weapons.

"Bring her back to the shallows!" Kevon yelled back, and turned to make his own way back to the flooded entrance.

Bertus helped the Blademaster tow Mirsa over to where the water was merely waist-deep, to a waiting Kevon.

"Hold her still," Kevon cautioned, taking a breath and lowering himself into the tepid gloom.

The Journeyman Mage closed his eyes and opened his mind as he submerged, gathering power from deep within himself before turning his attention to the darkened Water rune that pried at his awareness. Forcing the mass of accumulated power into the shadowy form, he pushed his consciousness after it as well. His senses occluded as he shepherded the magic across the mental threshold of the rune.

Time stretched. Within the runic construct, and beyond the barriers that siphoned off the bulk of the stored energy, Kevon was free to guide the remaining Water magic unimpeded. He expanded his awareness, taking care to avoid the shards of hungering darkness that lay submerged nearby. A moment's examination yielded no trace of the Orclord in the nearby waterways.

Kevon returned to the situation at hand. He sensed the water choking Mirsa, and drew in magic from nearby to channel the fluids away and out of her throat and lungs. With the force already in motion, Kevon relaxed and drifted up and out of the Water rune.

Ending the spell was not as simple as Kevon thought. As his focus drifted to the boundary of the rune in his mind's eye, the darkness surrounding it leeched away the magic that he had drawn in from the surrounding water. He drifted closer, and was suddenly afraid of what would happen if he made contact without a protective wrap of energy.

Kevon reached back down toward the center of the Water rune, grasping for a trickle, a droplet of power to reawaken the magic. Finally, he grasped a small bead of magic, and used it to reach out once more to the surrounding stream, to wrap himself in borrowed magic, and swim back away from the horrific boundary. The frantic Mage pulled layer after layer of energy from his surroundings and cocooned his will until he felt as though he would drown in it. He flicked a tendril of awareness through his defenses to reassess his physical surroundings.

Mirsa's lungs had not yet cleared, but a small geyser of water billowed from her mouth in slow-motion. Large bubbles were bursting in the water just in front of her.

Right where…

Kevon whisked his focus to his own body, where a jaw that had been tightly clenched when he began sinking now hung slack, agape. Panicking, he rushed magic to force water out of his own body as he had Mirsa's, wrapped a few more layers of Water magic around himself, and sped at the barrier of the construct as fast as he could manage.

The Mage lunged out of the water, sputtering the vile liquid and coughing before daring to take a breath. Mirsa stood nearby, supported by Bertus and Carlo, doing much the same.

"How…?" she asked, as her breathing steadied. "I felt Water magic, for just a moment…"

"It's not something I would recommend," Kevon answered. "I'd rather not even discuss it until we're far away from here."

Mirsa peered at him for a moment, then nodded. "I'm sorry that I behaved... so rashly."

The darkened Water rune loomed large in Kevon's mind, pulsing larger and hungrier as the waves lapped against his waist. It was as if the waiting magic was daring him to brave its depths once again. Shivering, Kevon spoke up. "We need to leave here, now..."

The dimmed Water rune slammed into Kevon's consciousness as the Mage swept his gaze across the room. "Wait," he gasped, fixing his eyes on one of the points toward the middle of the chamber where the sensation seemed strongest. Kevon sloshed out into the center of the room, until he could feel the presence of the shadowed rune close to his feet.

Drawing focus from one of the orbs near his companions, Kevon directed a cone of light downward toward the source of his apprehension.

A fragment of the shattered stone arch lay less than a pace from where Kevon stood. Leaning closer, the Mage half-saw, half-felt the runes carved and empowered in the smooth rock. Elemental runes linked with Concealment, and another rune that Kevon did not recognize curved along the face of the broken portal stone. The dark, devouring images that swam through his mind seemed to be coming from the broken edges, where some of the runes were incomplete. Kevon focused on the unfamiliar rune, fixed it in his mind without giving it any power, and returned to his friends.

"I have a few questions about magic to ask you later," Kevon said as he passed by Mirsa, taking the lead as he waded out of the chamber. "For now, I just want to leave this place."

"What of the Orclord?" Mirsa cried after him.

"It is not here, nor is it as far as this water reaches," Kevon replied over his shoulder. "Let us hope it has not escaped."

CHAPTER 18

The aura of Light that diffused up the stairwell wavered, and Kevon shifted his attention to stabilize it, focusing on the orb down the hallway that he was filtering the power through. The ensconced crystal flickered, lighting of its own accord from the barest leakage of magic.

His companions lay arrayed on the stone landing below him, shaded from the majority of his Light spell, which he had been maintaining for the last two hours. The Mage watched Mirsa slumbering peacefully, and wondered if his strength would hold until dawn, if he should wake her for her shift maintaining a light bright enough to discourage the creatures of darkness. His concentration flagged again, the exertions of the afternoon weighing down, pressing him into weariness.

Half an hour later, Kevon gently shook Mirsa awake, unable to keep the spell steady enough to feel comfortable that the light would deter unwanted visitors. Dark circles under the Master Mage's eyes, and an unfamiliar crease in her forehead spoke the volumes her cheerful response did not.

The remaining hours before the outside world brightened were strewn with horrific memories of the things he had witnessed in the years since leaving home. Kevon's fragile snatches of sleep were punctuated with twisted visions of events that had never even happened. Sometimes it was Waine dying at the hands of the Orclord, sometimes himself or Mirsa. Variations of the battle that took place just outside ended with the Mage Pholos stabbing Kevon in the back with a knife, instead of Kevon slaying Gurlin in the same fashion. Marelle lay bound in the hideout far to the north where Kevon had rescued Carlo, brigands looming over with filthy, reaching hands. The darkness between the fragments of dreams swam with warped faces and chitinous limbs.

◆ ◆ ◆

"Kevon."

The Seeker found himself shook to wakefulness, a small share of stale bread and cold dry fish thrust into his hands.

"We need to leave," Mirsa said, lowering the light levels once she saw everyone had finished with their provisions and secured their belongings. "There is nothing here for us, we can hope the Orclord has perished below, but I will convince the Prince to build a garrison here nevertheless."

"It would strike at the heart of this blight of darkness, even a small force of competent men," Carlo agreed, turning and starting up the stairway.

Chaos erupted as the party neared the surface. Carlo rounded the last corner into the faint natural light of the morning, the rasp of his blade winning free of its sheath in the cramped passage mingling with his strangled battle cry.

Kevon leapt into the corner as the Blademaster charged forward, Light magic gathered, and a Movement rune readied as he strained to ignore the corrupted Earth sigil that threatened to overwhelm him as he worked other magic.

Kevon made out the figures of an Orcish female and at least two of the smaller child scouts scrambling back toward the entrance, shrieking with panic. He dropped his concentration so that he could follow Carlo up the litter-strewn stairs at best possible speed. He burst out into the full light of morning, nearly colliding with the Blademaster before stopping to squint.

"Where did they go?" Kevon asked, peering around for a few moments before following Carlo's gaze toward the west, to where the rubble of the broken tower was piled deepest.

The ground quivered, a nearby puddle scattering waves of light as the rings on the surface crisscrossed and interlaced.

The female orc and three scouts broke from the rubble pile, the younger ones squealing in terror, ushered forward to the north by the older, agitated female.

Kevon started after them, but Carlo held out a restraining arm as the Mage tried to rush past.

"No," Carlo growled, eyes locked on the still-shimmering puddle. "Back down the stairs!"

Kevon turned and rushed to the stairwell, motioning for Bertus to turn back. As he closed the distance on his return to the downward passage, the Seeker saw movement looming above the broken walls to the west.

Carlo charged down after Kevon, nearly crashing into him and Bertus. Mirsa stood further down the stairs, ready to descend if needed.

"We found it," the Blademaster commented wryly, "Now how do we kill it?"

Kevon shook his head, edging closer to the entrance to peer out. "It was going to be difficult enough with the beast trapped underground, behind a magical shield. With it roaming free..."

"We have to kill it before it moves on," Bertus said, checking his crossbow over, counting his ammunition. "North to Kron, endangers the food supply. East to the Inner Cities, it would eventually be stopped, but after how many more were killed? And if it turns south..."

Carlo nodded slowly. "If it were allowed to break through the Southern Frontier, rally the orcs in the Barrens... It would take all the force we could gather to bring them down."

The Blademaster sighed. "And I don't know that the peace treaties are sturdy enough to survive the full commitment of our forces to the southern border."

"Are we going to stand here discussing politics," Mirsa snapped, "Or are we going to act?"

Carlo crept back up to where Kevon was still scanning in the direction the Orclord had gone.

"Has it..."

Grotesque laughter warbled through the ruins, and the Warriors turned and saw the beast through the broken remains of the tower. Not too distant from the boundary of the debris-filled moat, the gigantic Orc hoisted its prize, one of the scouts that had fled from the stairway moments earlier. Shrill cries rang out above the deep laughter, but both silenced as the bull stuffed the younger orc into his mouth and began chewing.

"Left?" Kevon finished Carlo's question. "Not yet." The Warrior-Mage craned his neck higher, trying to get a better angle to survey the ground around the Orclord. "I don't know if he's finished, or just getting started, though."

"We need to move." Mirsa whispered, creeping past them, circling wide around Carlo and his weaponry. "We are at a grave disadvantage here. If we could only lure it far enough away to where our magic is not constrained..."

Kevon stood upright, eyes gleaming. "Run," he said calmly, pointing to the southeast, away from the Orclord, back the direction they had come from. "I'll bring him along after you."

CHAPTER 19

"Illusion may not fool it this time," Mirsa whispered as she passed Kevon, hurrying to follow Carlo away from the Orclord.

Kevon nodded, and winked at Bertus as the boy passed him, never taking his eyes off the behemoth in the distance. "I have a few ideas," he chuckled.

The Seeker watched as the orc devoured two more of its smaller brethren, then chanced a backward glance to see how far his friends had retreated.

They're not moving as quickly as I'd hoped, he thought, turning his gaze back to his giant foe. Perhaps it will take a nap.

As if in response, the Orclord yawned, scratched itself, and glanced about slowly. Its sleepy gaze locked on Kevon.

Kevon threw up an obscuring haze, drawing the Illusion enchanted rod from inside his tunic. The spell, focused through the short staff, was nearly effortless, and would buy the Mage precious time to think.

The orc swiveled his field of vision about, searching for where Kevon could have gone.

He's going to spot them.

Kevon sprinted off toward his friends, maintaining the wrap of illusory waves around him, while sending a crude representation of himself running down the stairs to disappear.

The Orclord roared, and began running, its frantic pace shaking the ground more violently than before. It crashed through part of the dilapidated outer wall, sending large chunks of stone debris flying, some landing yards ahead of Kevon.

The Mage chanced a backward glance, in time to see the gigantic orc sprawl, one foot kicking out and almost hitting him, raising a cloud of dust as the Orclord jammed its arm down the stairwell.

The dust cloud enveloped Kevon, complicating his illusion, sending brown sparkles across his concentration, as well as his vision. Distracted, he choked on a dust-laden breath, and coughed.

The Orclord's frustrated rumblings quieted, and its meaty arm rasped free of the stairwell.

Kevon wrapped himself in an envelope of silence, frustrated that he had not done so sooner. He then duplicated the veil and the aura of silence around his friends for a few moments, then dropped it. After repeating it once more, Mirsa understood, and raised wards of her own. *Less organized*, Kevon thought, *but serviceable.*

The Orclord knew something was happening, and the general direction. It advanced haltingly, but its size allowed it to catch up while stopping every few steps to look, listen, and smell.

If this continues, we lose. Kevon realized. He was not tired from his brief sprint, but Mirsa could not maintain the pace they would need to keep eluding the beast, and without access to Wind magic to mask their scents, the Orclord would surely find them before long. *Might as well try something different.*

Kevon whirled around to face the gargantuan Orc, drawing forth the Movement rod that he'd had stored with the Illusion rod he was focusing his spells through now. The Warrior-Mage backpedaled, allowing his illusions to fragment enough to draw the Orclord more his direction.

Satisfied with his positioning, Kevon stopped, and dropped his concealing spells. He summoned all his focus, and drew it through the Movement rod.

The orc, fixated on his newly visible prey, did not see the man-sized shard of stone that lifted to stand on end in its path.

It lunged forward, nearly in range to grasp Kevon, and put all its weight down on the jagged spike that Kevon was struggling to keep hoisted upright with his Art. The stone sank a yard into the leathery foot, then shattered under the pressure as it struck bone. Fragments of rock pelted Kevon, and the Orclord howled in pain and rage.

Kevon shifted focus from the orc and the stone to himself, and renewed the veils he had dropped. Using both rods to full capacity, he sprinted with unnatural speed to reach where his friends were retreating east at a hasty, if measured, pace. He widened the scope of his Illusion spell to encompass the entire party.

Mirsa relaxed as she released the magic that was no longer needed. "Do you think you've slowed it down enough...?"

Carlo snorted, and Kevon was grateful he'd kept the sound dampening portion of the illusion active.

"No," the Mage said, stretching muscles ill-used from his brief run. "It's hurt, angry, and half starved. We can't possibly outrun it at this pace. Our magic can barely deceive it as it is, and there's precious little of it left." Kevon handed the Movement rod to Mirsa. "I'm going to ask for a bit more of yours, and hope it gets us out of this."

Mirsa nodded, and Kevon felt the Aid rune form in her mind. Kevon formed a Movement rune, and began jogging in circles around his friends, drawing power from Mirsa to augment his speed.

"Easy enough?" Kevon asked, returning to the group. "Carlo and Bertus can keep up a quicker pace if you can. Stay with them, run to where you can use elemental magic safely, and burrow to safety if I haven't returned."

"Trade me," Mirsa suggested, holding the rod Kevon had given her out at arm's length. "I'm more skilled at Movement than Illusion."

The Warsmith took the offered focal rod, and gave Mirsa the other in return. He smiled. "With this one, I won't even need to use Illusion." He stopped, and began releasing the Illusion spell that maintained the concealing cloak about them. As the magical shield passed over him, Mirsa took control. "See you in a few miles," Kevon called, his voice ringing clearly without magical interference.

Kevon closed his eyes and allowed himself one moment of pure relaxation; no magic, no worries, just the feel of the cool breeze and warm sun wrestling good-naturedly on his skin.

The Orclord roared at the sight of its prey, so exposed and immobile, bringing Kevon back to the situation at hand.

He gripped the Movement rod easily, like a baton in a Feastday relay, and let the focal enchantment sharpen the rune in his mind to crystal clarity. With the barest outlay of magical energy, the Mage sprinted back toward the Orclord, swerving to avoid a predictable lunge by his pursuer turned plaything. He turned and struck out in a northeasterly direction, leading the beast away, but not too far away, from his friends that were headed almost due east.

The chase went on for the better part of an hour. Kevon would speed ahead, then stop to catch his breath. Not truly winded, nor low on magic, Kevon did need the frequent stops to rub the aches out of his muscles. The breaks also ensured that his magic would replenish enough to draw the pursuit far enough away from the source of the mystical corruption that Kevon and Mirsa would eventually have the upper hand in the inevitable confrontation.

The Orclord stopped, as it had several times before, and seemed again like it was ready to give up. Kevon sped around his giant foe, in a tightening spiral, waiting for the response that signaled a renewed interest in the chase.

Minding the terrain and trying to gauge where the Orc's attention had been diverted, Kevon nearly smashed into a striding foot as the Orclord began walking. The Mage ducked and skidded to a shaky halt yards away from the newly motivated giant. Once he was positive which direction the orc was headed, he looped wide around the Orclord with great haste, speeding, he assumed, to where his friends had been spotted.

A five minute sprint left Kevon nearly drained, both physically and mentally. His muscles burned, and he wobbled shakily on his overtaxed legs. A backward glance over his shoulder saw his pursuer in the distance, perhaps ten minutes away.

"Kevon!" Mirsa called as she dropped the illusion that nearly concealed the rest of the party. "Why are you...?" Her voice trailed off as she saw the horror bearing down on them from the north.

"You're both spent, then?" Carlo smiled grimly, drawing his broadsword.

"All but," Kevon admitted. "And I imagine Mirsa feels much the same, else she would not have let the illusion falter." The Mage sighed. "The corruption is less here, but it feels too great to overcome with the strength I have left."

"Let us continue," Mirsa suggested. "By the time it draws near, we may have gathered enough power between us to give a suitable accounting."

The four continued eastward at an easy pace, each quietly preparing for the coming battle in the best way they knew. Carlo stretched out, shaking muscles numbed by the long run. Bertus drew and loaded his crossbow, jogging to catch back up. Kevon held Mirsa's hand as they walked, twining his fingers with hers and squeezing gently. "We're going to be all right," he promised, but he wasn't sure who he was trying to reassure.

Shortly, Kevon could hear the orc's frenzied howling, and feel the earth tremble at its footfalls. He stopped, and turned toward the oncoming Orclord. "It's time."

His companions stopped and faced the oncoming threat. Bertus raised his crossbow, and Carlo rested his hand on his sword hilt.

Mirsa stretched a palm forward, and Kevon could feel her magic lancing through the latent elemental corruption. A slight upward trickle of Earth magic twined with the Master Mage's own stored energies before flowing outward. Kevon fought the urge to add his own magic to the spell, still wary of what had happened in the cavern below the tower.

The orc stumbled, and went down. The earth before it had given way in just the right spot, causing the fall.

Lacking the reserves to press the attack further, Mirsa marshaled the energies around her, trying to attract enough sympathetic magic to make a difference. The corruption leeched energy as fast as she could gather it, and she directed her attention downward, to delve deeper, gather more power that she could use to overcome the chaos that taxed her magic as well as her concentration.

Seeing her intent, and hoping that they could work greater magic, or even simply escape once they were deeper in the earth, Kevon lent Mirsa his strength.

The ground Mirsa stood upon sank until the Mage was waist-deep in the circular depression. Kevon could feel the energy swirling around her, gathering until she focused and lashed out with it again.

The earth beneath the Orclord groaned, and gave way. The beast cried out, then dropped from sight.

Mirsa slumped forward as the last of the magic left her. "It wasn't enough..." she whispered as Kevon whirled to catch her. "Run."

Kevon threw the exhausted Mage over his shoulder, easily lifting Mirsa with unfatigued arms that were used to a Blacksmith's work. His legs protested, but he set out at a trot, turning ever eastward, Bertus and Carlo falling in behind.

Bertus's crossbow *twanged*, and moments later the Orclord bawled, as the boy shouted in triumph.

Kevon could not waste the time or energy to turn, but Carlo's barking laughter was assurance enough that they had just won another small victory.

Five exhausting minutes later, Carlo spoke again.

"Well, now it's just angry, lad."

The Seeker heard Bertus sigh and stop briefly to reload his weapon.

Mirsa stirred, groaning, and the fatigued warrior stopped and lowered her to her feet.

"Can you walk?" he asked, "Or better, run?"

Her gaze drifted back behind him, to where Kevon had not looked since he had scooped her up. Wide eyed, she nodded, and turned to flee.

The Warsmith followed closely behind Mirsa, with limbs that felt as sturdy as Feastday pudding. His mind felt little better, having been constantly taxed the last few hours. Nevertheless, Kevon pushed outwards with his magical senses, and still felt the slight corruption affecting the elemental magic.

But only just... Kevon thought, horrified and elated at how near the Orclord must be drawing, and at how close they were to having the means to destroy it. He weighed the meager amount of energy he had accumulated in the minutes since he'd spent himself helping Mirsa, and judged it was not enough to delve more than a foot into the earth, and he was sure Mirsa had recovered even less than he. *If only there were some other place I could...*

A frenzied roar from the approaching Orclord, and a sudden shift in footing as one of Kevon's steps coincided with a shockwave from his pursuer pushed the unreasonable hope into a frantic search. In that moment of panic, Kevon expended all of his magic to reach out in all directions, searching for anything to latch onto, anything that could save them.

Kevon drank deeply of the power he found, right in the palm of his hand.

Or near the palm of my hand, He thought, smirking as he turned to face the charging Orc. Giddy with power, Kevon unleashed a surge of magic. The ground before him buckled, and an earthen wave flowed forth, gaining in size and speed as it traveled.

"Hah!" Kevon shouted, gesturing upward as the wave

crested to slam, chest high, into the oncoming Orclord. Suddenly aware of what he had just done, he released the power. "Is it dead?" he asked, peering ahead at the newly shattered landscape.

As if in response, the rubble shifted. After a few moments, it shifted again.

"What do you think we should...?" Kevon stopped short as he turned and spotted the expressions on his friends' faces. Carlo, weapon still in its scabbard, nonetheless appeared to be sizing Kevon up as a possible adversary. Mirsa's face was a mask of shock and confusion. Only Bertus's grin and eyes shining with excitement and hope seemed in character.
"How did...?" Mirsa whispered, backing away.

"I'll explain after!" Kevon snapped. "Right now we need to deal with..."

The broken earth he'd turned his back on shifted audibly. Kevon turned to look directly at Carlo.

"You seemed to be doing fine," the Commander grunted.

Kevon sighed, and turned to face the Orclord, who was struggling into a sitting position. He cleared his mind, and wrenched more Earth magic from the ring. He wrapped himself in the energy, readying a strike larger than the last, when the well ran dry.

The power that he'd gathered began diffusing, ebbing swiftly below the amount of magic he'd used for the previous spell. Seeing no alternative, Kevon used his swiftly frazzling reserves to sink into the earth. To his waist. To his neck. Six feet under. Twelve. Sympathetic magic flowed inward, punching through the disarray of the broken enchantments, offering, then forcing its way into his mind. He wrestled with the forces, and as he mastered them, brought his friends down to safety, covering the shafts above them as he merged their passageways into his chamber.

Mirsa drew a Light orb from her cloak pocket, and lit it, but Kevon's senses were elsewhere, as he pushed the stone chamber they were now encased in through the earth to the east.

The strain of managing the power was wearing him down, but he paused long enough to direct his attention back to where they had left the Orclord, He flung his palm toward the west, unleashing all of the forces that he had drawn in. He pushed back against the renewed influx of Earth magic, and ended the spell. Grasping his sword hilt for relief, he smiled, and fell asleep.

CHAPTER 20

Kevon awoke to a flurry of jabs in his leg. Before he could steel himself against it, the pain from his overtaxed muscles washed over him. His head throbbed, and copious amounts of Earth magic threatened to cascade into his mind.

"Wake up," Bertus pleaded, whispering. "We let you sleep about an hour, but Mirsa is *not* well."

The Mage peered over to the other side of the chamber, where Mirsa crouched, holding the flickering Light orb, eyes closed, rocking back and forth on her heels. He knew what she must be feeling, trapped here, mind being crushed by the magic, afraid to wield it even this far from the source of the corruption. He rose and walked stiffly over to Mirsa. "I told you it will be all right," he said, cupping the side of her face in his hand. "And it starts now."

Not willing to wait any longer, Kevon formed an Earth rune in his mind, and accepted the power that was bearing down on him. He siphoned the energies he felt gathered around Mirsa, actively drawing from that direction, while passively absorbing whatever other magic that presented itself. Shortly, he had gathered more than enough to begin propelling their stone chamber toward the surface, and the ascent began.

Mirsa stood, and Kevon adjusted the flows to compensate for her change in position, and hastened the chamber upward. He could feel her mind reach out and touch the torrents of magic that writhed past her, and then withdraw. Moments later, the stone overhead split, opening to the sky and light rain. The floor of their temporary sanctuary had almost reached ground level when the magic gave out, and the spell ended.

Carlo and Bertus both turned their faces into the oncoming rain, no doubt thankful to be free of an underground prison they had no chance of escaping on their own. Color started returning to Mirsa's face, and Kevon breathed deeply of fresh air that did not smell of sweat and fear.

Kevon vaulted over the partially formed wall to the west, and leaned back against it, peering at his handiwork in the distance. Several hundred yards away, standing, half slumped forward, was the Orclord. Supporting its still form was a field of stone spikes that thrust up at an angle toward the west. Some of the rock formations extended above the height of the lifeless orc, and at least four of them pierced completely through it.

Bertus climbed the wall and sat next to Kevon, letting out a low whistle of approval. "Fortunate that I slowed it down for you back there," he commented, shoving the Mage playfully.

"Yes, it was," Kevon agreed. "Waine would have been proud of you... Of all of us."

Mirsa climbed out of the depression at a notch in what remained of the wall, and walked around to where the others waited. She regarded the slain orc in silence, then turned to Kevon. "You've been able to bend great amounts of power to your will. As much as I've seen any Master work, at least." She locked her gaze to his. "By now you must have realized the potentials for power, as well as disaster, when using borrowed elemental magic."

Kevon grimaced.

"Even with the corrupted state of magic in this area," Mirsa continued, "It's safer to use large amounts of elemental energy, where there are no other Magi, to speak of."

"Why is that?" Bertus chimed in.

"All another Mage would need to do would be to gather magic from a source you are using at the wrong time, and the results could be... Well, you've seen them for yourself."

"Hmm?" Bertus asked, face scrunched in disbelief.

"The wastelands of the Southern Frontier?" Mirsa asked, eyes widening. "The final battleground of the War of the Magi?"

"Miners and blacksmiths wouldn't normally speak of such things, even if they knew them," Kevon offered. "I must admit, I've only seen brief mention of the War, myself."

Mirsa drew her cloak tighter about her as the wind picked up. The rain was no more than scattered droplets by then, and clothing seemed to dry as fast as it dampened. "This is as much of a shelter as I expect we'll find today?" Mirsa asked, nodding to the broken chamber. "I don't fancy going underground any too soon."

"The orc's dead," Carlo grunted. "As far as I'm concerned, the Leapers can eat us."

Bertus laughed, the weariness showing in his young face perhaps more than the others.

Hours later, they sat gathered around a small fire in the waning light. Carlo perched atop the rim of one of the lower walls, inspecting his blades. Bertus was wedged into a corner, quietly dozing. Kevon and Mirsa sat, backs to another wall, quietly conversing.

"The Magi of long ago were more powerful, unafraid to wrest their spell energies from the elements." Mirsa explained. "Before the Realm of Kærtis was even formed, smaller nation-states battled for control of the northern and southern ends of the continent. Few settled the middle part, for nothing grew well, and even then, orcs roamed in abundance. Then, as now, Magi were reluctant to become involved in political matters, territorial disputes. They preferred to be left to their studies, lending aid as they could when the other races threatened to rise against Men."

Mirsa remained silent for a few moments, lost in thought. "Power on the continent stabilized, the Monarchy consolidating its forces in the north, and a federation of states formed an uneasy alliance in the south. Hostilities ebbed for a number of years..."

"Until?"

"Word reached the two nations at about the same time. Someone living in the middle-lands had unearthed a relic, a thing of myth. Some say it was a Seat of Power."

Kevon shook his head. "I don't..."

"The oldest legends tell of the making of Ærth," Mirsa sighed. "That the creators walked among us, and ruled different areas of the world. More people had faith in the old tales then, and acted upon their beliefs."

"M'Lani..." Kevon breathed, recalling a story he'd read what seemed a lifetime ago.

"The goddess of Light," Mirsa nodded. "You do know some of the Old Lore."

"It was something I read in a children's storybook," Kevon explained, "Something about it seemed..." Kevon searched for words, but couldn't manage to find the right ones.

"Believers of the Old Lore are often persuasive, eloquent," Mirsa agreed, "But I've researched magic for years, torn at the fabric of the world and the planes that lie beyond. I've seen no proof." She paused, as if she expected Kevon to continue interrupting. When he did not, she proceeded. "A Seat of Power would have been an incredible find, not just ideologically, but the magical potential would have been incalculable. Neither the King in the north, nor the Council in the south, could allow the other side to have such an advantage. Troops were deployed. They met in the Middle-lands, skirmished back and forth, killing each other fruitlessly. According to the legends, the Council was the first to convince the Magi to join the battle. After all, if the King held the Seat, his subjects would prosper, and the southern states would be overrun. The King, fearing a similar fate, enlisted Magi from his own lands. Once the Magi had tasted battle, what was left of the regular armies fled. For days the storm clouds gathered, and flashes of fire were seen for miles. No one knows which side did it, but it was felt across the Realm, some say even across the sea. Years later, when people ventured back, the landscape was forever changed."

"So the Seat was destroyed?"

"If it ever existed, it wouldn't have survived the cataclysm." Mirsa affirmed. "None of the soldiers knew the location, just rumors. And none of the Magi from the final battle survived."

"How many Magi would it have taken to do that?" Kevon wondered aloud.

"If one could delve deep enough, survive the power long enough to misuse it..." Mirsa shuddered. "One would be all it took. Add another Mage to disrupt or try and divert his focus..."

"Our second night away from the Company..." Kevon began, surprised at how difficult it was trying to recall the recent events. "I was sensing almost the whole valley, drawing power from the mountain cave we were in. I thought I felt a group of orcs on the move. I knew that it would only take a thought to kill them all, but the power scared me."

Mirsa nodded. "You would be better able to handle it now, with the experience you've gained in the last few days. But, the more you use the elements, the more you draw from sympathetic sources, the more power you attract from those sources. Powerful Elementalists often have to retire to places where the elements are balanced, preferably away from their element of choice. The Geomancers that caused the cataclysm would have been best off living among the Sea Elves, atop one of their islands. Open to the sky, surrounded by water."

"A high mountain village, next to a stream?" Kevon asked, tensing up.

"More ideal for a Pyromancer," Mirsa responded. "Why do you..."

"Holten..." Kevon spat. "What better reason for a Master Mage to move to somewhere so out of the way? Maybe he was hiding from himself, as well as others."

"It's possible," she whispered.

"Would..." Kevon frowned. "Would a Mage that needed to isolate himself from Fire... Would he be able to open a gateway to the Plane of Fire, summon a dragon?"

"With the right tools, bonfires lit nearby, anywhere near midday, and the skill to focus the magic..." Mirsa pursed her lips. "It may be possible. But there is no record of such a powerful Pyromancer in ages. Having access to the Royal Library has its benefits. Court Wizards keep meticulous track of all known Magi that reach Journeyman status." She giggled. "Except you, of course."

The Warsmith stood and leapt out of the circular depression. The pounding of his heart was mirrored by the pulsing Earth rune that rasped at his awareness, whispering to be used.

Mirsa followed, clambering over the low wall, summoning a globe of Light after she stood and dusted herself off.

"Life is strange," Kevon mused, kicking at pebbles that he spotted by Mage-light. "If my suspicions are correct, not only was Holten conspiring to unleash the Orclord on our Realm, he could have been the Mage that summoned the dragon that killed my father."

"More revenge, eh?" Carlo called from his nearby perch.

"I'm going!" Bertus gasped, now half awake. "Where are we going?"

CHAPTER 21

"I'm still going," Bertus sniped, riding past Kevon and Mirsa to catch up with Carlo.

Kevon smiled. He knew the boy was right. Bertus was the logical choice, as Mirsa and Carlo both had obligations in Navlia. *Obligations that lay less than an hour's ride ahead,* he thought, furrowing his brow.

The return trip had gone smoothly enough, after they had retrieved the horses. There had been one attack by a trio of Leapers the second night, and well clear of the hindrance on elemental magic, Kevon and Mirsa had made short work of the beasts. A lone imp harassed them for three nights, finally drawing close enough that Bertus could skewer it with a bolt. The remaining weeks had served to heal wounds, replenish provisions, and rest weary muscles and minds.

Kevon glanced at the Guardsman riding behind them, and sighed. He'd been unable to talk openly with his friends about magic for the last few days. The four companions had been rather tight-lipped about the defeat of the Orclord, not wanting to chance the spread of rumors before Alacrit had been briefed on the encounter.

"By your leave, Mirsa Magus," Kevon said politely, and at her nod, rode ahead to join the others.

"I don't envy your paperwork," he said, pulling alongside Carlo.

"Recounting Mirsa's triumph against the Orclord should be more amusing than most of my reports," the Commander replied, giving Kevon a sidelong glance. "Have you decided where your next assignment should be?"

"Unless I hear differently, I should head back to Eastport to settle affairs there."

"I can have orders drawn up to that effect by the morning, should you need them." Carlo glanced askew at Kevon. "Settle affairs, or scores?"

"Whatever needs settling, I suppose." Kevon let his mount drift to the side of the road, and did not speak until they reached the city.

"What was it like?" Xæver pressed, as Kevon straightened up his belongings and readied for the evening banquet.

Kevon shrugged. "We just protected the Wizard," he sighed. "She did all the work."

"Just back from the greatest battle in generations, and rumor has it you're being reassigned to a post in the north?"

"I *will* have dinner first." Kevon smiled, and finished changing into his dress uniform. The overly talkative Warsmith kept jabbering as Kevon stood in front of a mirror and scraped away the remaining few whiskers he'd missed earlier with the edge of his knife.

Carlo and Bertus arrived as he was finishing up, and escorted by a ceremonial guard, they made their way to the Great Hall.

The four guardsmen that flanked Kevon and his friends halted at the entrance to the room, and motioned them ahead. Carlo, Kevon, and then Bertus entered single file, each expecting something far grander than their last meal with the Prince.

Instead, Mirsa and the young monarch sat at one of the smaller dining tables, while the rest of the room sat quiet and empty. Plates and utensils for over a hundred lay on the other tables, which were otherwise barren.

"Your Highness?" Carlo bowed as they approached the

table.

"Come," the Prince stood and motioned to the others. "Sit."

To Kevon's surprise, the food was exquisite quality renderings of simple tavern fare. No servants approached to serve them or pour wine. The Prince himself picked up a bowl heaped with large flaky biscuits, took two, and passed them on.

"My advisor told me," he began, "That she and her companions would appreciate something far simpler, more personal than I had planned." He chuckled. "Many in the court are very displeased, but we are here to honor you, not them."

"Your Highness," Carlo rumbled, a hint of gruffness in his voice. "We did only what we were able, as have so many before us."

Alacrit smiled, nodded, and ate in silence for a short time.

"You four intrigue me," he said at length. "Great deeds, greater humility. It seems the only proper reward for such loyalty and service... Is more difficult service."

Carlo grunted in amusement.

"It won't do to keep such talent and skill here, where the perils number fewest," the monarch continued. "I would like to grant you, Commander, the title of Knight Protector, and send you to train my other officers in the arts of strategy and tactics, as well as the blade. You, sir Warsmith," he said, eyes resting on Kevon, "Have a great talent with weaponry for one so young, I'm told."

"I've bested my betters, on occasion," Kevon admitted. "I manage to find enough strength to win."

The Prince laughed. "That is exactly what people look for in their heroes. Do you realize the people have named you so already? 'Heroes of the Western Vale', they are saying. You four are exactly what the Realm has been needing."

Kevon stopped in mid bite, the gravy smothered morsel of bread suddenly losing its appeal. The last thing he needed was to lose the advantage of anonymity.

"I would like to make you a Warsmith Comman..."

"Begging your pardon," Kevon interrupted, "If you intend to use me in the same capacity as Carlo, I think it would be best if I did not have a contingent to look after."

Prince Alacrit bit his lip, looking equal parts irritated and amused. "And you, Sir Bertus?"

"I wouldn't mind being a Knight," Bertus admitted, "Though I don't think I've earned it yet. Besides, someone needs to watch out for the 'Warsmith Commander'."

"I suppose that settles it," the Prince continued. "Carlo will begin selecting and training a special tactics unit within the week. He'll leave for the Southern Frontier by the end of the Season. We have greatest need of military advantage there. Mirsa shall remain here, in the palace, as I have great need of experienced advisors, rather than those who have never left the city walls. And the two of you..."

"I have business in Eastport, your Highness," Kevon said, pushing his plate away and standing. "If it pleases you, I would like to begin my duties there."

"Nothing pleases me more than skill, coupled with loyalty. Please, each of you, see me before you depart."

The ruler of Kærtis stood and took his leave of the companions, guards that Kevon had not noticed during the meal rising to escort Alacrit out of the room.

"Hadn't seen them..." Kevon muttered under his breath.

"Almost choked on my biscuit when I spotted them," Carlo rumbled in agreement. "I may have to enlist one or two of them in my training squad."

Mirsa started to rise, and Bertus and Carlo swiftly stood. "I understand you have preparations to make," she said, her voice slipping into an affected, haughty tone that was not too different than when Kevon had first met her. "But please, make time to see me before you leave, as well." she finished in her normal voice. She turned to leave, and two of the ceremonial guard that had escorted the men in separated to follow her back into the residential quarters.

"This should make things much easier," Kevon growled. "Extra attention from nearly everyone. I'm going to the Guild-hall. They should be least impressed with our new status."

CHAPTER 22

Kevon found it hard to measure how less impressed his fellow Warriors were through the pounding headache he awoke to. He remembered that both he and Bertus had tested for advancement, and the beginning of the resulting celebration. He could only assume that the palace staff had brought him back safely; though the room did not look familiar, he could see his belongings from his barracks stacked neatly about.

Poking his head out the door to try to get his bearings, he spotted a page stationed nearby.

"Excuse me…" he called softly. "Do you know…?"

"I'll alert Mirsa Magus," the page said, bowing and disappearing into a hallway.

The Warsmith sighed and closed the door. He finished making himself presentable, and waited the few minutes until he heard a knock on his door.

"What does she want with…?" Kevon stopped short as he opened the door and saw Mirsa standing there instead of one of the servants.

"I suppose she wants a proper goodbye," the Master Wizard said, pressing a palm to Kevon's chest, pushing him back inside the room, steering the scabbarded sword on his left hip away from her. "She's going to have to stay here, while the other 'heroes' are off adventuring."

"I was planning on seeing you before we left," Kevon mumbled as Mirsa closed the door behind her. "There's no way I would…"

"I'm aware of the things that you would not do, sadly." she whispered, putting a finger to his lips. "Let's discuss what you are willing to do."

"Mirsa, I..." Kevon stammered. "You know what I've been through, I can't...."

The Wizard shrieked in frustration, storming across the room to flounce onto Kevon's bed. "The scheming and intrigues here at court used to amuse me, before I knew the truths you've all shown me. Now I see they've always been petty, trivial plays at the shadow of power. There are forces far from here that care nothing for these silly games, but have plans of their own in motion that could destroy us all. I need to be out there fighting them."

Kevon pushed aside the urges that surfaced against his will. "I cannot go against Alacrit's orders," he said, sitting beside her. "I would like to have you with me." Kevon sighed. "But maybe the Realm needs you here."

The Warsmith stood, kissed the Wizard atop her head, and strode quickly away, seeking an audience with the Prince.

◆ ◆ ◆

Minutes later, Kevon knelt before the monarch of Kærtis.

"Enough," Alacrit chuckled, helping Kevon to his feet. "Heroes of the Realm are afforded the luxury of more casual courtesy."

"Thank you, my Prince," Kevon responded, looking Alacrit in the eye.

"Ready to depart so soon?" Prince Alacrit asked. "Is there anything I can provide that might help you on your way? A new suit of chain mail from the royal armory? A better sword?"

"Thank you, no," Kevon answered. "My weapons are more than suitable, and I wouldn't know how to move in armor. My horses are healthy, and one of the best cooks in the Realm is accompanying me. There is little that could improve my situation."

"Are you certain you won't take an attachment of Guardsmen?" Alacrit asked again. "It wouldn't do to have anything befall a Hero of the Realm…"

"The only companions I would accept without hesitation would be Carlo and Mirsa, Your Majesty." Kevon replied. "But for a few fallen comrades, they alone have my complete trust."

Alacrit nodded. "I understand your loyalty, but you must understand my position. We must pray that no danger befalls us that is dire enough to require all of your services again. It is to that end that I send you to strengthen our weaknesses throughout the Realm. You are all, however, welcome to visit at any time."

Even though the Monarch was disbanding his group of friends, Kevon could not help but admire the conviction he heard in the young Prince's voice, saw in his eyes. "Thank you, milord," he mumbled, inclining his head slightly.

"Since you want for nothing," Alacrit chided, "Perhaps I can meet your needs, should they arise." He drew forth from his tunic a thin scroll case, tastefully inlaid with semiprecious stones. "Should you require anything on your journey, use this to procure it, in my name."

Kevon thought back to the last time he'd been sent on a quest by someone he admired and respected. *I'll check the scroll later,* he thought, accepting the ornate vessel with a smile.

"I will take no more of your time," Alacrit announced. "Depart at your leisure, with my blessing."

"Thank you." Kevon bowed, and hastened from the audience chamber.

"Ready?" Bertus asked as Kevon passed by his open door.

"I've already spoken with Prince Alacrit, if that's what you mean," Kevon answered, eyeing the young man's dress uniform.

"No, so have I," Bertus retorted, pulling a scroll case part-way out of his tunic. "Our last night in the only town they know us as heroes?"

The Warsmith could feel his head pounding again, echoing the questionable choices of the night before. "I think I'll finish getting things together and relax for the rest of the evening. I'd like to be able to ride in the morning."

"I see." Bertus grinned, straightening his collar and moving toward the door. "Plenty of entertainment under this roof, as well. I'll have your things from the Guild sent over."

"Thank you," Kevon replied, turning to his own room.

He had his belongings unpacked, sorted, and was beginning to repack them when the chest from the Guild arrived. The two palace guards bearing it waited outside for Kevon to unload it before carrying it away again. As he had grown accustomed, Kevon sorted his gear into Warrior and Mage piles, and packed them accordingly. Anyone discovering his magical equipment while he traveled as a Warrior would believe that it was all spoils of combat. Now that Bertus was a Guildsman, excess gear could be hauled on the packhorse and attributed to him, should Kevon need to appear as a Mage.

With the magical implements tucked into his newest set of saddlebags, and the rest packed away in the two remaining sets, all hung over the bedpost, Kevon breathed a sigh of relief. A solid night's rest, and they would be on their way to Eastport, *and Justice.*

CHAPTER 23

Kevon struggled within the dream, knowing the images that flashed before him were unreal, but unable to awaken. Shadowy figures chased him across a barren landscape, and he fled in terror. He knew that he should stand and fight, either steel or magic should be more than a match for the faceless enemies that pursued him. His dream-self would not listen, and gibbered hysterically as it ran. He crossed bridges over canals, and came to a closed gate. Pounding, screaming, his dream-self pleaded for entrance. The pursuing shadows drew closer, slowing to savor the fear.

The gate creaked open, and Kevon threw himself into the enveloping darkness within. He pulled the gate closed behind, and helped drop the bar to secure it. Turning to thank his rescuer, he gasped at the cowled figure that reached out for him, a single emerald spark gleaming from beneath the hood. He felt a Fire rune form, and braced for the spell, flinging out his arm to shield his face.

Dream gave way to reality, but the nightmare had merely changed forms. The Fire rune still burned brightly in Kevon's mind, fueled by a figure standing silhouetted in the doorway to his room. Kevon's shielding arm flared with pain, enveloped in a burst of flames. The magical fire reached the iron ring on his finger, and faltered.

Kevon's surprise and anger latched onto the already formed rune, and fed on the heat still in the air. A bolt of Fire lanced out and struck the surprised assailant before Kevon could restrain himself. Shifting focus, he formed a Movement rune, and shoved the screaming Mage from behind, into his waiting grasp. Ignoring the pain, he drew his sword from its resting place and pressed the tip to the Mage's chest.

'Blasphemer!" the hooded Mage screamed.

Kevon pressed the sword more firmly, and the screaming stopped.

"*You!*" the attacker hissed, as Kevon felt a twinge of recognition. The Mage was one of Tarska Magus's acolytes from the gathering at Gurlin's tower. "No matter," he laughed. "You'll not survive the night."

Before Kevon could react, the Mage grasped the sword blade with both hands, his convulsion pulling the tip into his flesh to scrape against bone before he collapsed, dead.

Shadows in the hallway stretched and danced. Kevon swore and pried his blade from the fallen Mage's hands. Lights grew brighter, and Kevon rushed the door, sword at the ready.

A black-robed figure whirled into the room, staff ablaze, followed by two guards. Glancing at the still form crumpled on the ground, she quelled the flaming staff. "With me!" Mirsa commanded. "There may be others!"

The Warsmith followed the Master Mage, her reignited staff blazing ahead of them. He fought the urge to sheath his sword so that he could feel the magic that she was tracking.

Mirsa led the brisk march through the residential quarters toward the Great Hall, pausing only briefly at intersections to concentrate. When they reached the Hall, Mirsa navigated around the overturned tables and chairs to the entrance of the south wing, where the Royals kept residence. "Be ready," she cautioned, plunging ahead without pause.

A few quick twists and turns, and Kevon burst out into a small meeting hall, sidling into place beside Mirsa.

"No…" she whispered, audible only to Kevon above the fracas before them.

Tarska Magus and two other hooded Magi had Prince Alacrit, two of his Court Wizards, and a single injured Royal Guard backed into a corner. "All your victories are hollow!" he shrieked, his aged voice quavering. "The Masters will not be hindered by your feeble attacks!"

"Really?" Kevon asked, drawing his sword from the spasming acolyte he'd sheathed it in. "What would hinder them?"

"Ahh, the 'Hero'", Tarska sneered, turning to face Kevon. "And the *Heretic*," he added, glancing past the Warrior to Mirsa.

"In my experience," Kevon whipped his blade in a flourish, spattering Tarska with flecks of his student's blood. "People who use that word often don't know what they're talking about."

The flicker of motion from the tip of the Wizard's staff was all the warning Kevon had, but it was enough. He reversed the grip on his sword hilt, and swung it into a figure-eight that wrapped him in a blurring shield of steel.

The first blast of flame seared Kevon's hand before contacting the iron in the hilt. The Warrior grimaced, not expecting to escape unscathed, but still trying nevertheless. He shifted his pattern, lurching the center of the flashing barrier to and fro, trying to stay ahead of Tarska's attacks.

The Wizard changed tactics, weaving Wind and Fire in short bursts that terminated before they reached Kevon's blade, but carried the scorching heat to their target regardless. Tarska Magus retreated as Kevon advanced, evenly, with measured steps, always two sword-lengths away.

Kevon slowed for a moment to wipe the sweat from his eyes. The Wizard's attacks had heated the medium sized room to nearly that of the frontier smithy that Kevon had abandoned almost a season ago. Uncomfortable, but not unbearable.

That instant was enough for Tarska to land another searing blast to Kevon's sword hand. Swearing, the Warsmith shifted hands, his left clumsier, and inherently more unpredictable than his right as he focused his entire being on maintaining the speed of the blade.

"What?!" Tarska cried, stumbling into his remaining acolyte. The younger Mage was squaring off against Mirsa, who had edged around to get a clear view and prevent the Journeyman from flanking Kevon. "Fool!" the Master Mage shoved his remaining assistant forward toward the left edge of Kevon's blade barrier, still between himself and Mirsa, but close enough to concern the Warrior.

The reeling Mage managed to deflect a blast of Fire magic from Mirsa before an almost intentional slice from Kevon's sword dropped him to the floor, convulsing.

The shallow slice from the desperately whirling blade was enough to kill the Mage, and wrest the weapon from the unpracticed grip of its wielder. The sword clattered off to the side toward Alacrit and his surviving retainers.

"Now!" the Monarch commanded, and the guard stepped aside to allow the Court Wizards to work their Art. Alacrit's Magi unleashed blasts of fire, no doubt drawing from the latent heat in the room.

As Kevon expected, at the last moment, Tarska Magus deflected the magic toward him. Or rather where he had been. Kevon leapt and rolled, swatting at the oncoming flames with his burnt hand, and the ring upon it. The maneuver that squelched the flaming blast threw him off balance, and he knew he was going to end up short of his goal, the fallen blade. Drawing focus from the momentum he already had, Kevon pulsed the trickle of magic he'd wrenched from his surroundings into a Movement spell, speeding and extending his roll to his weapon.

He leapt to his feet and whirled to face the Wizard, trying not to show his weakness, but slowed considerably by the pain. He held his sword at the ready, not close enough to his foe now for the tactics of a moment ago to make sense. Alacrit's guards rushed forward, their blades and armor closing in front of him, providing a much needed pause in the frantic battle.

The guard, learning from Kevon's tactics, now advanced toward the lone Magi instead of letting himself be pushed into a corner. He leaned into the attacks against the oncoming spells, laughing now, protected by far more iron and steel than Kevon could bring to bear.

"Stop!" the embattled Wizard cried, blasting a fiery bolt that landed at Mirsa's feet, then spread to encircle her. "Or your *Hero* dies."

Kevon could not imagine Mirsa allowing herself to be threatened in such a manner, and readied himself for her response. The guard looked back to the Prince for direction, but Kevon drew his sword back, wide eyed, and crouched as though he was going to place the weapon on the ground.

The temperature in the room dropped from the stifling haze it had been, to that of a crisp fall morning. The flames surrounding Mirsa dwindled to nothing as her hair shone like strands of glowing embers, and flames blossomed from her outstretched hands.

Kevon felt the heat wash over him as though he was standing before his Master's forge in the badlands. He raised his hand to shield his face, and shifted his grip on his sword.

Tarska shrieked as he turned toward Mirsa, now aware of his mistake. The column of fire that rushed toward him was too tightly controlled by the Master Wizard he had thought weaker, and without the ambient heat Mirsa had used to help fuel her magic, the older Wizard had no chance.

Kevon realized that after the blade left his hand, spinning toward the distracted Magi in a wobbly arc.

The hilt of the sword slammed into Tarska's head two heartbeats after Mirsa's rage-fueled inferno, putting a swift end to the Wizard's shrieking agony, and dousing the magical fire in one stroke.

No longer buffeted by her magic or her anger, Mirsa whimpered and slumped to the floor.

Forgetting everything else but her safety, Kevon rushed past the smoldering carcass to her side. He could see no visible burns, and the Master Wizard reached out to grasp him by the collar to pull him close.

"Heroes," she whispered. "He said Heroes…"

"Carlo and Bertus!" Kevon cried out, tearing free of her shaky grasp as he stood. "Guard her with your lives!"

Alacrit and his retinue moved to surround and support Mirsa, but Kevon was already in the north hallway, sprinting out into the Great Hall. Stopping only long enough to slash strips from a tablecloth to bind his burned hands, the enraged Warsmith sheathed his recovered sword, wrapped his wounds with practiced efficiency, and snatched up a broken table leg. As he reached the far end of the banquet chamber, he pressed outward with his senses. Two others were doing the same, from the direction he had just come, but he felt runes of Fire and Movement flickering further to the north. He squeezed the end of the makeshift club until he wanted to scream from the pain the burns continued to inflict, then eased back, confident in his grip even with his wounds.

Kevon stalked through the hallways, pulsing his awareness outward, guessing at where the spell casters were when he could not feel any magic in use for any length of time.

After passing through two long hallways, Kevon had felt enough to surmise that the battle was taking place in the barracks adjoining Carlo's office. Confident that the attacking Magi had not waded through the ranks of sleeping guardsmen to get to the Commander, Kevon changed direction and headed to the alternate entrance to Carlo's office, rather than the barracks.

The nearer Kevon came, the more convinced he was that the struggle was actually taking place *in* Carlo's office. When he came around the last corner before the doorway, he was somewhat relieved that the door was closed. Opening it quietly, he surveyed the ongoing fracas.

Bertus was lying face up between Kevon and Carlo's desk, clothes charred and streaked with blood. Carlo appeared better off only in that he remained upright. The Commander leaned against the wall near the doorway into the barracks, sword at the ready, markedly unimpressed by two blasts of flame that angled through the narrow portal.

Spotting Kevon, Carlo motioned for the Warsmith to enter quickly, move to the sheltered area of the room, and attend to Bertus.

The Warsmith slipped into the room and dove behind the desk without seeing anyone through the barracks entrance. After making sure that Bertus was merely unconscious, and his bleeding was superficial, he moved the youth further behind the obscuring desk before joining Carlo by the door.

"Took care of yours already, I see," Carlo grumbled as Kevon slid in beside him.

"A Master Wizard and three students," he replied. "I had help..." he added, noting Carlo's dubious glance.

"Mirsa?" the Blademaster asked, shifting position as the bursts of flame coming through the door straightened visibly in angle.

"Yes, we were both targeted, as well as Prince Alacrit." Kevon motioned for Carlo to retreat, and switched places with his mentor, sidling up to the door, club in hand.

A tongue of flame spewed into the room, nearly straight on. Feeling the spell release, Kevon shifted his weight, swinging the club in a wide arc, focusing on the motion, pairing it with the Movement rune newly formed in his mind. He released it, at the edge of the doorway, spinning end over end, propelled by a surge of power, to where he felt the Fire spell end. A sickening crunch and a smattering of cheers and whoops from the far end of the next chamber let Kevon know his ploy had worked.

Another barrage of Fire magic poured through the doorway, and Kevon backed away, urging Carlo further along the shielding wall.

"Just one left now, lads!" came a reassuring bellow from one of the veteran guardsmen. "We three can hold him for now, someone run and fetch a crossbow!"

Kevon groaned. A good strategy, to be assured, but announcing it gave the cornered Mage nothing to lose, and precious minutes to act. Assuming the Mage would act sooner than later, Kevon directed Carlo to retake his position at the door. He scrambled over to where Bertus lay behind the desk, and pulled the boy's feet out from behind the sheltering object until they would be plainly visible from the doorway. Crouching low behind the desk himself, Kevon waited and hoped that the enemy Mage would only be expecting two people in the office, and try to break for the open door that was only a few panicked strides away.

Kevon pointed to the door over the desk as he felt the Fire spell forming, giving Carlo a few seconds of preparation, and drawing his hand back down before he could be spotted.

Flames played along the edge of the doorway, then sloshed in as the Mage wielding them wheeled into the room. The strength of the Fire rune Kevon sensed from the spell guttered and flared as Carlo broke the magic with rapid sword swings.

"No!" Carlo cried, and Kevon saw flames splash across Bertus's outstretched feet. The youth moaned, awakened from his torpor by the fresh pain.

Turning his attention to the stream of flames directed at Bertus, Carlo let a blast intended for him slip though his guard.

Pleased with the damage he had inflicted, the Mage nevertheless had to turn to run as the guardsmen from the barracks crowded the doorway behind him.

Seeing his chance, Kevon leapt from behind the desk, sword flashing as he drew it free from its scabbard. He cleft a bolt of flame that spewed raggedly from the tiring Magi's outstretched hand, and shifted to launch a sidelong kick that caught his foe under the jaw. The impact lifted the lighter man, sending him crashing headfirst into the stone wall.

"Wait!" Kevon cried as the guards rushed in from the next room, swords drawn. "He's unconscious!"

The guardsmen slowed and looked to Carlo. The Commander's eyes narrowed as he looked at Kevon.

"I have an *idea*," the Warsmith said, turning back to study the limp form on the ground.

CHAPTER 24

Carlo's desk was *exactly* the right size. The single living Magi from the attack was bound atop it, leather straps tethering his wrists and ankles down to the sturdy wooden legs below. A leather helmet affixed with ropes served to immobilize the captive's head, to keep it from inadvertently swaying into the daggers buried in the polished desktop less than an inch to either side at eye level.

"You're sure this will hold him?" Carlo asked.

"It won't prevent him from using magic, I would imagine," Kevon answered, "but it'll make him think. There's nowhere for him to go, Even if he could use magic to free himself, he'd die as soon as he tried to get up." The Seeker motioned to the three guardsmen that still hung close, watching the sleeping Mage's every breath. "Besides, there's three swords that will be ready to fall at the first hint of trouble."

Carlo nodded. "He's not going to kill anyone else, that's for sure. But do you think you'll be able to get anything out of him?"

"Honestly, no." Kevon confessed. "One of his friends practically impaled himself on my sword earlier. But he's all we have left. We have to try."

Carlo opened his mouth to respond, but the prisoner began moaning.

Not three, but five blades sang free of sheaths, and the Warriors jostled for position around the captive before Carlo hollered at the three guardsmen to make way for Kevon.

"Have you made your peace with whatever gods you worship?" Kevon asked, moving into the Mage's field of view. He could see the man's eyes flitting back and forth from the daggers near his face to Kevon and one of the other nearby guardsmen.

The Mage slowly tested each limb's restraints, evened his breathing out and closed his eyes. "I have indeed made my peace, and have all that I need. It is you that will soon have to reconcile your own beliefs with the way the world really is, where the future lies."

"We have futures," Kevon said, smiling at the Mage. "Yours is forfeit."

Beads of sweat formed on the prisoner's forehead, a smile formed as he began trembling.

Kevon's eyes narrowed as he noticed the flames from the torches in the room were dancing higher than normal, without putting out any more light. "What..."

The door from the hallway slammed open, wood cracking around the hinges.

"No!" shouted Mirsa, sweeping into the room, brandishing her blazing staff.

The captive Mage managed a wheezing giggle. "*His* will be done!"

"Kill him," Carlo said to the nearest Guardsman, stepping around the desk toward the doorway into the cleared barracks.

Kevon whirled around to see what Mirsa was fixated on in the next room. A mixture of shock and relief struck him as he saw the Dark portal swirling in the next room. His sword had shielded him from feeling its twisted presence, but had concealed it from him at the same time.

The bound Mage gurgled as two blades pierced his chest. The flames from the torches dropped to natural levels, and the room grew suddenly darker. Unsupported, the portal began to close.

Kevon's sigh of relief caught in his throat as two leapers bounded through the far side of the distortion into the barracks. The room brightened for a moment as the tear in the world collapsed upon itself, but bunks rattled and cracked on the other side of the threshold as the torches in the next room were quickly snuffed.

"You! Around through the hallway! Secure the Barracks door!" Carlo shouted, pointing to the only guard who hadn't buried his sword in the Mage. "You two, torches! Flank this door! You! Extra light only! There are only two of them!"

Mirsa scowled at the familiarity of Carlo's order, but extinguished her staff and pulled a crystalline orb from a robe pocket, activating it and holding the piercing brilliance aloft.

"Shall we?" Kevon asked, edging toward the darkened doorway.

Carlo led the way into the barracks, Kevon close on his heels. The torch-bearing guardsmen entered and slid along the walls to the side, clearing the way for Mirsa to follow.

The Adept kept his back to the light, knowing that Carlo was watching the other half of the room. As Mirsa stretched the glowing orb upward, the beams of light threw eerie shadows amongst the broken bunks, giving the impression of movement where there was none.

One of the shadows moved of its own accord beyond a pile of splintered planks.

"There," Kevon pointed with the tip of his blade, and began circling around the edge of the room, alert for any sign of the other leaper.

Drawing close to where he should have a look at his target, Kevon slowed, unsure of what he saw. Torn blankets lay wrapped about the other wreckage, but Kevon saw no sign of the leaper he had spotted before, nor had he seen it move since he'd spotted it.

One of the blankets near the mound of destroyed bunks twitched, and Kevon moved closer, and extended his sword to lift a corner to expose the beast beneath.

The blanket launched itself at Kevon, the beast's color returning to a sickly-white sheen as it moved. The leaper was larger and faster than the ones the companions had seen before, and its aerial rush caught the Warsmith off guard. The tip of Kevon's outstretched blade *clacked* against the beast's hide and clattered to the floor as he jumped back.

The leaper lashed out with one of its spindly-looking forelegs and struck at Kevon with a glancing blow that felt like a war-hammer strike. It landed near a wall, crouched down, and appeared to vanish.

The Warsmith recovered his weapon and turned to where the leaper had disappeared. It looked as though there had been an impact against the wall, and the mortar joining the bricks had been smudged over.

Then the patch Kevon was observing shifted.

"It's changing its skin!" Carlo cried, ducking under an attack from the other leaper. "It's not perfect! Pay attention!"

Kevon focused, and discerned the outline of the creature in front of him, tensing for another attack.

The leaper's appearance shifted just before it launched itself at Kevon. The Warsmith dodged to the left, and aimed a slashing counterstrike at the beast's throat.

Instead of lashing out to strike Kevon as it had before, the leaper swung its arm up to protect itself. The blade bit deep into the creature's arm and stuck, wrenching free from Kevon's grasp as the leaper sailed by.

He grabbed a splintered plank that lay nearby, and turned to give chase. A Movement rune formed in his mind, but he had no magic to fuel it with. He brandished the makeshift weapon, glared in Mirsa's direction, and advanced, hoping she would get the message.

The injured leaper was unable to hide with the sword lodged in its unreasonably tough hide, and hissed at Kevon and the torch-bearing guardsman that was also closing in on it.

The Journeyman Mage felt the Aid rune form in Mirsa's mind, and he latched onto it. He wrapped himself in the barest amount of magic, siphoning only enough to keep the link open, and his movements controlled. As soon as the leaper crouched, Kevon pulled more aid from Mirsa, and swung the broken timber with everything he had.

The impact rocked Kevon back on his feet. The plank crashed through the leaper's uninjured arm into the side of its face, and heaved it sidelong into a nearby pile of debris. The end of the improvised club shattered, sending splinters flying.

The Warsmith rushed toward the fallen creature, hefting his shortened weapon, maintaining the Movement spell at half-strength. The leaper twitched, one leg convulsing to full extension, its neck twisted oddly to one side. Spider-web fractures radiated from the two points Kevon's attack had impacted, marring the beast's oddly glossed outer skin. One eye swiveled to fix on Kevon, and the Seeker swung again with overwhelming force, striking the leaper at the same spot in the neck. The stricken creature's hide buckled, the cracks of the previous wound more than doubling. A gruesome *POP* sounded, and the downed leaper lay still.

Kevon turned, and unable to see where the other enemy was, relinquished control of Mirsa's magic. One of the torchbearers was whirling about, sword at the ready. Kevon could not see the other guardsman. The light from Mirsa's spell increased as she assumed full control of her magic, but was still only just brighter than a torch. Carlo stood at alert, sword held as though an afterthought, unable to discern his prey in the lowered light.

Advancing toward the far corner of the room, Kevon kicked at debris as he worked down the possible area that the leaper could be hiding. Carlo began moving toward the same corner, prodding at obstacles as he walked past them.

The guardsman checked his fallen comrade, laid down his weapon, and picked up the extinguished torch that lay nearby. After lighting the spare torch, he held both high and wide, throwing fitful illumination into even the furthest corners.

Mirsa made her way to his side, and with a gesture of her staff, doubled the brightness of the lit torches before placing herself between the guard and the most probable location of the remaining creature.

The perimeter of the search narrowed, until Mirsa called a halt.

"It's here," she warned. "It's beaten. I could open a portal and let it escape."

"After it killed one of us, you would let it live?" the remaining guardsman spat.

Mirsa turned to regard the man, "I said let it escape, not let it live."

Kevon felt the Master Mage begin her spell, and weaken. The energy he had drawn from her to fuel his Movement rune had taken its toll. He used his minimal reserves to snuff the torches the guardsman held, and pressed his attention outward to the darkness surrounding him before drawing it in and adding his energy to Mirsa's spell. As his mind contacted the rune, and the portal began to open, Kevon staggered, more dizzied than nauseated at the touch of the twisted symbol. There was a flurry of movement, a whistling of wind, and Kevon felt the portal ripple as the leaper soared through it. The spell collapsed, and the tip of Mirsa's staff shone, bringing light back where moments before, darkness had clotted the air.

Carlo glared at the Master Mage. "Did you kill it?"

"The portal I opened back to its realm was far above where even imps can be summoned." Mirsa smiled. "It's probably still falling."

The Blademaster nodded, and turned his attention to the fallen guard. After checking for any sign of life, he shook his head. "Form two details. One to clean up the barracks, one to bury Rophel." He patted the other guard on the back. "We'll see justice done. See that he is honored properly."

"You two, with me." The Commander continued, pointing to Kevon and Mirsa. "We're not resting until we've been over every inch of the palace grounds."

CHAPTER 25

Kevon grumbled, and pulled the blanket up over his head. The knocking at his chamber door resumed, louder this time. Resigned to the fact the rapping was not going to stop, the Warsmith sat up and rubbed at his eyes. "What!?" he yelled, hoping his attitude might win him a brief respite.

"Pardon my intrusion," Prince Alacrit declared as he opened the door and stepped in. "I have come to apprise you of the changes in our plans."

The Warsmith took a deep breath and tried to open his eyes. He, Mirsa, and Carlo had not slept until well after the sun had risen. A dozen more palace residents had been slain in the incursion, but nearly twice as many of the intruders met the same fate. The fighting was all finished by the time the trio, flanked by half a dozen crossbowmen, began their final sweep. The grisly images were not lessened by their stillness. Soldiers Kevon had served with on the first foray to Gurlin's tower, Guild brothers he had trained with since then, lay lifeless, some burned almost beyond recognition.

"All right," Kevon whispered, taking a deep breath, and looking at the waiting Prince.

"Bertus is recovering," Alacrit began, "Though he will need re-branded. Carlo gathers troops as we speak, readying for his journey to the south."

Kevon nodded, confused. "This is what we had already discussed, correct?"

"Yes," Alacrit assented, "However, Mirsa Magus also prepares to travel with you and the boy, to Eastport."

Mirsa? Kevon wondered. Why would she be going...?

"We felt that the three of you would be at greater risk apart from one another. You seem capable enough to handle your own defenses, and Carlo will be safe enough with the troops." Alacrit's eyes veered briefly to the side as Kevon gazed at him.

"And we'll be more of a target to draw focus away from the Palace." Kevon added. "I understand, I think we all do." Kevon stretched and stood up. "I, for one, am looking forward to the challenge. I wouldn't doubt the others feel the same."

"I can assign troops..."

"No," Kevon interrupted the nobleman with a smile. "We're better off by ourselves. I can't explain it, but I just feel our chances are better."

"As always, should you need anything, you have only to ask," Alacrit continued. "Mirsa has already sampled from the reliquary." He chuckled. "Nothing but the best for my Heroes."

"I'll keep that in mind," Kevon replied, "Perhaps Bertus and I will look through the armory later. I would like to leave tomorrow, or the day after, if at all possible."

"I would almost feel safer if the four of you stayed," Alacrit offered, "You were the main reason last night's attack failed. Mirsa is questioning local Master Magi, and looking for extra Court Wizards during her absence."

"I will be able to focus wholly on this matter once I return from Eastport," Kevon reassured the Prince. "If things here worsen, I have allies I may be able to contact from there."

Alacrit's expression showed only momentary surprise before returning to normal. "As I have said before, you have the gift of Adnoros, and we are blessed to have earned your loyalty, rather than your enmity." The Prince regarded Kevon's sleep-starved countenance for a moment before adding, "I have other pressing duties to attend to, so I shall take my leave." He bowed slightly before exiting, closing the door behind him.

Kevon awoke again to a loud pounding.

"C'mon!" Bertus jeered through the door. "I almost died, and I'm already up!"

"If you don't have food, go away," Kevon shouted, throwing a boot toward the noise.

"Sleep then," Mirsa called. "We're leaving."

The Adept dragged himself out of bed and pulled on his tunic and boot. He hobbled over and opened the door before grabbing the other boot. "Where are we headed?"

Kevon was unsure what amused Mirsa the most; the lavishing of attention from the Guildsmen as she sat at the main table, or the scowls of the serving maids that were accustomed to having it for themselves. He and Mirsa ate while the brand heated in the fire, and Bertus sat quietly, contemplating the pain to come.

Carlo emerged from a knot of Warriors that had moved to the table, brandishing the glowing implement. "Look familiar, boy?"

Bertus raised his tunic sleeve and leaned toward the approaching Blademaster. "*My* memory is just fine, old man." The Seeker clenched his teeth and forced a smile as Carlo pressed the sizzling brand into his flesh. He yelped only when one of the barmaids sloshed some clear liquid from a wooden goblet over the burn, and handed the remainder of it to him to drink. He took a swallow and sputtered. "Not sure which way burns more," he gasped when he found his voice again. He held still as the wound was bound with clean strips of cloth, and once he had rotated his arm around to check the wrapping's effect on his range of motion, the crowd dispersed.

"A re-branding is only amusing for a short while," Bertus explained to Mirsa over the surrounding conversations that were surprisingly courteous, due no doubt to her presence. "It's a trade-off. The pain of the brand is supposed to purify the weakness that required Healing."

"It's barbaric," Mirsa scolded, "But I'm learning to appreciate the way things are done here. The brand is shared pain. That experience ties you together, much as shared magic binds Magi, helps them to know one another." Her gaze drifted to Kevon long enough for him to notice.

"I had better get back to the Palace," Kevon said, standing. "Prince Alacrit wanted us to look through the armory before we leave."

"A new sword would be nice," Bertus said, standing and flexing the fingers of his branded arm. "Shall we?

Prince Alacrit's eyes danced as he watched the two Warriors survey the contents of the room. They were the only ones outside of the royal family to lay eyes on any of the treasures contained in this private vault since before the completion of the palace, shortly after the beginning of the Wars of Men. More than two thousand years of history sat displayed here, serving no purpose other than to amuse and comfort generations of his family. Alacrit had decided that was no longer acceptable. If his heroes stood a better chance of surviving with aid from heroes from the past, tradition would have to change.

"A little more extravagant that I would like," Bertus called over his shoulder to Alacrit as he hefted a wide-bladed short sword with a hilt inset with jewels, "But it is a fine weapon."

"That is the sword my own blade, and in turn, those of my personal guard, is based on." Alacrit explained. "It belonged to a king whose name, and kingdom, has been lost to history. It is only fitting that it now defend this Realm."

"And this?" Kevon asked, lifting a strange looking hammer from the stand on which it had been resting. Ignoring the shock that tore through him at first contact, he traced his fingers over the top, a four-edged spike that speared through the weapon's head. The hammer head was balanced by an axe blade, reminding Kevon of a halberd, the blade less wicked, and more regal.

"The only weapon ever to have been recovered from any of the Dwarven Lords," the Prince explained. "The metal is unknown to us, and as you might imagine, we have not asked the Dwarves about it." Alacrit smiled. "So you have chosen, then? I will personally oversee their preparation this evening, and you shall have them in the morning."

Kevon nodded, replacing the hammer on its stand, and moving to join Bertus, who had already started for the exit. A jagged, rusty length of greatsword caught his gaze as he walked by its display case, seeming out of place amongst the rest of the treasures. He blinked and shook his head, thinking there was something he should remember, but continued on out after Bertus and Alacrit.

"Mirsa thought it best that you leave early in the morning, unescorted," Alacrit remarked as they crossed from the royal quarters back into the common hallways. "It would let you get well clear of the city without drawing too much attention to yourselves. You could easily outdistance most pursuers at your normal pace."

Kevon found himself wondering what manner of forces might give chase. *Magi, for certain, but have they recruited others?* He could think of no Warriors in the local Guildhall that would move against him, but if the coin was great enough, loyalties could change. There was always plenty of riff-raff in the slums to the north, past the market quarter. He chuckled to himself. Those undesirables would be as likely as not to cut down a Mage offering a job for the gold in his purse rather than accept a job from one. He and his friends might have less to worry about than they feared.

"You seem amused," Alacrit observed, stopping to address Kevon. "Care to share?"

The Warsmith thought for a moment before he answered.

"Running... Hiding... Fighting..." He shook his head. "There used to be a point to it all. I could see the life at the end... Now?"

"Because of *Her?*" Alacrit asked.

Kevon stood, silent, unsure of what to say.

"The Merchant's daughter?" the Prince prodded. "Your business in Eastport?"

"I..."

"There is little that escapes me where my inner circle is concerned, Warsmith." Alacrit laughed. "Your love, his parents, Mirsa's training..." He waved an astounded Bertus off as he resumed walking. "We have no time for this at present. Your journey to the north will provide what you require to choose your paths."

At the next intersection in the hallway, Alacrit stopped and gripped each Warrior in a firm, but familiar handshake. "Rest well," he advised, "A new adventure begins upon the morrow."

Kevon and Bertus stood and watched the monarch stride out of sight down the hall.

"My parents?" Bertus whispered after the departing prince, face scrunched in bewilderment.

Kevon remained silent, wondering what other information Alacrit held in reserve, what methods he used to collect it. Deciding that the prince could not possibly know *his* secret, he jostled Bertus as he started back to his quarters. "*Begins upon the morrow...*" he teased, exaggerating Alacrit's lofty accent and staid bearing until he needed to duck a punch thrown by the younger Warrior.

CHAPTER 26

Kevon rolled out of his bunk, ready, at the first light knock on his door. He'd slept earlier, but as the night dragged on, he'd tossed and turned. Deciding to put his waking hours to good use, he'd shaved and dressed, prepared everything he could so that there would be no delay when the others arrived.

One of the two men flanking his door was from Alacrit's personal guard, the other a guardsman that Kevon had fought beside during the recent attack. He hefted his packed belongings, glanced around the room once more, and followed the escorting officers down the hallway.

The detail led him to Carlo's office, where the Commander greeted him at the door.

"You thought to leave without orders from your superior?" the Blademaster grumped. "Get in there."

The Adept peered past his comrade to the office, where the desk had been moved into a corner, making room for the tables laden with breakfast foods. Mirsa, Bertus, and Alacrit were already filling their plates. He sat his gear next to the pile by the door, and joined the others.

"You really think you can handle it?" Mirsa asked Bertus. "It's not to be taken lightly."

"I learned a few things when we ran with the patrol to the tower," the Novice reassured her, "And I've worked around them for years."

"He does have a way with the beasts," Carlo agreed, eliciting a grin from the younger Warrior. "That's not to say it's a wise idea."

"As I said before, I can spare a hostler," Alacrit interjected. "It's no great..."

"No!" the four chorused.

Alacrit sighed. "You're hiding something, I understand." He looked from face to face, locking eyes with Kevon. "And it's about you, Kevon. Or Anton, whichever you prefer."

Kevon's gaze faltered under the monarch's steely glare. He was unsure how much more the prince knew, and began weighing the possibility of telling him everything before the royal spies found out on their own. "It's..."

"Sire," Carlo interrupted, "If I may, something that I learned not so long ago?"

"Speak," Alacrit assented.

"With all due respect... You're not ready."

Bertus chortled, nearly choking on a strip of bacon.

Prince Alacrit's expression shifted from one of displeasure, to mild amusement. "I will find out," he cautioned.

Kevon nodded. "I pray you will be as accepting of the truth as the others."

Alacrit shook his head. "This is a farewell, not an interrogation." He motioned to a guard by the door. "Bring them in."

The guard exited, and returned a few seconds later, followed by two others bearing a long crate. The two soldiers placed the crate at the Prince's feet, bowed, and left. The guard resumed his post without a word.

Alacrit lifted the crate's lid, and pulled a scabbarded sword from it. "For Bertus. I could not bring myself to have the gems removed, but they are now all but hidden by the new leatherwork. A regal blade, disguised as commonplace... It's almost..." Alacrit smiled and handed the sword to Bertus. "May it serve you well."

Next, the Prince retrieved a thick leather-bound tome from the depths of the crate. "This book has not been seen by Magi for over five hundred years. It was once studied by all the

Royal Wizards of this House, but was stored away generations ago when my ancestors began to fear another War of the Magi might arise. The Arts described within are thought to be dangerous, but they may be needed in the days to come." He handed the book to Mirsa, whose eyes shone with excitement, and hands trembled as she held the tome close to her.

"Kevon," Alacrit said, lifting the Dwarven warhammer from the crate, holding it out for the Warrior to examine. "The old inlays have been replaced with ebony, the handle was rewrapped."

"The strap is new," Kevon observed, thinking it could be useful if he lost his grip on the weapon in the heat of battle. "It is beautiful." He admired the inlaid strips that showed no gaps between the dusky wood and the creamy grey metal for a few moments longer before taking the weapon from Alacrit.

"And for my Knight Commander," Alacrit began, reaching once again into the container.

Kevon snickered, and Carlo groaned as the Prince began lifting an iron-rimmed shield from the crate. The Warsmith was well aware of the Blademaster's disdain for shields.

"Before you judge the gift," Alacrit growled, "Consider it." He spun the shield around to face the others, revealing the decoration on the front. Sunken into the shield-face, outlined by more hammered iron and held fast by steel bands, was the rusted greatsword that Kevon remembered seeing in the Royal armory the day before. Beneath the jagged point of the sword, he recognized the indented 'x' that was Xæver's artisan's mark.

"Is that?" Carlo asked, dumbfounded.

"The sword is not fit to attack, the shield is not the best defense," Alacrit answered, "But the men will rally to our cause, follow wherever you lead. It is indeed, *that* sword."

Carlo looked more shaken than Mirsa had at her gift of ancient magic as he accepted the shield. "From Keldin's Reach, The Twisted Spires, to the Southern Shore..." the Blademaster whispered, looking down at the captive relic.

"Rode the mighty Bartok," the Prince added, "Behind him... followed War."

Kevon's head spun, memories of an evening of strong drink and singing more than two years gone by flowing through his mind. "The song?"

"How will they know?" Carlo asked Alacrit. "I can believe... I want to believe... but the people?"

"Messengers are already on their way to the Warrior's Guild." The Monarch drank deeply from a goblet filled with juice. "Timed properly, the commotion should cover the exit of our other Heroes. Unfortunately, that means breakfast is over."

The Adept ranged out ahead of the wagon, and was not quite a mile from the western gates of Navlia when he heard the faint clanging of the bells in the main square. He reined the stallion back, and wheeled around to see Bertus looking over his shoulder back toward the city. Mirsa alone spared no attention for the abandoned Capitol, urging her mount on, passing the wagon.

"This may only distract them for a short time," the Master Mage said as she pulled alongside Kevon. "We cannot slow. If any of them know who I am, they could be scrying for me even now."

"We may have destroyed their leadership, disrupted their organization" Kevon replied. "There is no way to know for sure, but we may not be followed at all."

Mirsa shook her head. "*His will be done...*" she quoted, and the hairs on the back of Kevon's neck stood on end. "It seems that they were connected with Gurlin. But... where we were led to believe in our mission of containing the evil, they may have been told differently, told the truth. Such fanaticism... could hardly be limited to such a small group."

"So we're almost certainly going to be followed."

She nodded.

Fragments of Kevon's nightmare from days earlier spun through his consciousness, the mad rush to the gates of Eastport, the horrific greeting once he reached 'safety'. He knew it was just a dream, intensified by the events that followed it. The knowledge did little to comfort him.

"Best possible speed, then," he decided. "We have extra supplies, feed for the horses. No larger force could catch us, no smaller force would want to."

"Unless they were *Sent* ahead of us," Mirsa countered. "We cannot rule out that possibility, given who we might be facing."

Would they know we were headed to Eastport? Kevon wondered. Very few knew, but there was still a risk of someone letting the information slip. *Or having it pried out of them.*

The rumbling of the approaching wagon started to drown out the conversation. Mirsa slowed, to fall back to her position alongside it, as Kevon spurred his stallion ahead.

CHAPTER 27

"The book is useless," Mirsa declared, brushing crumbs from her morning meal off of her robes and rising from her place at the fire. "I looked through it last night. All of the runes are fragments, and it's written in Dwarven script. Of all the languages..."

"Maybe not useless, just not simple?" Kevon asked, after cinching up his saddle and scratching the stallion behind his ears.

"Of course! I'll learn the entire Dwarven language while we travel to Eastport." Mirsa huffed. "Shouldn't take more than a few years."

"Or you could find a dwarf," Bertus suggested, adjusting the canvas that covered the supplies in the wagon.

"What do Dwarves care of magic? It's not as if they could use it." she retorted.

"We could convince one to care?" Kevon asked, more to frustrate the Mage than help.

"Have either one of you ever seen a dwarf?" she snapped.

Both Warriors shook their heads and mumbled.

"They are foul, violent creatures that..."

"How many Dwarves have you met?" Kevon interrupted, peering at the Mage.

"That's not the point," Mirsa huffed, climbing into her saddle. "It's well known that..."

"You might have used those words to describe Warriors not so long ago." Kevon took his time checking the fastenings on his own saddle. "And yet you trust us with your life now. Might the same be true of others?"

"No one would expect us to go that far north," Bertus added, hoisting himself up to the wagon's bench and taking the reins. "As far as anyone knows, even our allies, we're headed straight for Eastport."

"We'll assume the entrances to the city are being watched, and that riding with Mirsa may give our position away." Kevon chewed his lip for a moment. "Correct?"

"I can try and fashion a charm to protect against scrying," the Master Mage offered, "But for now, yes."

The corners of Kevon's mouth twisted up into a grin. "Can you have such a charm ready in a week?"

"This is good for the night," Kevon announced, directing the wagon off the track just before it crossed a small stream. "We'll double back in the morning, after we test Mirsa's enchantment."

The Mage pulled a necklace from a robe pocket, and swept her hair aside to fasten the leather tie around her neck. The carved wooden charm that hung from it settled against her skin, but she could not sense it as she would have another powered rune. The other enchantments that she felt about her dulled in her mind's eye, causing a measure of concern, followed by a rush of relief as she realized the charm was functioning.

"It's working," she told Kevon, stepping down from the saddle and handing off her reins to Bertus. "It's a crude enchantment, hurried far more than any other I've even assisted with. I can sense the power draining from it, much like the barrier beneath Gurlin's tower, only faster." She ran her fingers across the raised rune on the surface of the charm. "As long as we're adding to the spell daily, until the enchantment is strong enough to hold on its own, we should have nothing to fear."

Kevon climbed up into the wagon and removed his weapons, placing them in a chest that he'd pulled out from under the seat. He stood for a while, looking up and down the road, scanning the tree-line for unwanted observers. Confident that no one was watching, he formed an Illusion rune and threw up a vision of wooden walls closed in around him while he changed from his Warrior's garb to his Mage robes. He dropped the illusion, and put the medallion he wore around his neck in the chest with his other equipment, replacing it with the seashell necklace gifted to him by the Myrnar.

"Our journey should be much safer now," Kevon announced, stepping down from the wagon. "Our pursuers must not have great resources, if they have been unable to Send forces directly to us. There may be other places that are better prepared to Send to, ahead of us. If they are watching the entrances to Eastport, I'll wager they're not looking the direction we'll be coming from."

"You think the coastal roads are in good enough condition to travel that quickly?" Bertus asked.

"If they're not," Kevon answered, reaching deep within himself and downward into the ground beneath him, causing a low rumbling with the minor shifts the spell was effecting. "We'll fix them ourselves."

Bertus waited for the noises to stop and the horses to calm before leaving them picketed near the stream and returning to the wagon to dole out provisions. "Do you think we'll see some of the Sea-Folk?" he asked, eyeing the necklace about Kevon's neck.

Kevon shrugged. "Marelle seemed to think..." He choked on the words as he realized what he was saying. "The Myrnar do not usually have anything to do with Men. So, no."

The Mage took a deep breath and continued. "Two Magi and a single Warrior will not be what they are looking for, though the wagon might draw attention."

"I don't have any reason to go back there," Bertus confessed, "Other than to help you out. We still need to find a dwarf for Mirsa..."

"You don't need to find me..." Mirsa yelled, quieting and narrowing her eyes to slits when she saw the Seeker's smile.

"Yes," Kevon mused. "The two of you will continue on past Eastport, to the Dwarven Hold in the northwest. I can find out what Liah knows, and decide what to do from there. Most likely I'll need help, so I can catch up to you before you even see a dwarf."

CHAPTER 28

Kevon's predictions about the Myrnar held true, but it seemed as if everyone else was travelling the coastal road. They had met over a dozen groups headed south since they had made the turn northward. They had also overtaken four wagons and two other bands of adventurers making their way toward Eastport.

The highlight of the journey thus far had been spotting a trio of Elves camped off the road one morning after beginning their daily trek. Kevon had been checking the road ahead, and noticed the camp being struck, and one of their hoods had fallen back, revealing the brilliant yellow hair, pointed ears, and fragile features for a moment before the covering was replaced. All three elves had turned to watch him ride past, but Kevon turned his head, obscuring his own features within his robes. *If they want to travel in secret,* he thought, *I'll not begrudge them the same courtesy I wish for.*

Only days later did he mention it to the others, bringing a surprised expression to Mirsa's face. "What reason would they have for going south, on foot?" she asked.

"They may have had horses," Kevon added. "I didn't see any, but I wasn't really looking."

Mirsa shook her head. "They can travel nearly as fast through the woods as we can on the road with the wagon." She thought a few minutes more. "The only thing of interest to them would be the capital," she decided. "But it's strange that they would take this route, rather than a direct one."

"What would they want in Navlia?" Bertus asked, throwing another stick into the evening fire.

"Something they could not get in Eastport," Mirsa answered. "An audience with the Prince, perhaps. They are almost certainly not going to the Southern Frontier, all of their weapons are made from wood or bone. Elves avoid metal nearly as much as Magi do."

"Maybe they were looking for a boat," Bertus suggested, pointing at one of the more frequent sail-clad vessels they had seen as they neared the port city. "That would keep them on this road."

"Why would they not meet a boat in Eastport?" Kevon asked. "It's the only safe place to land a craft on this half of Purlon."

"I can think of people and things that I would not want anywhere near Eastport," Mirsa grumbled, gazing out over the water. "Myself included."

Kevon chuckled and finished the last few bites of his dinner. "Agreed. I may only be there a few hours, depending on Liah's information. There's really nothing left for me there."

"Judging by the ships we have seen, we're no more than three or four days away now," Bertus estimated. "We need to be ready in case we're challenged by those fanatics again."

"I think we've been more than a match for the ones we've come up against," Kevon said, grinning. "You two together should be able to handle anything that comes your way, as long as you stay alert. I've still got my advantage over most Magi, too. They have all relied mainly on Fire and Darkness..."

"They would not have been able to use Earth magic in the Palace in Navlia, because of the wards built into the stone of the castle," Mirsa advised. "There will be no such protection here." She shot a piercing glance at Kevon. "We've seen what one using Earth magic can accomplish, with only the barest of instruction."

He nodded. His dreams of late, in addition to the ones about the destruction of the tower, had been about the defeat of the Orclord. *Well, the running away before its defeat, mostly,* he amended inwardly. "That could be a problem."

Hours later, a lancet of flame lit the darkness, and Kevon moved out of its path as he focused his will to deflect it enough that his movement would be effective.

"You're moving again," Mirsa snapped, and Kevon felt the magic building around her for another spell.

"I don't want to get hit," Kevon retorted, smirking and unleashing his Art moments before the Master Mage's spell bloomed.

Unable to sense the magic Kevon worked, Mirsa called a fireball into existence, but as soon as it formed, it was batted downward, exploding with a dull *whump* at her feet. "Better," she admitted. "But what would you do about..."

Kevon felt the connection form between Mirsa and the sea that lay a few dozen yards from their practice battleground. He formed the rune of Negation that Mirsa had shown him, paired it with his own Water rune, and began attacking the bond, trying desperately to sever the influx of power before she could manage to bend it to her purpose. The swift attacks interrupted, but did not collapse the flow of power, which seemed to grow thicker, more resilient. He tapped into the energy himself, and swung the runes like an axe, cleaving the link again and again, until it finally sputtered to a halt.

"Hah!" he laughed, sides heaving from the effort. "You finally ran out of..."

The wave pounded him to the ground, cutting his taunt short, along with his breath. The salt stung his eyes and the brackish taste seeped into his mouth. Sputtering, Kevon stood and studied Mirsa, who still held a looming ribbon of sea water in a magical grip that he could not feel.

"You split your focus," he said, spitting brine and smoothing his drenched hair back. "You made me deal with the power I could feel, while preparing an attack I couldn't."

"I didn't make you do anything," Mirsa laughed. "If you'd looked, rather than trusting your mystical senses, you might have been able to counter me."

"Lesson learned," Kevon acknowledged, wringing out a corner of his robe. "Can I dry off now?"

Saying nothing, Mirsa turned and strolled back to camp, and the fire Bertus was cooking over. Kevon followed, boots squishing as he walked.

CHAPTER 29

"We'll camp here," Bertus informed Kevon as the Warsmith returned to the motionless wagon. "Eastport is only an hour away, you might be able to reach it before you lose the light."

Kevon scratched his stallion's ears, hoping to quiet the animal's restless stamping. "All right," he agreed. "Sunrise, then, each morning, I'll remove my ring, and you can search for me?" he confirmed with Mirsa. Seeing the Master Mage's slight nod, he wheeled his mount back toward his destination. "Two, three days... A week at most. Good fortune to you!"

The stallion took no urging to break into a gallop toward the city, but slowed as the light waned faster than Kevon anticipated.

The Mage's heart beat faster as he crossed the bridge over the canal that flowed from the city, and saw the closed gate. He shook his head, and pushed aside his irrational fear, drawing nearer to the entrance to the city.

"Hullo!" he called, when no one challenged from the gatepost. Moments later, a face and a torch peeked over the high wall.

"Who goes there?"

Kevon called forth a glowing sphere of light, revealing his station to the guard. He looked up enough so that the bottom half of his face was visible, but his eyes remained shadowed by his robe's hood.

"Let him in!" cried his observer, and the gate began creaking open.

Kevon rode slowly in, avoiding eye contact with any of the guards around the gate, and keeping aloof, which was to be expected. *So much for my nightmare*, he reassured himself, riding for the nearest inn. The streets were empty of all traffic, and any threats would be immediately visible. He reined the stallion to a halt under a sign with a bird of hammered metal depicted on it. *'The Copper Canary'?* He wondered as the door opened and he stepped down from the stirrups. Stablehands and servants surrounded him, taking his saddlebags and leading the stallion around the corner.

Too many... he thought, as they pressed in on him. *There were only three at the* Maiden, *and it was respectable...* The dress of the brigands surrounding him was not consistent, as would be the case if they were employed by the inn. Runes flashed to mind, and he prepared the correct combination that would allow him to break free from the pack, distance himself from them and return to the gate to beg for help in recovering his things.

Jostled for a moment from behind, it seemed the world spun as a voice slick with hatred uttered two words that chilled Kevon to the bone.

"Die, Mage."

Panic flared along with the Fire rune that Kevon readied, but the spell fluttered into darkness as the pain lanced white-hot into his back, and he knew no more.

CHAPTER 30

Bertus stirred the crushed leaves into the hot water already in the fragile-looking cup, and waited as his companion sat, seemingly lost in contemplation. The light brightened, and the warmth of the morning sun played across her face, casting a glow through her auburn locks that disturbed the Seeker's sense of propriety.

"Nothing," she said, opening her eyes, and taking the offered tea.

"It's only been two days, Mirsa." he reminded the Master Mage, "He might have solid information he could act on. We need to trust him."

"I don't like it," she protested. "He knew what dangers we feared in Eastport. For him to not even allow us to know that he is still there?"

"Between the two of us, we should be able to convince the Dwarves to help us," Bertus said, starting to pack away the rest of the supplies. "Besides... If anything has happened to Kevon, it's probably too late to do anything about it." He looked Mirsa squarely in the eye. "Without him, we may need whatever's in that book to keep ourselves alive."

Mirsa ruffled the Novice's hair with a velvet gloved hand. She had seen Bertus grow in confidence in the season since she'd met him, and was growing to appreciate his presence more than she cared to admit. At times, she saw shades of Pholos in the young Warrior, a naïve goodness she'd been unable to appreciate in the Journeyman Mage she'd studied with when she was wrapped up in her own bitterness. The things Bertus had seen and done had given him perspective, without changing him for the worse. "We'll see what the Dwarves have to say."

The Master Mage retrieved her charm from the seat of the wagon, and placed it around her neck, dulling her extra senses, but keeping her nearly as safe as Kevon's ring kept him. She gathered her things from around the sparse campsite, and stowed them in the wagon. By the time she was ready, her horse was already hitched to the back of the wagon, and Bertus was climbing up to the seat and readying the reins.

A week further north, the salt air of the sea to the east faded for the more familiar pine scent of the evergreens the road now twisted through. As the terrain steepened, Mirsa could feel the power in the mountains poking into her awareness, even through the protection of the charm she'd enchanted.

The energy feels different, she thought, as she probed the aura of the mountains with her mind. *More organized, guarded. I'm not sure if it would be easy to draw from or not.* She decided against trying. Not only was there no need, as there had been on the other side of the Realm, but the difference in the way the power *felt* was unsettling.

"Another week, you said?" Bertus asked as evening settled in over their campsite.

"You need to sleep," Mirsa admonished. "It's a third night, you deserve the extra rest." The Master Mage tossed another log onto the fire, and shrugged deeper into her robes. She watched as the young Warrior drifted off in his customary spot beneath the wagon near where the horses were hitched, for the first decent sleep he'd had in over two days. She smiled as she watched his hand clench reflexively around the scabbard of the ancient sword that rested by him. The Seeker had taken the extra responsibility of night watches on when Kevon had left them, only taking more than two hours of rest at a time every third day.

Mirsa placed the last log onto the glowing remains of the

fire, and watched it crackle back to life. She would wake Bertus when it had burned down more than halfway. Shadows thrown by the flames danced against the side of the wagon and the sur-rounding trees in a hypnotic fashion, almost as if...

The sound of restless horses woke her at the same time as Bertus. The youth rolled out from under the wagon, drawing his sword and casting aside the scabbard. Standing with his back to the conveyance, he peered out into the newly illuminated gloom. A globe of light hung over him, bringing an eerie almost-midday glow to the surrounding area. The flaming tip of Mirsa's staff provided the warmth and color the sterile light above lacked. She swept in alongside him, leaving adequate room to maneuver, adding her eyes to the search for the disturbance.

The log on the fire still burned, not even halfway con-sumed. "Only minutes," she whispered in Bertus's direction. "I fell asleep... I..."

A rustling in the wagon further alarmed both the horses and humans. Bertus leapt back, brandishing regal steel at his unseen enemy, while Mirsa stepped out and away, leveling her weapon toward the noise, the eager runes begging her for re-lease.

In a flurry of motion, several burlap sacks flipped out of the back of the wagon and hurtled with unnatural speed from the light into the surrounding trees.

"Gnomes." Mirsa unleashed a torrent of flames skyward before regaining her poise. "The wagon was in the way," she said, justifying her outburst.

Bertus climbed into the wagon and surveyed the loss. "They only took food," he called down to Mirsa. "But they took it all."

The Master Mage set aside her staff, and relaxed as the urge to use the power within it subsided. She reached up and took the bag that Bertus handed down to her, and unwrapped the book within, taking great care to avoid damaging the ancient text. "It's unharmed," she said after looking over it for a few moments.

"Kevon's fancy hammer-thing is all right, too," Bertus called down, pulling the weapon free of its fastenings and brandishing it indelicately.

"The food..."

"We'll be fine," Bertus assured her. "There's plenty of game, and we're close to our destination anyway." The Seeker returned the weapon to its place, and snugged their remaining belongings closer together, lashing them down with leather ties. "It's not as if I couldn't afford to miss a few meals, either."

Mirsa frowned. Her familiarity with the Earth-aligned creatures was minimal. She'd read volumes on the creatures of the sea, but the libraries she'd frequented had little to do with the Dwarves and Gnomes. "And what should happen if they come for food, and we have none?" she wondered aloud.

Bertus shook his head. "We'll press on, and reach the Hold in five days," he decided. "I can make it five days. Besides..." he grinned in the eerie shadows of the remaining Magelight, "If the Dwarves aren't friendly, it won't matter how rested I am."

CHAPTER 31

The room swam into view as the pain in Kevon's side sharpened. He struggled with the bonds holding his wrists to the back of the chair he sat in before realizing they were forged iron clamps, unlike the ropes that held his legs to the chair. He grimaced at the taste of the gag, but was relieved the blindfold was pushed up onto his forehead so that he could examine his surroundings.

Kevon ran his thumb between the slats of the chair, feeling the dressing and binding on the wound in the back of his right side. He experimented, breathing deeper until the agony threatened to return him to the peaceful darkness he'd just emerged from. While the pain was considerable, it was less than he expected from what little of the attack he could remember. *Healing potion,* he thought, wondering why his attackers would go to so much trouble to keep him alive.

Who are they? What do they want? Questions flooded a mind already filled with dull runes that could have freed him from his bonds, had they not been made of iron. Unable to voice his queries, he set about trying to learn as much as he could by viewing his makeshift prison.

The room was smallish, and not the sort of place Kevon would imagine one would normally leave a bound and gagged prisoner. Next to him was a neatly made cot, overhung by several small paintings. An array of knives and a short sword lay on the table by the head of the bed, not more than six feet from where Kevon sat. Opposite the cot, to his left, was a table with a pitcher and washbasin. Beyond that was the side of a wooden cabinet that could have been a wardrobe. The left wall held more weapons. Throwing knives and crossbows hung from pegs above a bin of bolts only served to make the dainty writing desk next to the arsenal look even more out of place.

He tested the slack in the ropes around his legs, wondering if he could shuffle his way to the weapons, or move from the corner into the center of the room to try and break the chair apart and free himself.

The door opened, and one of his attackers from outside the inn entered. Seeing him awake, the brigand drew his sword and smiled.

The hooded figure that entered just behind him touched his arm, and murmured something too low for Kevon to hear. The swordsman grunted in disgust, and stormed past the newcomer, who closed the door behind him. Kevon's captor turned, and looked up to meet his stare.

Strands of blonde hair escaped from the hood, framing a somber gaze. A patch covered her left eye, and a crescent scar rode low on her right cheek. Her lips parted, as if to speak, but trembled for a moment.

"Are you a Mage?" she whispered, in the venomous voice that had preceded his near mortal wound.

So it comes down to this. Kevon's heart sank. All the running. All the hiding. To wind up being blindsided by a thug with a grudge... He did not move, only waited, eyes defiant in the absence of words.

His captor pulled back her hood, and sighed. She started toward him. Through his pounding headache, the thought that there was something he should remember, but he could not grasp that particular memory. "I'm going to release you," she said, moving in close and shifting around to his side to access the iron clamps. *"Don't hurt me."* Her lips brushed the edge of his ear as she spoke.

Kevon's mind recoiled. He gasped, choking on the gag, and turned toward her. Recognition dawned and new questions pushed older ones out of the way. The curve of her neck, the line of her jaw, he could see it now, undistracted by other details. His freed hand shot up to tear the gag away. "Marelle!"

"Shh…" she cautioned, nuzzling his neck as she worked at the other clamp. "It's Alanna now."

"But how?" Kevon pushed, wanting to understand. "I heard that you were…"

"Marelle *is* dead!" she whispered, loosing his other wrist, and pushing back to stand and look down at him. "She was weak. Always afraid of assassins and Magi." A slight chuckle escaped her lips. "Alanna leads assassins, and kills Mages."

Kevon shook his leg free of the last remaining restraint, and looked up into Marelle's face. Dread and attraction tore at his very being. He'd come here to avenge her death, and was unsure if she would even spare him if he told her the truth about his abilities.

"Your father? Your plans?" he asked her, stalling while he tried to decide what truth to tell her.

"Another time," Marelle, or rather, *Alanna*, snapped. "I have to decide what to tell the men who have been watching over you for the last few days. What's most likely to keep them from killing you, preferably."

Kevon rose and took Alanna by the shoulders. "I am a Mage," he admitted. "I'm sorry I didn't let you know before. Things were… complicated."

Pain intruded on the void, goading Kevon to wakefulness. He found himself back in the chair, shackled once again. His head pounded, and his neck and throat hurt as never before. He groaned, and Alanna moved back into his field of vision.

"I'll tell the others what I plan to do with you as soon as I decide," she chuckled. "Things are… complicated."

CHAPTER 32

T he horn echoing down the canyon road prodded Bertus to full alert. He handed the reins to Mirsa, and readied his crossbow.

The Mage let the team slow, flicking the reins only when they dropped below half the speed they had been traveling at. She scanned the canyon walls, and continued to marvel at the structure of magic in the area.

This was not a near impenetrable murk, as the elements had been bound with beneath, and around Gurlin's tower. Earth magic surrounded them, more evident and plentiful than she had ever felt. But not only was the power not crushing in on her, she could not use it at all. It was as if the magic was distilled into bricks of pure energy and stacked all around, behind thick panes of glass. She had used Earth magic since coming closer to the mountains. It was in no way hindered, and in fact was easy to use since the surrounding power's rune was constantly in her mind. But there was not even a hint of sympathetic energy flowing back to use for the spell, and as such, she'd ended it promptly.

"Ho there!" Bertus called, waving to the dwarf that edged out from behind a rock about fifty yards up the canyon. He shot Mirsa a glance, and she slowed the team even further. He set the crossbow behind him in the wagon, and turned back to appraise the curious being.

The dwarf carried a crossbow that was twice as large as Bertus's in nearly every dimension, and undoubtedly better made. The weapon was nearly as long as the dwarf was tall, but he carried it with an easy grace in one hand beside him, ready to use at a moment's notice. The handle of a long axe stuck out above his back, and he was garbed in stout looking ring mail.

"What business have ye at the Hold?" he challenged, and Mirsa drew the reins back to halt the wagon perhaps thirty yards from the sentry.

"We seek the counsel of your scholars," Mirsa called.

"We intend you no harm," Bertus added.

The sentry guffawed, nearly dropping his bow in the process. "Ye promise not te harm us?"

Bertus looked around at the half dozen crossbows trained on himself and Mirsa from concealed battlements in the valley walls above. He smiled. "We promise."

"It'd take more than a Wizard and a whelp te make trouble here, fer sure." The sentry gestured with his crossbow. "Follow me in."

Around the next turn in the canyon, the entrance to the Hold came into view. Large stone double doors lay beyond a trio of rock slabs that lay jumbled across the path. Bertus guided the team to the highest clearance of each of the obstacles. He and Mirsa had to duck to make it under the last one, and glancing backward the Seeker noticed the walkway cut into the second stone slab they had passed under, also manned by crossbow-wielding Dwarves. He reached up and ran a hand along the spiral ridge of the stone above him. His eyes traced a path upward, following gouges up the canyon wall to the broken formations above, and the one remaining spire that was still intact.

Mirsa observed their surroundings with other senses, and felt the doors ahead beginning to open before the rumble reached their ears. Sections of the pent-up magic surrounding them twitched in her mind, and her inability to grasp the mechanism of the energy release grated her ego more than the sound that assailed her ears.

"Wait here," their guide ordered, not waiting to see if his guests were going to comply before turning to march down a hallway from the antechamber, deeper into the mountain.

"Ye can come down, if ye please," another dwarf suggested as soon as the rumbling of the closing doors ceased. He offered a leather-gloved hand to Mirsa.

The Master Mage pulled back her cloak's hood and smiled as she took his hand and his help stepping to the marble floor below. "A most agreeable welcome," she commented, turning to take in the magnificence of the chamber surrounding them. Small iron baskets bolted to the walls held stones that glowed brightly with a slight green cast, and the ceiling was dotted with crystal formations that both diffused light around the room, and sent shafts of brilliant light to the glowing stones, or near to them.

"Yer animals will be taken care of," the dwarf assisting Mirsa assured them. "We've sent fer fodder. Our stables are rarely used."

"One moment," Bertus cautioned. He unstrapped some of the supplies in the back of the wagon, and handed the bundle with the book down to Mirsa before sliding Kevon's Dwarven axe from under its cover. He shouldered the weapon, and hopped down lightly to the floor.

The two handlers that had come to take the wagon and team stood speechless, gaping at Bertus as he slung the axe into a loop on his belt. "Get... Get ye to the stables!" stammered the other dwarf. As soon as the wagon was almost out of sight, their new companion ventured a question. "And just what right have ye to wear that axe?"

"I'm a Hero of the Western Vale," Bertus replied, doing his best to appear bored. "Am I to be questioned about the rest of my equipment as well, then? This is a sword of ancient kings," The Seeker lifted the weapon a few inches in its scabbard and let it fall back into place. "The shirt, I bought in Navlia."

"We are honored to have such a young Hero among us," the dwarf said, bowing to Bertus.

"*Heroes*," the Warrior corrected, gesturing to Mirsa. "Master Mirsa, Advisor to Alacrit du Kærtis, and slayer of Orclords."

Their Dwarven companion sputtered in surprise, missing the withering glance Mirsa shot at Bertus. "And yer name?" he asked, a hint of reverence creeping into his voice.

"Just Bertus," the Seeker shrugged.

"Bertus the Bold, I name ye," the dwarf retorted. "I'm called Kylgren-Wode. I'm what passes fer an Ambassador around here, not that we've had need fer one since I got the job." Kylgren grinned. "Let's make sure we do this good and proper, take our time. As long as yer here, I'm not hauling trash or water fer no one!"

"How does one become an Ambassador, Kylgren?" Mirsa inquired.

"Speak Common," the dwarf grunted, "And be awful at everthing else."

Bertus laughed. "I'm sure we can make your next few days interesting enough."

"After all, there are the proper formalities to be observed," Mirsa added.

"Proper formalities..." Kylgren-Wode scratched his beard, then looked to Mirsa, who shrugged, a coy smile turning the corner of her mouth.

Understanding washed over the Ambassador's face, and he stifled a laugh as the sentry reentered from the hall.

"The King will see them now!" the sentry announced, gesturing back down the passage he had emerged from.

"The King will wait," Kylgren said, waving his kinsman off with a smirk. "There be formalities that need observing fer Heroes such as these. Make ready chambers, beds, hot baths, and refreshments." When the sentry's expression changed from one of surety of command to mild confusion, Kylgren-Wode jabbed a stubby finger in his direction. "What are ye waiting fer?" he shouted. "My apologies yer graces," he said, turning to take Mirsa's gloved hand in his own and kiss it. "Some of my brothers have no manners." The Ambassador winked before turning to glare at the bewildered sentry. "Now!" he yelled.

The sentry turned and fled back down the hallway.

Kylgren-Wode straightened up, and smoothed out his beard deliberately. "I think I'm going te like this."

CHAPTER 33

"I told them you were an old lover I was teaching a lesson," Alanna chuckled as she slipped the last shackle free of Kevon's wrist. "It's not the whole truth, but they'll accept it." She smiled, the familiar look of mischief in her eye reminding Kevon of the times they'd spent before she had been *Alanna*.

The still-tender bruise on the side of his head was elegant proof of just how much had changed since the last time they'd been together. Aside from a misunderstanding with a crossbow, he'd never seen her harm anyone. She'd only raised her voice a handful of times in all of their travels before.

"How could this happen?" he asked, standing and rubbing his wrists. He touched the bruise at his temple and winced.

"I kill Mages," Alanna shrugged. "And I needed a little more time to think about it."

"Not that," Kevon shook his head. "All of this? What happened to you? Your father?"

"I have no time for this," she snapped, turning toward the door. "More Magi have been gathering here, so I have work to do."

"Wait, more?" Kevon reached for Alanna's shoulder, but stopped short.

"The few who were here fell quickly," she answered, abandoning her withdrawal, turning to sit at the writing desk near the doorway. "Perfect practice for a fledgling assassin. Two or three others arrived in the season that followed, more prepared. By the time I'd finished... 'reorganizing' the Merchant's Guild, and cleansing the streets of common thieves, they were the perfect targets to solidify my control here." She frowned. "The first Magi to be seen in Eastport in over half a year were spotted two weeks ago. They didn't come in through the gates, or my informants would have known. They've been running in groups of three or more, being very careful. You..." Alanna laughed. "You were the first one stupid enough to ride into town alone."

"They're here for me," Kevon thought aloud.

"Well then," Alanna purred, her eye narrowing as she stood to close the distance to Kevon, "I'm even more pleased that we didn't kill you. I knew you had one or two Magi out to get you... Why the army?"

Kevon remained silent, unsure how much he wanted to tell *Alanna*.

"Oh..." Alanna's expression softened, and she moved in, resting a hand on his chest, burying her face in his neck. "You'd tell Marelle, wouldn't you?" she whispered.

"You said yourself she was dead," Kevon countered. "I came here to avenge her death, not to be used by something wearing her face."

"They did tell everyone I was dead," Alanna giggled, pushing away from Kevon and fidgeting for a moment. "The Merchant's Guild. They couldn't have seized Father's assets, and mine, if I was still alive." She sniffed. "You wonder what would happen if you went home. I've stared down the length of a loaded crossbow and been told what would happen."

"They knew?"

"Four weeks from the time we left, I crawled back to my doorstep, filthy, bleeding, and starving. My Father's steward saw a chance to take my birthright for his own gain, and turned me away. He's dead, but there are always more greedy profiteers to step into such a void." Alanna shrugged. "Mages and thieves are more of a problem, only not as common."

Kevon stared at the harsh expression on the woman's face before him. *Death has followed me on my travels, reared its head in spectacular fashion on occasion. But it has taken her as its lover.* The thought chilled him, made him want to reach out to her, and crushed, all at once, the hopes that had glimmered through the pain and confusion since he had realized she was still alive. He had mentally outlined the actions he would have been willing to take to punish anyone who had been involved in her death, but now only chaos remained in the space his devotion had occupied for so long. He was not completely sure what role she played in the shady underbelly of the city, and what was bluster or overconfidence. The others he had seen her with had been deferential, at least. *Will I be able to save her from this, from herself? What about Bertus and Mirsa? Are other Magi tracking them by now? Will Alanna's followers attack them as they did me, should they return here?*

"Dear one," Alanna fussed, guiding Kevon to the bed. "You have much to think about. Rest. I have matters that need attended." She stroked the side of his face, looking as sincere as he'd seen her since he woke in shackles.

If she wanted me dead, I would be dead. Although not the most comforting sentiment, it helped him drift into an uneasy sleep, where he dreamt of a woman that was sometimes Alanna, sometimes Marelle, surrounded by people who were either Magi or farmerfolk.

"They're not positive you're here," Alanna commented at Kevon's first sign of wakefulness. "But they're still looking." She waited for him to sit up and rub the sleep from his eyes. "I've lost several men to attacks on the Magi over the past week, and we've only managed to kill two of them."

"I'm sure I could take two or three myself, getting in close and surprising them," Kevon mused, "If they're moving in groups as you say."

"Three. That's good…" Alanna agreed. "But what about the nine or twelve that are watching from a distance? Are you strong enough to face them, or fast enough to run from them?"

Kevon frowned. Unless I can isolate groups of the enemy Magi, I have no chance of surviving the first attack. "No," he admitted. "What did you have in mind?"

"We don't have the numbers we used to, not enough for a surprise attack that would take them all at once," she admitted. "If they were focused on something else, and on the move, we might be able to destroy enough of them that we could face the others without the advantage of surprise."

"Focused on *me*, you mean?" Kevon grimaced. He did not relish playing the role of bait, but had been successful at it before, against arguably a fiercer opponent. "I suppose we have little choice."

"It will take a few days to scout out their movements, pick a time and place that will work to our advantage," Alanna mused. "There might be openings for crossbowmen to thin their ranks a bit further."

Kevon nodded. "They wouldn't know who I am in this outfit," he told her. "I'll need new clothes, wooden weapons, and some paints."

Alanna furrowed her brow at his request, but nodded, turned, and left.

CHAPTER 34

Bertus startled awake at the pealing of the gong. He'd grown used to the deep horn that signaled sundown in the outside world, but the morning alarm rattled him to the bone, set his teeth on edge.

Mirsa stirred in the bed alongside his, wincing, then relaxing as the penetrating *thrum* tapered down to silence.

"I don't know how you stand it," Bertus complained, sitting upright and rubbing his fingers at the base of his ears. "Every morning, my head is ringing for hours, and you..."

Mirsa lay still, eyes closed, the corners of her mouth turned up in a smile.

"Hey! You're... That's not fair!" He launched a pillow that *smooshed* into the side of the Master Mage's head, disrupting her concentration.

"You think it wise to anger a fellow Hero on the morning of our formal presentation to the Dwarven King?" She rose from her blankets and stretched, the shimmering, nearly translucent fabric of her nightclothes draping in ways that made Bertus avert his eyes.

"That wasn't what I..." he began as Mirsa turned to pad off to the adjoining bath chamber. As he turned to watch her leave, the pillow he'd thrown leapt back to strike him in the face. "You'll pay for that, Wizard!" he bellowed as she dashed around the corner to the bath.

Bertus put the pillow back behind his head and stretched out, awaiting his turn in the giant recessed stone tub. The last three days had been a whirlwind of activity interspersed with

unexpected stints of luxurious relaxation. Things that the no-
bility in Navlia would have marveled at were commonplace
here, hundreds of yards deep in the mountain. The bath chamber itself was a perfect example. Two miniature sluice gates
fed into the polished granite tub, and one led out. No servants
bearing pails of hot water like in the palace. He was unsure if
every Dwarven dwelling had such conveniences, but the earlier
tour of the river led him to believe it was possible. Waterwheels
turned millstones, ran pulleys that lifted water filled vessels
through the ceiling to the upper levels. Workers walked along
sturdy causeways, checking for frayed rope and cracking boards.
Mirsa had been impressed and disappointed at turns, alluding
that there was no easy way for her to duplicate the processes
through magic, and that the simple machinery was superior to
anything she could accomplish on her own.

It did not stop her from enjoying it immensely, it appeared. Bertus woke what must have been an hour later when
Mirsa, fully attired for a regal audience, shook him. "The tub is
filling," she announced, "and I'm going for a walk. Meet you in
the dining hall for a late breakfast?"

Bertus nodded and yawned. Mirsa ruffled his hair and
headed toward the doorway. The Seeker smiled and lingered in
thoughtful repose a moment longer. Daily he saw more of what
Waine had in the Wizard, and he hated himself for it. The Adept
had been his brother, his friend, even more of a *father* than Bertus had ever had, excepting Carlo. Spending so much time with
the increasingly attractive Mage was bound to affect him, but
he still felt as if the feelings were an affront to the memory of his
dead companion.

He shook off the worries and the covers. Today, of all days,
I need to be the Hero I've been branded. Anything less could
cost lives. Even the delay of the last few days may have rendered
our mission pointless... Bertus hurried to the bath chamber and
scrubbed himself clean, dressed, and set out to find Mirsa.

Kylgren-Wode and Mirsa were in the dining hall near the kitchen, conversing over half eaten plates of food. The Dwarven ambassador signaled to one of the kitchen staff, and a bowl of the customary morning gruel, along with a plate of thick sliced crusty bread and crisp vegetables were brought out and set before Bertus shortly after he sat down.

"We were just talking about yer meeting with the King," Kylgren said, laying his fork down. "I'm not sure how he'll take yer request to help out with anything... *magical*," the last word whispered after a quick glance around the room. "Not that there's much difference either way. But... Yer the first Mage that's been in the Hold since anyone ken remember."

Mirsa nodded and clasped Kylgren's hand, squeezing it as she spoke. "I appreciate how quickly you've all adjusted to my being here," she laughed. The first day, all of the iron and steel fixtures that they might have come in contact with were covered over with bright red cloth, and the following day were replaced with copper, silver, or brass; metals that were magically neutral. "Any help or advice he might give would be more than we could have hoped for."

"We'll see..." Kylgren moped.

He's important now, Bertus thought, *as he has never been before. He'll miss it when it's over.* Knowing how he would feel if his journey with Kevon, Mirsa, and Carlo was coming to an end, the Seeker decided to try to do something that would give the kindly dwarf something to remember their time together.

Bertus finished his meal while Mirsa and Kylgren conversed quietly about last minute points of etiquette for their upcoming meeting. They had spoken of it at length during the previous days, but everyone wanted things to proceed as smoothly as possible.

"Bargthar-Stoun, Master of this Hold, and King of all the Dwarves... grows impatient." Kylgren-Wode admitted, as Bertus finished his meal. "He has no great love fer Men, and even less fer Magi. Staying calm the last few days has taxed him, and his household. He's ready te be quit with ye before ye even meet."

"We may be able to use that to our advantage," Mirsa reassured the dwarf. "Let us worry about the King."

Kylgren grumbled some more in Dwarven under his breath, but did not speak of it further.

The morning gong sounded again. Bertus, Mirsa, and Kylgren-Wode all stood as some of the kitchen staff peered out into the dining area. "It's time," the Ambassador announced.

Dwarven guards, almost looking comfortable in their new leather armor, appeared at the entrance to the hall, and waited until Kylgren-Wode led his charges into their midst before forming up around them and marching through the hallways to the throne room.

The path they took led through a part of the tunnels they had not seen before, by a handful of forges that Dwarven smiths were working, pounding out odd-looking pieces of armor. *The hammering...* Mirsa had grown used to the oddly restrained Earth magic that had surrounded them for the last few days, but as they passed close to the forges, she could feel the energy pulsing and ebbing with each *clang* of the hammers. *Dwarves cannot use magic...* she thought, remembering her studies at Gurlin's tower, and before that at the feet of Tarska Magus. *What is happening here?*

Kylgren-Wode did not slow as they passed through the smithing district, and no one spoke at all.

At last, they came to a large set of marble doors inlaid with gold and silver etchings, runes that Mirsa recognized as Dwarven, but could not comprehend.

"Beyond lies the throne of the Lords of the Earth," Kylgren announced, pointing at the runes. "Enter ye who would marvel at the bones of the world."

The front two escorting guards each placed a hand on one of the doors, and pushed. The massive stone slabs groaned, but moved steadily inward.

Mirsa felt the same sort of fluctuation in the surrounding

Earth magic, but slighter, more steady and drawn-out than the quick pulses accompanying the hammer-blows of the Dwarven smiths they had passed earlier. Just when she could almost tell where the magic was being drawn from, where it was going, the doors creaked to a stop.

Roaring fireplaces lined the sides of the regal chamber, heating the room and throwing faint shadows over the muted glow of the light-stones. Tapestries with action-filled scenes hung separated by no more than a foot or two each, hinting at the rich history that the Dwarven people alternately cele-brated, and tried to live down. The flickering firelight brought out the best in the lighter tapestries, the proud face of a Dwar-ven noble and his love renewing their partner-bonds. It also deepened the darkness in others, chained humans and gnomes seemed to writhe under a taskmaster's whip in a masterful de-piction of a cruel age long ago.

Kylgren-Wode led the procession at a pace that allowed the humans to take the spectacle in, but not study anything too closely as they moved through toward the throne at the far end of the room. Stout Dwarven guards surrounded the steps lead-ing up to the focus of power in the Hold. They bristled with weapons, in full suits of armor that seemed to be made of the same metal as the war axe that Bertus carried.

Mirsa slowed as they neared the end of the chamber, the magic flooding her senses as she approached the Dwarven King. "I can almost *see* it..." she whispered, noticing how the lines in the caged power seemed to echo the cut marble slabs and their polished gold seams, the flawless obsidian columns where their warped, dark reflections slid by in an eerie parody of their movement. The focal point of the increasing energy was the throne itself, pulsing with unseen power.

I wish Kevon were here to see this, Mirsa thought, nearly passing out from the intensity of the magic, even though it was not crushing in against her as it had when she and Kevon had used the sympathetic energies on their way to Gurlin's tower.

The unadorned basalt seat appeared to her to be shifting like quicksand, the inexorable pulsing of the magic manifesting visibly to her as one layer of reality began to overtake another. *A Seat of Power?* She wondered.

The armored Dwarves moved apart to the sides of the steps that led up to the throne, but their demeanors left no doubt that any hostile movement would be met with deadly force. The guards escorting Mirsa and Bertus also parted, taking up station alongside the last two obsidian columns. The Ambassador sank to one knee and bowed his head.

Bargthar-Stoun began speaking, but Mirsa could not understand a single syllable of the Dwarven ruler's words. He finished, and looked at Kylgren-Wode expectantly.

The Ambassador stood and turned to his guests. "Bargthar-Stoun greets ye on behalf of the Dwarven nation. He trusts yer stay here thus far has befitted yer station."

Mirsa bowed to the ruler. "These halls have provided as much as any Hero could hope for. Your hospitality has been most welcome after our long journey." She elbowed Bertus, who merely nodded.

"Yer journey, to this Hold, puzzles our King," Kylgren continued, after conversing with Bargthar-Stoun once more. "What brings champions of Men to the Throne of the Earth?"

"We've battled darkness to the west, defeated an Orclord and staved off the Magi that sought revenge for it. My companions and I are charged with strengthening the Realm against these continuing threats, and our path has led us here."

Kylgren-Wode thought a moment before translating, and Bargthar-Stoun frowned before answering. "What could the Dwarves offer ye that the royals in Navlia could not?"

"Your language." Mirsa explained. "An ancient text has been entrusted to us, which may help ensure the continued safety of the Realm. Its author was presumably a Mage, but the script is Dwarven."

"We don't know a thing about yer magic," Kylgren translated. "Ye'll have to take yer things and we'll be done with ye."

"No." Bertus said, in a calm, yet forceful tone. "You will help us," he continued, taking a step forward and drawing the battle-axe.

Spears and crossbows leveled at the young Hero's chest.

"You will help us because you know the merit of our claims." He held the weapon in upturned palms, showing it to the Dwarven King. "This weapon was gifted to another of our companions, a sign of our worthiness that you would be a fool to ignore."

Kylgren-Wode cringed, and stammered a hasty translation to his enraged ruler.

"If the Magi behind the destruction to the west are allowed to continue as they wish," Bertus continued, not waiting for an answer, "They will not stop with Navlia. The Orclords of old were kept in check by the wastes to the south. If these Magi are unleashing them in the north, how long do you think you will remain safe, even here?"

Mirsa, who had stepped aside at the first sign of the weapon, stepped forward as well. "While I do not agree with my companion's behavior," she said, glaring at Bertus, "He has seen the devastation firsthand, and lost friends to it. We all have."

The Dwarven Ambassador calmed and continued interpreting, but Mirsa was not waiting for a response. "This boy has fought those who seek to bring this land to ruin, while you have hidden here, sharpening your axes." She laughed. "And you quibble about looking at a book. We *are* done here."

Without further hesitation, the Master Mage turned on her heel and marched back toward the massive entry doors. Bertus shook his head, twirled the axe, and slid it into the loop he'd pulled it from at his back. Giving a mock bow, he followed Mirsa out of the chamber, the guards who had escorted them looking to their King for instruction. Kylgren-Wode rushed through the translation, and waited, breathless, for his Lord's response. After several moments of waiting, the Ambassador threw his hands up in frustration, and chased after his errant charges.

Mirsa stopped to wait for Bertus at the beginning of the smithing district. It was far enough away from the restrained potency of the throne room that she could concentrate once more. The hammering, made somewhat alien by the acoustics of the Hold, nevertheless served to make the underground warren a bit closer to the world above that she was familiar with. The rhythmic pounding beat a strain that syncopated with her heart and breath. She closed her eyes, and could feel the waves of magical disturbance spreading like ripples in a pond from the forges, following the lines of force built around all the surfaces of the Hold's passageways. The longer she listened and felt, the further she could detect the ripples traveling. She stretched her senses, and rested a hand against one of the walls. Several waves passing by her distorted at her touch, ruining the effect. Curious, she anticipated one of the next waves passing by, and trailed her fingers behind and through it, and the section she disturbed intensified and accelerated with her motion. She could sense it careening down the hallway, around corners, nearly reaching the throne room. Waiting a few heartbeats, she caught another wave, and focusing her intent, launched it after the other.

The very act of focusing kept the ripple intact, causing it to speed up as a whole, brightening in her mind, winding down the hallways into the Throne Room. For an instant, she could see the whole room as the wave refracted around and over the stone walls and obsidian columns, a phantom image in her head. Then several parts of the ripple struck the Throne.

The power pulsing from the throne absorbed and disgorged the wave, amplified beyond anything she had expected. Instead of a rapid ripple bouncing along the walls and floors at odd angles, the discharge from the throne room was lightning-fast sheets of the same energy, mapping out everywhere they had been in their brief stay, part of the springs and waterways, and all the residences and other chambers they had not been through. The thing that surprised Mirsa the most was the passage hidden behind the Throne, doors twice as large as the ones they had passed through led down a wide stairway to a chamber that had tunnels leading straight for many miles in several directions. The Master Mage felt very small and exposed, and shook free of the sensory assault before she could see just how far and where the passages led.

"Are you all right?" Bertus asked, catching up to her.

"I'm fine," she said, steadying herself before taking her hand off the wall she was leaning on. "We just need to leave here before I'm not."

"I'll have the wagon readied, you see to our things, we'll be on our way within the hour," the Seeker assured her. "We'll be back with Kevon before we know it."

They hurried through the twisted passageways to the main entrance, garnering more than a few strange looks from the locals, who had never seen them unescorted.

"Ten minutes," Bertus said, grasping Mirsa's hands and squeezing a reassurance. "I'll have them ready and here in ten minutes, and meet you back in the residence to..."

"Heroes!" Kylgren-Wode called as he burst into the chamber, wheezing, at a dead run. "Heroes... Wait..." The Ambassador stumbled over to them. "I apologize fer our King's..." He snorted. "Not just fer our King. Fer all of us. Yer right te be angry. Since the Wars, we've been hiding, training fer another battle with Men that never happened. Mining, hoarding weapons and armor, and pretending all Men were good fer was growing our food. I'm..."

"Kylgren-Wode!" Bargthar-Stoun shouted from the entrance to the room they had all just passed through.

The Ambassador snarled a few abrupt phrases to the King, and turned to face his ruler, face twisted in a fiery glare.

Bargthar-Stoun smiled, nodded and advanced toward the trio. His fatigue was not as pronounced as Kylgren's had been, but he was in no great hurry to cross the last few yards to where the others stood. As he drew close, he punched Kylgren-Wode in the shoulder, barking in Dwarven, and laughing.

Kylgren nodded and turned to Bertus. "I'm not te speak te him like that again, unless I mean it."

Mirsa peered toward the passageway, expecting a contingency of guards to burst through at any moment. The King followed her gaze, shook his head, waved his hands in front of her, and spoke to Kylgren once more. He pulled the rings from his fingers and began putting them in a pouch as the Ambassador translated.

"The guards remain in the Throne Room and..." Kylgren-Wode slowed as Bargthar-Stoun extended an upturned palm to Mirsa, and kissed the back of her offered hand. "They wait fer our return."

The King gestured at Mirsa's feet, then up to her face, talking through his laughter before turning to shake Bertus's hand with an iron grip.

"I won't be translating that fer ye," Kylgren-Wode said soberly. The Ambassador shook his ruler's shoulder, questioning him in Dwarven.

"*Boka!*" Bargthar-Stoun exclaimed, still pumping Bertus's hand with an almost childlike exuberance.

"Aye. He wants te see yer book," Kylgren-Wode explained.

"Ahhh..." The King said as Mirsa drew the text from her robe pocket, and unwrapped it. "*Boka anch...*" he whispered when he saw the runes inscribed on the cover, extending a hand slowly, as if asking permission.

Mirsa untied the fastenings, bowed and handed him the book. He leafed carefully through a few pages, and shook his head. "*Anch mo...*" he decided, showing a page to Kylgren. "Rhysabeth-Dane!" he shouted.

Kylgren-Wode put a hand on Bargthar-Stoun's shoulder, speaking a few calming words before taking the book from him and returning it to Mirsa. "There's someone you need te meet."

◆ ◆ ◆

After some convincing by the Ambassador, Bargthar-Stoun returned to the Throne Room to reassure his guards that nothing had happened. The King's absence also allowed the Kylgren-Wode and his guests to continue without undue disruption.

"I must warn ye..." Kylgren paused outside the door he had led Bertus and Mirsa to. "She's... *zarray*... ahh..." he fumbled for the right word. "Odd?"

Bertus chuckled, recalling their ordeal only minutes before with Bargthar-Stoun. "I'm sure she'll be fine."

The library was lit with the same light-stone sconces as the outside passages and chambers, only smaller and hung at closer intervals, as well as on the lower hanging ceiling. Thick cut slabs of dark polished wood were joined in severe but serviceable bookshelves that were crowded with volumes of all sizes and shapes.

Though gloved and covered by a thin cloak, Mirsa wove a deliberate path through the stacks, watching for the occasional metal-clasped book and other obstacles that had not been marked for her safety due to the relative suddenness of their visit. Years of practice made it seem like occasional steps to an elaborate dance, to halting music that only she could hear.

Stopping at the end of a row and peering along the walls to either side, Kylgren-Wode grumbled loudly. "Ye'll find her downstairs, then." He motioned back the direction they had come from, to a recessed stairwell near the entrance. He followed Mirsa and Bertus back to the opposite end of the row, then moved around them to lead the way down the narrow stairwell.

After the staircase doubled back on itself, the passage opened up to reveal a space with a far different feel than the level above. The group passed by rooms that were filled with dusty, broken items, and another chamber that was a meeting hall, or classroom, filled with chairs both stacked to the side and arranged in a large circle. Past those rooms and more bookshelves was another door that Kylgren rapped on three times before turning back to the others and waiting.

The door opened a crack, and a dwarf poked her head out, looking over the Ambassador and his charges. She disappeared for a moment, returning with a stumpy tallow candle on a dish, throwing more light into the hallway. "Mirsa 'ap Briltor, Bertus Orcslayer, this is Rhysabeth-Dane.

Kylgren-Wode spoke to her while she continued her inspection of Mirsa and Bertus. She nodded at several of the Ambassador's comments and questions, and at length asked questions of her own.

"She would like te see the book, if ye would," Kylgren-Wode announced.

As Mirsa produced the book, the tiny librarian hooted gleefully at the sight of the rune on the cover. After placing her lit candle back inside the room and peering wide-eyed at the Master Mage for approval, she took the leather-bound volume and ran her fingers over the stitching on the front before gesturing for the others to follow her through the doorway.

Rhysabeth-Dane set the book down on a low table, and set about arranging the lighting. Several freestanding lamps made from the metal-caged light-stones were moved well away from the immediate area, and other candles were lit and positioned close around. After admiring the cover a moment longer, she checked the book's spine and binding before opening it with something akin to reverence. After leafing through several pages, she squawked something at Kylgren-Wode, and began rearranging the candles in a wider pattern. She left the room, and returned with two other books that she laid out beside the grimoire. These she flipped through with a casual familiarity, stopping frequently to compare symbols, shake her head, mutter, and continue.

"The words she is able te translate make no sense put

together," Kylgren relayed to the others after Rhysabeth-Dane closed the book and spoke with him, rubbing her eyes. "She says she thinks there is a pattern, it could be a code, but it will take weeks te figure it out."

"We don't have weeks," Bertus sighed. "We need to get back on the road, find our friend."

"And we trust you," Mirsa added, "But we dare not leave the book behind to be studied."

"I'm sorry we could not do more for ye," Kylgren-Wode apologized. "At least ye know a bit more about yer book."

"Would ye be able to stay one more night?" the Ambassador asked, turning back after the few steps he'd taken toward the door. "I'm certain Bargthar-Stoun would want te have a feast in yer honor. As ye've pointed out, we've had no Heroes in an age, and little cause te celebrate. It may be that this generation of Dwarves needs te learn from the courage of Men."

"We would be honored," Mirsa answered. "And thank you," the Master Mage said, placing her hand on Rhysabeth-Dane's before collecting the book and following the others out of the library.

The Dwarven librarian sat, staring at the volumes of research material arrayed before her. She looked out of the room to see the others around a corner, out of sight. She shook her head, muttering, and picked up two of the books. Halfway through the door on her way to return them to the shelves, she stopped. A smile curved the corners of her mouth, and she returned the books to the table she'd been working on. She searched the bins in the corner shelf until she found a sturdy leather knapsack, and stacked the small pile of books into it. Whistling a cheery tune, she prowled back into the main area of the library, searching for more.

CHAPTER 35

It had taken Kevon two days to mix the paints into colors that were believable enough at a distance to even think about painting the sword he had whittled to something resembling sharpness. The flat grey was somewhere between steel and weathered silver, without the sheen of either. He hoped the lacquer that Alanna's lackeys were supposed to be fetching him worked to pull the look together enough to be believed.

"I don't see how a fake sword is going to help at all," Alanna teased, as Kevon brushed color into the corner of the joint of the blade and the crosspiece.

"I don't expect you to, or even need you to understand it," Kevon answered, frustrated with the familiarity of her behaviors the last few days. He had done everything he knew how to let her know he was not interested in the woman she'd become, but it seemed to make the game that much more interesting in her eyes. "Just as I don't want to know what your part in this is, as long as it's *done*."

"My men will do their part," she said, walking toward the door, trailing her fingers along his shoulders and neck as she passed behind him. "*All of them*," she whispered in a husky tone before sweeping out of the room, giggling.

Kevon pushed the unfinished project away, nearly spilling the container of paint he'd spent so much time getting just right. He buried his face in his hands and tried to calm his breathing. Being around Marelle when he was attracted to her had been frustrating enough. Adding fear and loathing into the equation, without being able to wholly remove the attraction was tilting him toward madness.

He gathered his wits and made himself pick up the painted sword once more. If Alanna happened back in while he was struggling with his emotions, there would be no end to the gloating and teasing. Kevon was looking forward to confronting the enemy Magi, and was hopeful that with more help this time, the city would not be pulled down around him. He wondered if once they were done, Alanna would let him leave, rejoin his friends without further delay.

If I can keep my magic limited to Movement, a few small illusions, and stay away from Fire, he thought, it might not focus her rage on me. That should improve my chances.

The Warsmith patted the scrolls he had hidden in a tunic pocket. He'd scribed them with the paints he hadn't mixed in with the colors he'd needed for the sword, passed them off as color tests for mixing the other paints. Although the runes were mottled, garish monstrosities that seemed to mock the severity of the situation they were created for, Kevon could still feel the power humming in the Concealed Movement runes when he touched the dried symbols, and could not detect them as soon as his skin no longer made contact. He thought he might have need of them in the coming days.

"The lacquer is here," Alanna announced, leaning through the doorway, holding a covered ceramic vessel. "Is your blade ready to polish?"

Kevon glared at her, and shook his head. "The paint is still wet in places. It'll take a few hours to dry, then the lacquer can dry overnight."

"So we have time for... other things?" Alanna teased, setting the container down on the desk and moving in closer.

"Plenty of time to talk," Kevon answered, peering closer at the detail work on the painted sword. "If you want."

"I don't know why you think you have to try and figure out what's *wrong* with me," Alanna hissed. "I know how the world works. That's all. *Marelle* didn't."

"Every time I see something of her in you, you push it down, hide it away," Kevon mused. "Are you afraid that if you let go of the anger, the control, she might come back?"

"Do you know what the men Alanna controls would do to Marelle? What they did?" Alanna's eye flashed wide with anger before she recovered her composure. "She's better off hiding while I take care of things."

"What they *did*?" Kevon turned and grabbed Alanna by the shoulders. "Your father? Your eye? Some of them did this to you?"

"There's only one left," she whispered. "The others have paid with their lives. None of them knew until the end. The last one is one of the few keeping the rest of the Guild in line, and I need him to finish this mission, at least. I don't know if Marelle will come back when he's gone or not. Either way, I lose."

Alanna's madness spun into perspective for Kevon. Having to depend on your father's killers for support all this time, keeping up appearances to stay in their good graces, and stay alive. Learning at the feet of your worst enemies, and becoming capable enough to lead them?

"I am so sorry."

"Save your pity for some-" Alanna's voice cracked. "Save your..." Her breath quickened, and her eye fluttered, blinking away the beginning of a tear. "*Save me.*"

CHAPTER 36

The room seemed to spin as Mirsa's feet beat a rhythm in time with the choppy music, a difficult task made near impossible by the amount of wine she'd had with her dinner. The room *lurched* as Bargthar-Stoun finished his circuit and grabbed her hand to twirl her around to Bertus's waiting grasp. Three quick steps and she was matching palms with Kylgren-Wode, then pushing off to fall back into line and hoping her footwork held up to the continued scrutiny of the rest of the gathering.

Seconds later, the Dwarves present shouted in exaltation, and the music stopped. Mirsa tottered a bit before bowing to the other dancers. She endured the rough congratulations of the now rowdy Dwarves, and made her way back to her seat.

"Not bad, for a Mage," Bertus whispered as he came up behind her, serving as a buffer against the still-jostling crowd. "It's almost like you'd done this before."

"In my village, before I was chosen," Mirsa laughed, still gasping for air. "I loved the Feastday celebrations. Until I was twelve, there was not a dance I could not do."

"And since?"

"Magi have a higher standard to uphold," she sighed. "Mingling with the commoners is frowned upon, dangerous. You never know who might have an iron bracelet or earring, dagger hilt. It seemed frivolous... the potential danger for so petty a pleasure. This has made me rethink things a bit..."

Bertus smiled and eased the Master Mage into her chair, pushing it in as she sat. "It suits you, I think. Perhaps not every day, but often, I would hope."

"This place makes me believe it is possible," Mirsa admitted. "But for now, we have other concerns at hand."

"Yer prayers have been answered," Kylgren-Wode announced as he reached the table, followed by Bargthar-Stoun. "Perhaps," he added as the companions looked to him, and then each other.

"Our King has asked, and we have both agreed te accompany ye on yer way," the Ambassador explained, "Te figure out yer book, and help ye with whatever else ye might need."

"Both?" Bertus asked.

"Rhysabeth-Dane," Kylgren answered. "She is gathering books te study as we speak. We'll get extra supplies loaded in yer wagon before morning, and be ready te leave as soon as ye like."

"Knowing us is not the safest thing, outside these walls," Mirsa cautioned. "You may want to reconsider."

"Rhysabeth-Dane is eager te get te studying the book," Kylgren said, with a half-shrug. "I have my suspicions it was all her idea. I'll need to be there te translate... but..." the Ambassador leaned in closer, dropping his voice to a whisper. "The worst day since yer arrival tops the best day before it, fer me anyway. I like *being* an Ambassador, not being *called* one."

"Well then," Bertus said, extending his hand in greeting, "Your words, and your axe, are welcome in our company. May we all find what we seek."

"Agreed," Mirsa added, pushing her chair away from the table to stand. "And I think it best we leave at first light. The sooner we begin, the sooner we find out what happened to Kevon."

CHAPTER 37

The 'sword' looked almost too perfect from a distance, gleaming in the firelight across the room from Kevon. As the Warsmith drew closer, he could tell it was a fake, at no more than half a dozen yards. He hoped that his experience as a Warrior and Blacksmith gave him a better eye when it came down to it, and that in the heat of battle, a Mage would not realize the difference at all.

Or at least not until it's too late, anyway. He smiled, and picked the weapon up, running his fingers along the blade to check once more for uncured spots that might stick in the scabbard, or collect dirt and ruin the illusion. Finding none, he scabbarded and drew it several times, noting only minor scratches in the clear finish, and only a slight difference in the sound between the fake blade and a real one.

One of Alanna's henchmen watched from a darkened corner with something less respectful than disdain. Even though their leader's position on Kevon had softened the last few days, none of her subordinates had been anything even approaching civil to him since his abduction.

There had been no more discussion of Marelle's transition to Alanna since the other night. The half-sane leader of the Assassin's Guild had limited her interactions with the other Guild members in Kevon's presence. He was not sure which was the remaining assailant that Alanna intended to dispatch as soon as their usefulness came to an end, but two men were at the top of Kevon's suspect list. The man in the corner was one of them.

He's younger, more savage than the other, less calculating. Kevon's mind raced, comparing him to the other man. They both hold sway in the Guild, but this one I can believe might not recognize a past victim. The other assassin was older, almost the equivalent to Carlo in the Warrior's Guild. Where the younger used fear, he led with experience and wisdom. To have survived so long in the company they kept, however, he must have done things to earn a reputation that would retain influence over the noise of all the brash newcomers.

His vision darkened and a red haze filled the space between Kevon and the young assassin. The Warsmith forced himself to calm down, evened his breathing, and made his way back to the quarters he was sharing with Alanna.

The Guildmistress was not in, and he was not sure when she would return. Kevon drew the painted blade, and began sword practice.

It was evident he had foregone his workouts for the last few weeks. Muscles groaned and knotted with the unfamiliar motions, his arms heavy with the unworked muscling of a Journeyman Blacksmith. His actions were painful, sluggish. A powered Movement rune corrected his speed, but redoubled his pain. Kevon stopped and stretched out, not something he was used to having to do. His stint as a Mage, coupled with his recent captivity, had taken their toll.

Half an hour into his workout, drenched with sweat, laboring to breathe, Kevon whirled around and stopped the painted sword's blade just shy of where Alanna's neck *had* been. The assassin rebounded off the wall, having cartwheeled away from the initial swing with a lilting burst of laughter. She slapped the flat of the blade down and away as she dove into a rolling kick that swept one of Kevon's legs out from under him.

Kevon turned with the kick, recovering his control of the wooden sword, pulling it in and whipping it around to the side to shift his center of gravity to recover from Alanna's attack. He turned to look in the direction she'd rolled, to find nothing. He scanned quickly to both sides before turning his gaze upwards.

She hurtled from the low rafters like a catapult stone,

striking the exhausted Warsmith in the right shoulder with an outstretched heel. Something twinged, and his arm went numb, spasmed, his hand twitching to cast the replica sword aside, clattering to the floor. Using the stricken shoulder as a stepping stone, Alanna kicked Kevon lightly alongside the head with her other foot, and launched herself into a backflip before he had even finished falling to the bed behind him.

Determined to push through the fatigue and let her know who she was dealing with, Kevon rolled forward to the floor, scooped up the wooden blade, and sprang at Alanna. He fell short, slamming to the floor with a sharp pain in his back where she had stepped while leaping over him. He regained his feet a bit slower, turning to face her as she leaned against the bedpost, smirking.

The runes formed easily, Movement and Illusion danced through his mind, and he latched onto them, fed them reserves he had not yet touched. The Movement spell settled over Kevon, and his muscles relaxed. He returned the crooked smile, and the sword he held appeared to burst into flames.

Before he could take a step forward, Alanna was halfway across the room, daggers appearing in both hands as if from nowhere. Kevon spent a moment forming a Light rune as he blinked, expending a ridiculous amount of energy for a brilliant flash of light between himself and Alanna. Opening his eyes, he shifted the focus of the Illusion rune from his sword to his feet, muffling his steps as he dodged to the left, but the soft padding noises shuffled off to the right.

The rushing flurry of Alanna's feet stuttered for an instant, long enough for Kevon's sidestep to work. He swung the blade and thwacked her smartly across the buttocks as she slashed crosswise with her knives at the empty air in front of her. She twisted and lashed a foot out to kick at the wall she had been running toward, stopping her mad rush before writhing around into a defensive crouch, blinking and bristling with fury. She took a step toward where Kevon wanted her to believe he was, and he smiled.

The dagger she hurled caught his cloak beneath his arm and *thunked* deep into the wardrobe behind him, pinning Kevon loosely to the large wooden cabinet. He shrugged his shoulders and dropped, releasing the wooden blade as he did so, slipping out of the cloak as Alanna planted a foot where his chest had just been.

Kevon's concentration blurred as he hit the floor and the door of the wardrobe reverberated into his head several times from the impact of Alanna's foot. He retained enough presence of mind to aim a kick upward at her outstretched leg, reinforcing the strength of the blow with his Art.

The force of the attack flipped his attacker backwards, heels over head. For an instant, her feet touched down, and then she was flipping backward again with the grace of a court acrobat in the Great Hall in the palace in Navlia. Kevon picked up the wooden sword yet again, and climbed to his feet as Alanna finished another backflip to land in front of the door to the hallway outside.

"Need reinforcements?" he chided the squinting assassin, who then began a slow advance toward him, her neck craning at odd angles to take stock of Kevon and his surroundings. As she closed to within a dozen feet, she spun into an impossibly fast cartwheel, striking out to her right to try and outflank Kevon on his left.

Smiling, Kevon wound up and flashed the sword in a magic-fueled arc across his body to intersect with her advance.

Swish.

The momentum of the unimpeded stroke spun Kevon just enough to shift his field of vision away from the battle for a second, at best. Panic struck when he jerked his gaze back, and Alanna was nowhere to be seen.

Without the barest whisper of a warning, the knife was at his throat, his magic drained away. Alanna's arms twined around him from behind, precisely angled pressure forcing the wooden blade to the ground yet again. "We may not have the same understandings in place as we did before," she hissed into Kevon's ear, "But you should know better than to come into my house and do the very thing I hate the most." She shoved him away, barely removing the blade from his neck before sending him sprawling to the floor. "You'd best behave until we can get the situation outside under control. Do your part, and we'll discuss whether you have a future or not." Alanna paused at the doorway after she stepped over his trembling form. "Don't make me get the chains."

CHAPTER 38

The sky was overcast, an easy transition from the tunnels behind them to the wide open spaces that lay ahead. Mirsa held Rhysabeth-Dane's hand as they sat in the back of the wagon on sacks of grain, backs against tarpaulin-covered bales of fodder. The librarian, petite by even Dwarven standards, reminded the Master Mage of a curious child seeing her first Feastday celebration in one of the Inner Cities.

And we're not even clear of the mountains yet, she thought, smiling and squeezing her companion's hand reassuringly.

Bertus and Kylgren-Wode rode on the front bench, the Ambassador asking more questions about the outside world now that they were making their way into it.

"This 'Kevon' of yers," Kylgren inquired after a while. "Ye speak of him often, what's his part in all this?"

"Kevon is different," Bertus explained after a minute. "There are things about him that only he can explain. He's twice the hero I am."

"Yer quick te say that," Kylgren cautioned, "But I'm slow te believe it. Ye might want te rethink yer opinion of yerself."

"He leads us, after a fashion." Bertus continued. "We're all agents of Prince Alacrit now, but we were sent to Eastport on Kevon's say-so. He sent us on in case there was danger looking for us in the city."

"And ye expected him te meet ye by now?"

"If there was business he could finish quickly, or if he needed our help with something more difficult, yes."

"Yer likely worried about nothing," the dwarf reassured him. "He's-"

"We should have been in contact by now," Mirsa interjected. "I fear something has gone wrong."

Kylgren-Wode shrugged, and turned his attention back to the road ahead.

The mouth of the pass that led to the Dwarven Hold was hours behind them, and the strange Earth magic lingered only in the mountain to Mirsa's right as the wagon sped south down the track toward Eastport. Rhysabeth-Dane had withdrawn further into herself, clinging to Mirsa, burying her face in the Master Mage's robes as the sky above widened and the morning clouds burned away.

"Shall we stop for lunch?" she asked, clasping the clinging dwarf tighter to her side.

Calling out to the team, Bertus reined them in to a halt before leaping into the back of the wagon to dig through the supplies.

Mirsa stood to stretch her legs, and Rhysabeth-Dane squeaked and leapt over the side of the wagon to scurry beneath it.

"Should we...?" Bertus asked, leaning on the brake mechanism to make sure it was fully engaged.

"She's never been outside before," Kylgren explained. "Yer never quite sure how someone's going te take it."

After taking Rhysabeth's and her rations from Bertus, Mirsa stepped down from the back of the wagon and peered beneath it.

The librarian was sitting with her back to one of the wheels, head buried in her hands, rocking back and forth, moaning.

Taking care not to stir up the road dust as she approached

the panic-stricken dwarf, Mirsa crawled beneath the wagon. She leaned back against the wheel next to Rhysabeth, careful not to hit her head on the axle the Dwarven librarian was safely beneath.

"Here, now," she said, offering some of the bread and cured venison to her frightened companion.

Rhysabeth-Dane huddled up even tighter, groaning as if she had been run through with a blade.

Digging into her robe pocket, Mirsa fished out the book, and slid it into Rhysabeth's hands.

The librarian traced her fingers over the pattern on the cover, and seemed to calm down, breathe easier.

"Is it the sky? Is it too much to look at?" Mirsa asked, wrapping her arm around Rhysabeth-Dane, hoping even the sound of her voice would further calm the dwarf.

"*No*," Rhysabeth whispered. "*I cannot feel the mountain.*"

CHAPTER 39

The shadows of late evening stretched from building to building, cloaking all but small sections of the widest roadways in a darkened veil. Street traffic, less crowded and more wary than Kevon remembered from his time spent here before, was winding down to disappear as the last light did the same.

"Is it the Magi, or Alanna they're afraid of more?" he muttered under his breath.

"I'd love to take all the credit," the assassin said, beside him without a whisper of warning. "But I think it's both."

The shame he had begun to feel when surprised by Alanna's sudden appearances was all but gone. Some of the other guild members moved nearly as quietly as she, but no one else had caught him as completely off-guard as she was constantly doing. "What now?"

Her smile twisted past the point of charm. "Do I need a reason to check in on my favorite heretic?" She sighed. "Our scouts are getting less information, and putting themselves at more risk than usual. We've lost another two, in as many days. Not full-fledged assassins, mind you, but still..."

"Why bother me with this?"

"We did find one of theirs, burned to a cinder in the middle of the street last night," she chuckled. "Your work?"

Kevon shook his head. "It's all I can do to get within twenty yards of them without doubting the strength of my illusions. And seeing one alone?" He snorted. "That's a trick I'd like to learn."

"One is easy to surprise," Alanna mused, her cool green eye sweeping slowly across the empty street before them. "But getting them to split up after the first few times... Not even *I* can do that anymore. Something else must be at play here."

"How many are there now?"

"Thirty is our best estimate," Alanna sighed. "Twelve black-robes, at least. I barely have a dozen assassins left, and only a handful of loyal informants."

"Which area are they sweeping tonight?"

"Near the south gate. They should be going through the safehouse you first woke up in shortly, if their pattern holds." Alanna turned her gaze to meet his. "The real battle may begin tonight."

The Warsmith nodded. The traps he had helped set might tilt the odds more toward their favor, but they would certainly mobilize the rest of the Magi that were not patrolling.

"You realize that we haven't been able to keep all of the gates under constant watch," Alanna reminded him.

The previous week had been bursting with frantic activity. Amidst the usual opportune ambushes, the Magi had begun clearing out sections of the city using small teams moving in tandem, never in numbers fewer than nine, and up to a dozen at times. Pretending authority granted by the Prince himself, they searched indiscriminately, and put to death any they thought were working against them. Kevon and his new allies had been forced to move twice already to avoid a confrontation they were not prepared to win.

The traps Kevon had rigged were a special surprise for the Magi. He'd scribed several small scraps of parchment, both sides with multiple fire runes, until the power was barely contained. He'd failed three attempts, scorching his fingers and losing inks and quills in the process. These he set in half-empty bags of flour, after slipping on his steel-laced armbands to shield the parchment from unintended magical attention. Over each of these, the assassins had upended pouches of Dwarven mining powder, and a double handful of horseshoeing nails. They were refilled with flour and stitched up to match the regular flour bags, and stacked around the warehouse side of the abandoned hideout. Seeing what Kevon intended, some of Alanna's men began pulling nails from support beams and shifting the placement of the rigged bags nearer to the sabotaged supports.

Not quite the same camaraderie as one sees at the Warrior's Guild, Kevon thought as he helped move the last few sacks of flour into place before they abandoned the place for good. But I can begin to see what Alanna is building here, harnessing one evil to balance against others.

Kevon snapped back to full awareness as the bells began clanging, and over the buildings to the south, a plume of black smoke began to roil upward.

"Let's hope we are all as prepared for this as you pretend to be," Alanna laughed, pulling her hood over and melting into the confused crowd that surged toward the fire.

CHAPTER 40

"You can't feel the mountain?" Mirsa repeated, mind racing as she pondered the possible implications of the dwarf's statement. My own discomfort with the change in local magical conditions has barely ended, and now this. Could there be a connection? Is she...

"You speak Common?" the Master Mage recoiled from the tiny librarian, peering at her through narrowed eyeslits.

"Some of the books in the library are in Common," Rhysabeth-Dane shrugged. "I wanted to read them."

"But who taught you?" Mirsa prodded, barely containing her excitement. "You don't have the accent that Kylgren-Wode or the others do."

The tiny librarian shook her head. "No one. I just read until it made sense. And I have been practicing *thinking* in Common since I met you. Kylgren probably is not doing that."

"I have some ideas about your connection to the mountain," Mirsa said, pushing the bread and dried meat at Rhysabeth-Dane. "We'll explore them once we are settled for the evening. For now, we eat."

◆ ◆ ◆

"Yer telling me ye have been able te speak Common fer years?" Kylgren fumed over the campfire once the horses were brushed and fed, picketed a short distance away.

Rhysabeth-Dane looked up from the book enough to glare at the Ambassador. "Was it something you needed to know?"

263

"Well!" Kylgren-Wode huffed. "It seems like it would have been good te know at some point before we-"

"Are you glad to be away from the Hold?" the librarian snapped.

"Ahem. I suppose..."

"Glad to be out in the world, being what you pretended for decades?"

"Aye. It is a wonder te be looked at with respect, te be useful fer a change." Kylgren took a bite of bread and shook the crust at her. "What of it?"

"Would Bargthar-Stoun have sent both of us, knowing I spoke Common?"

The ambassador stopped mid-chew.

"You are welcome." Rhysabeth-Dane returned to her study, mouthing out words in her native tongue.

Bertus chuckled, shaking his head at the Dwarves and continuing to secure the supplies the way Rhysabeth had shown them to prevent the Gnomes from taking too much. He left bits of food on the back of the opened wagon, and the rest of the rations were stored in tightly wrapped sacks stacked under the hay and grain for the horses near the front.

"Curious," Rhysabeth-Dane said, rifling through a satchel for a fresh sheet of parchment. "There is a pattern here. Every... Five!" The librarian began scribbling quick reproductions of the runes in the book into columns of five on her empty sheet. "Most of these runes are in a more ancient form of Dwarven. But beginning with the second..." she pointed down the short row of symbols she had scrawled, "These all appear more current. I could have a fifth of the book translated in a very short time."

Rhysabeth-Dane scowled at the other figures on the page. "There are more patterns here, I cannot tell for sure what they are."

"We know far more now than we did moments ago," Mirsa consoled the miniature scholar. "I'm sure in time, you'll decipher the rest."

Scowling, the dwarf returned to her writing, filling up the rest of her page and beginning another.

"She's odd," Kylgren-Wode grunted to Bertus as he climbed into the wagon to help check over the supplies. "But she'll figure yer problem out fer ye."

Bertus shrugged. "She seems to like you well enough."

The dwarf sputtered, yanking the corner of burlap he'd been tucking out of place. "I don't think tha-"

"If she hadn't held her tongue, you'd be back at the Hold, right?" Bertus snugged down the last bit of the rough covering and patted the bundle of food down with a handful of loose hay to complete the effect. "I thought she'd been glaring at you this whole time." The Seeker chuckled at the Ambassador's dumbfounded expression and hopped down from the wagon. "This makes more sense."

Kylgren-Wode clambered down and dusted himself off before taking up his axe and following Bertus to the clearing where the Warrior was beginning his sword practice. "I don't see it," he harrumphed, standing opposite from Bertus and beginning the abrupt, violent motions of ritualistic axe combat.

Bertus stopped after a few minutes, sweat beginning to bead on his brow. He crouched and continued to watch Kylgren-Wode. Every motion was a deadly close-quarters attack, with an added component. Some movements were advances, others sidesteps. There were kicks and stomps, but the axe was always flashing in a smooth, tight crescent, never at more than arm's length, never overextending its wielder.

"Would you be willing to teach me some of that?" he asked when the dwarf stopped for the evening and returned the axe to his belt loop.

"Yer looking te the wrong dwarf," Kylgren protested. "I'm no soldier. The Stoneguards would have a good laugh if they saw ye asking me fer lessons."

"My Commander would say that we all have things to teach, and to learn. I'm sure Kevon would agree." The Seeker slid his sword back into its scabbard and turned toward camp.

"I'll show ye what little I know," Kylgren-Wode assented. "And yer friend, too when we find him."

Nodding back over his shoulder, Bertus stalked back into camp.

CHAPTER 41

The frantic milling of the crowd near the scene of the explosions eased Kevon's mind, the distractions of the surrounding mob allowing him to throw simple illusions while keeping an eye on the few enemy Magi that he could spot on rooftops and balconies. Ducking into a doorway out of the press of bodies, in view of only one of the invading Magi, Kevon dropped his veil and nodded to the robed figure on the balcony across the street.

Feeling Fire magic build, and sure of his opponent's intent, he released the pent-up energy he'd set aside for the Movement rune glimmering in his mind. A flowerpot behind the distracted Mage struck with shattering force, toppling his foe over the railing and into the crowd below. Kevon threw up another concealing illusion, and moved back into the crowd.

Joining in a bucket line from a nearby canal, Kevon kept watch on the other wary Magi still patrolling. When a trio of hooded figures passed by, he watched until the red robed Magi were not looking toward their black robed superior before unleashing an invisible stream of force focused through the Movement rod strapped to his forearm. The Master Mage cried out as he sailed over the wooden railing into the canal. Tapping into the energy of the water in the buckets between himself and the canal, just a dozen yards away, then connecting to the canal water itself and the sea beyond, Kevon kept the currents pulling the Mage down. Severing the surprised Mage's attempts to use the power that surrounded him, he forced water into the floundering man's lungs, spinning the canal water into a miniature vortex to keep him disoriented.

"Mind your bucket!" the man next to Kevon shouted as their containers collided and spilled on the street.

Kevon retrieved his bucket and made sure that his arm brushed against the hilt of the painted sword at his side, in case the Magi were looking at him. He passed the empty vessel behind him to the return line and resumed the monotonous rhythm of the brigade. His diminished concentration proved to be more than enough to finish off the weakened Mage, before his companions could gather enough power to attempt a rescue.

With their superior defeated, the acolytes turned and fled toward the center of town, in the direction of the building the Magi had been using as a command center.

Past the burning warehouse, Kevon thought, a smile creeping onto his face. Into the sights of assassins with steel-tipped crossbow bolts...

The Journeyman Magi did not even make it halfway to the bucket line that they needed to cross before the sprint through the crowd to their destination. The hellish flaring of the ruined building dimmed, and a jet of flame washed from the outstretched hand of a bent, brown cloaked figure that steadied himself with a gnarled stick in his other hand.

The fleeing Magi were dead before they hit the ground. The fiery bloom that engulfed them was undetectable by magical means, but was spectacular enough to scatter the line of volunteers more than fifty yards away, and throw the rest of the containment effort into disarray.

Townsfolk near the attacking Mage panicked and ran, while Kevon could feel enormous amounts of magic being gathered by others approaching from all directions. The hooded figure threw his arms open wide, facing the still raging fire engulfing the warehouse and two other buildings. The flames died down to almost nothing, and a jagged red scar split the world between the Mage and the fire. Three hobbling steps, and he was gone, the tear vanishing as he did.

Taking advantage of the disruption, Kevon feigned panic

and abandoned his place in line. He cowered behind a boarded-up Merchant's cart, with a full view of the returning inferno and the approaching Magi. Three bursts of abandoned power to the west told him that the steel-tipped bolts of the crew of assassins had done their work. No magic flared in response, and he scored it as a victory in his mind. He estimated that between the explosion, the scene before him, and the assassins, half of the Magi in the city had been defeated.

I don't know who that Mage was, he thought, moving into a knot of townsfolk scrambling toward one of the meeting points Alanna had set for regrouping during the conflict. *I don't suppose he'll have enough strength to reappear after what he's just done, at any rate.*

"Seven in the warehouse, four at the pier", Alanna whispered as she slipped her arm into the crook of his. *"Four of them black-robes."*

"Three outside the warehouse, three more to the west," he mumbled, provoking a squeeze and a wink from the Mistress of Assassins. "Only one was mine," he responded, scowling.

A flash of light and a scream from a nearby rooftop preceded a flaming, falling underling of Alanna's, arms churning as though he might swim to the balcony ledge across the street.

Alanna squealed, hurrying around the smoldering corpse like a properly frightened citizen.

Calculating the odds with one less bow, the Warsmith assumed, fighting the urge to pick up the weapon as he stepped over the fallen assassin. His longer strides caught him up to his companion as she turned toward a narrow alley. She appeared to trip, and Kevon felt a magical *whump* as she stumbled into the passageway.

"Five black-robes," she smirked, twirling another throwing dagger once before concealing it in her tunic sleeve. In the relative concealment of the alley, Alanna sped along at a pace Kevon was hard-pressed to match. They burst out into an empty side street, and sprinted to another alley, racing halfway

down it before lurching into an opened threshold, slamming the door closed behind them.

Three familiar figures rose from their hiding places, two lowering loaded crossbows while the third sheathed a pair of throwing knives.

"*Counts!*" Alanna hissed.

"One."

"Two."

"Four."

"Mmmm," the Guildmistress purred, nodding to the knife-wielding assassin. "Five." She looked at Kevon, who stared back for a second.

"Oh. One." Kevon thought about the other Mage that had escaped into the fiery rift. "And, two?"

"If the others have done nearly as well as we have, there may only be a dozen of them left." Alanna stood straight and fierce. "They cannot remain here without reinforcements in so low of numbers. One way or another, this is over."

CHAPTER 42

"Something's wrong," Bertus said, looking to the south, and the dark ribbon of smoke that curled its way up onto the moonlit night. He wolfed down the last few bites of fish, wincing from the heat, and snatched up his swordbelt.

"Stay here with the Dwarves," he called across the camp to Mirsa as he dug his saddle out from the piled gear in the wagon. "I'll return, or send someone back with an extra horse when I know it's safe."

"That smoke is coming from Eastport?" the Master Mage asked, approaching Bertus as he began tightening the saddle straps down on the increasingly agitated mare. "Do you think Kevon has anything to do with it?"

"Not if he has a bit of sense," Bertus grumbled. "Still, I'd rather see what is going on before dragging you three into the unknown." He gave the mare a final pat of reassurance before climbing into the saddle and sidestepping her up to the roadway. "Keep them safe," he commanded, pointing to Kylgren-Wode with a stern glance.

The dwarf patted his axe with a smile and a nod as Bertus urged his mount toward the snaking darkness to the south.

Within minutes, the Seeker was out of sight behind the intervening terrain. The remaining travelers settled back around the campfire, sidelong glances at the ominous column of smoke punctuating the lack of conversation.

"Do you think he'll be all right?" Mirsa asked. "He had the last watch this morning, and was getting ready to sleep before he saw the smoke."

"Stoneguards in the Keep stay awake fer three days at a stretch at least once a season," Kylgren offered with a shrug. "I don't know what training yer Warriors endure, but I suspect sleep is the last thing that young fellow is thinking about."

◆ ◆ ◆

The mare loped along the road, seeming as excited about the increased pace as Bertus was to be back in a saddle after the long weeks of wagon benches. He could feel her trying to speed up to a gallop, but held her back again. The longer rolling gait would be easier on both of them before the night was over.

The chill of the evening seared his cheeks and clawed at his ears. It knifed up his tunic sleeves and down the nape of his neck in a rhythm that followed the motion of the mare. Frost glistened in patches alongside the rutted track, sometimes spreading onto the road itself, but never more than a hand's-breadth. Bertus focused and measured his breathing, leaned into the wind, and left the road to his eager companion.

More than an hour later, He drank from a stream that crossed the roadway. He chewed a strip of smoked venison while the mare drank the small amount of water he would allow. She nuzzled at the handful of oats that he pulled from the saddlebags as he chewed the last of his own snack. Aside from the occasional deep breath, and the thin sheen of sweat on her flanks, the horse showed no signs of undue fatigue.

"About halfway there," he told her, regarding the angle of the smoke plume beyond the intervening hills while scratching her muzzle. "Are you ready to go again?"

Minutes later, against his better judgment, Bertus allowed the mare to speed up to a gallop. The moon rose higher in the sky, better lighting the road ahead, and outlining the danger that loomed before them.

The mare slowed to a lope as they crested a hill and Eastport came into view. The smoke rose from the south section of town, muted flashes of yellowish-red making it clear that the fires were still burning. The road ahead wound around to the western gate, still a few miles distant. Bertus flicked the reins and urged the mare back to a gallop.

"No one in or out tonight!" the guardsman called down from the tower that loomed beside the massive gate to the city.

"By order of Prince Alacrit himself," Bertus shouted back, brandishing the scroll the monarch had given him like a weapon.

"Alacrit can go hang himself, sending those Magi here!" the response hurtled from the lofty guard shack. "I've half a mind to put a bolt through your... Bertus?"

"They must be desperate for guardsmen!" the Seeker shouted back. "If you shoot a bow like you threw rocks, do your worst, Alec!" Bertus dismounted and led the mare to the gate. Moments later, the doors creaked open enough for a single guardsman to slip through.

"What do you think you're doing, flapping your jaw about Alacrit at these gates in the middle of the night, *especially tonight*?" Alec hissed, glancing back through the gates as if he thought someone might be listening.

"Do Magi who burn down the city seem like the sort Alacrit would retain in his service?" Bertus spat to the side. "Honestly, Alec."

"It seemed strange to most of us from the beginning," the guard agreed. "But our superiors went along with it. There wasn't any questioning. They almost seemed scared."

The Novice could help himself no longer. He clasped his friend's arm in greeting. "How is the *Maiden* these days?"

"It's the best inn Eastport has to offer, now that Liah's back."

Bertus recoiled at the news. She'd been doing so well for

herself, and Kevon sent her back here...

"She's running the place now, hadn't you heard?" Alec chided. "Oh right, you've been dining with Prince Alacrit in the palace, eh?"

"Once or twice." The Warrior squeezed Alec's arm before releasing it. "These Magi were not sent by Alacrit. They were sent here to find my friends and I, because we killed their pet Orclord."

The guardsman's smile dissolved under the unflinching glare of his friend. "Get in here, let's sit down and talk about this."

Minutes later, his mare stabled by the guard barracks, Bertus looked out over the port city from the top of the gate tower. The fires appeared to be under control now, smoke no longer roiled upward from the south, but seemed to spread and blanket nearly half of Eastport in a ghostly haze.

"So, you really have other friends?" Alec jibed. "What's that like for you?"

"It was three of us at the start," the Warrior began, smiling at his friend's good natured ribbing. "They attacked the Palace because we were there, because we had meddled in their plans." He snorted. "As if raising an orc big enough to threaten Eastport was sane enough to be a real *plan*."

"We left the palace after we stopped the attackers," he continued. "I'm still wondering who is really safer with that decision."

"You, or the prince?" Alec asked, nodding. "Neither, I'd wager."

"We started to head this way, but Kevon sent us ahead to the north, while he stopped here by himself."

"The streets have changed since you were here last," Alec sighed. "They seem calmer by day, but people have been disappearing at night. Not that most have complained, thieves and crooked Merchants mostly. Magi, too. Until a few weeks ago."

"Alacrit's Magi?"

"So they said," the guardsman sniffed. "At first most of them 'disappeared' too. It wasn't until there were dozens of them that they started searching the city. 'Enemies of the Empire', they claimed they were looking for."

"And the fire?" Bertus asked, pointing toward the smoky blanket that appeared to be settling in for the night.

"A warehouse fire, from what I've heard. Someone said they heard thunder before it started, but there hasn't been a cloud in the sky for days." The guardsman snorted. "That's what they get for playing with magic. I think a few of them died in there."

A grin worked its way onto Bertus's grim visage. "I'd hoped my friend hadn't had anything to do with this, but it seems there's a small chance of that. We'd better go find him before they do."

CHAPTER 43

"They know we're tracking them by magic," Kevon whispered to Alanna as she peered around the corner of yet another building. "They've either stopped using it at all, or they're concealing it very well." His limited skill with the Detection rune Mirsa had shown him was proving useless. He had been able to more accurately pinpoint magic that he could already feel with it, but trying to use it to search out concealed spells had not worked at all. They had only accounted for one additional enemy casualty since they had split from the other assassins, and had not seen any of the other teams in over an hour.

"We may have missed out on all of the fun," Alanna pouted in Kevon's direction before transforming from lithe cutthroat to panicked townswoman to cross the street. The Adept followed, assuming an air of inept bravado before breaking step to scurry after her.

"There!" she whispered as he caught up, pointing to a closed door across another street that seemed far too wide in the deserted tension of the night.

"Is that where they are..."

"No, ours," she whispered, gesturing to an inconspicuously placed chalk smudge on the threshold. "We need to get in there and see what the others have managed to do so far."

They repeated their previous charade of incompetence, bumbling across the roadway and into the unlocked building. The windows were shuttered, and the faint moonlight from the mismatched joints in the wood was barely enough to make out the outlines of shapes in the room.

Kevon felt along the wall for torch sconces or lantern hooks, but the fireplace flared to light without even the barest whisper of power in his mind. The brown-robed, hooded figure from earlier in the evening stood near the hearth, leaning on a gnarled staff.

"Be at ease," the Mage whispered, the rasping an obvious effort. "Trying... to... help..." The mysterious Magi unclenched one hand from his supporting staff long enough to gesture to the table beside him where another staff lay. "Like... in... Palace..." he wheezed. "Destroy them."

The crippled Mage faltered, catching ahold of his staff with both hands again to steady himself before taking a deep breath. The fireplace dimmed to embers, and a flaming tear in reality appeared behind him. The heat emanating from the rift reminded Kevon of the forge, but the hunched Magi stepped backward into it, and the gash closed with a rumble.

"Friend of yours?" Alanna asked, resheathing her throwing dagger with a noticeable trembling of her usually steady hands. "From the Palace?"

"I don't remember him from the Palace..." the Adept scratched his head. "The most we dealt with Magi there was the attack..." Images of some of the skirmishes they had only seen the aftermaths of wheeled through Kevon's mind. Charred corpses of enemy Magi that none of the surviving Court Wizards had claimed credit for. *Has this Mage been following me, helping me out?* The possibility alarmed him more than it reassured him. *I don't know who he is, what he wants. What if he decides I'm not worthy of his help anymore? Does he know my secret?*

"He may have followed me from the Palace, or before that," Kevon admitted. "I have no idea who he is, though."

"*He seems to like you,*" she whispered in his ear, drawing uncomfortably close. "*I'm a little jealous.*"

Shrugging her off, Kevon walked to the table and picked up the staff.

The world spun madly, engulfed in a fiery cataclysm. The screams of the burning echoed in Kevon's ears, his face flushed with rage.

The staff clattered back to the table, and Kevon staggered, sweat beading on his face.

"Doesn't seem very helpful," Alanna offered.

The staff lay there, dormant, unnoticed by the Seeker's magical senses, but the power he'd just felt was akin to the torrent of flames he'd watched the mysterious Mage dispatch the other two enemy Magi with earlier tonight. It felt like the staves in the armory at Gurlin's tower, multiplied beyond his comprehension. The malevolence of the enchanter's intent must have transferred into this staff as the others had, to a degree approaching madness. Kevon was loath to handle the weapon, let alone use it, but at some point it might be his only advantage. He steeled his nerves against the residual emotion tied to the staff, and picked it up again.

The mental safeguards he'd erected seemed to keep at least a portion of the fury infused in the staff at bay. His pulse quickened, and the sweat already glistening on his face started flowing more freely. "Let's find the others," he snapped. "We're through hiding from these Magi."

The door slammed a bit too loudly for Kevon's liking, and he tripped over a chair, bruising his shins and smacking his elbow on a table. The fury that rose-

Isn't mine... the Warsmith reminded himself, pushing back at his connection to the enchanted staff.

From the shuttered window, Alanna tsk'd softly. "Almost brought that patrol down on us."

"*I did no such thing.*" The end of the staff Kevon held flared to life, lighting the darkened room.

Turning to gaze at the barely-restrained Mage, Alanna's glare softened, reminiscent of Marelle. "There must be a lot of anger in that, to change you so much." Scoffing, she turned back to the window and peeked out again as the sound of hoof-beats on cobblestone grew louder once more.

"Odd," she said once the noise quieted down to nothing. "Haven't seen him around in years."

"Who?"

"The boy from the inn," Alanna answered, tugging at her earlobe. "Bart…"

"Bertus?"

"Yes, that's him."

"Was there a Mage with him?" Kevon hurried to the door-way. "A black-robe?"

"No, a guardsman." She answered, twirling a dagger with a casual grace. "And two more following them. Is he one of the enemy?"

The Warsmith shook his head. "He's a good friend. And if Mirsa is in the city, she's in danger. We have to go warn them."

Alanna shrugged and followed Kevon's mad rush out into the night.

CHAPTER 44

"That's right, sir. The hostile Magi are not here on Prince Alacrit's orders." Bertus leaned forward over the Guard Commander's desk, tired of waiting for the man to finish reading the missive. "They are enemies of the Realm, to be dispatched on sight."

"So you say," the tired-looking man groaned. "And your friend is one of them?"

"He is a Mage, but not one of them!" the Seeker shouted, and hands around the room moved to sword hilts. "A Journeyman, Alone. From what Alec has told me, these others move in groups, always with a Master. I've been here all of half an hour, and I have it figured out. You've been dealing with this scum for weeks?"

"Now listen here, you *pup!*" the Commander snarled, slapping his hands down on the desk as he stood to shout into Bertus's face. "You can't just walk in here and tell me what-"

"That parchment you just read lets me do *exactly* that," the Seeker responded, quieting to his normal speaking voice. "Would you like to help me, or remain here, in chains?"

Thirty minutes later, Bertus rode at the head of a column of guardsmen that thundered down the smoke-filled streets. Three precinct Guard Commanders and over four dozen guardsmen and volunteers rode, crossbows at the ready. They had already slain a trio of the enemy Magi; a Master, a Journeyman, and an Apprentice, by the colors of their robes. That had been ten minutes ago, and not a soul besides the riders themselves had been spotted since.

The patrol rode into the Market Square, and Bertus turned to address the three ranking officers while the others fanned out, eyeing the rooftops and the side streets.

"Their supposed headquarters was empty, but they had been seen coming and going, at least in the area, for weeks?" The Seeker sighed, and glared at the precinct's Commander. "Do we need to swing back north and search building by building to the east until we flush them out?

"There are only a handful of places..." the targeted Commander shook his head. "I'll take two squads north and sweep them, to the east, as you suggested. The other two should ride east and fan out to the north and wait. If they're there, we'll get them."

The precinct Commander that Bertus had first spoken with motioned for the Seeker to follow, and twenty men rode east after them, leaving the other two Guard Captains and roughly thirty other guardsmen to begin the sweep north.

The choking fog still rolled in from the south, not quite strong enough to overpower the salt air as they rode closer to the sea. Five streets down, the Commander wheeled his horse around and addressed Bertus.

"We've enough men to stretch to the waterfront from here. You can wait-"

"I'd rather ride than sit," Bertus answered, edging his mount to the north. *The more ground I cover, the more likely I am to find Kevon*, he added mentally.

"Alec, stay with him."

"Yes, sir!" The young guardsman broke ranks and rode to Bertus's side.

The Seeker began leading the column up the darkened roadway, watching the shadows and the rooftops for any signs of movement. Crossbow at the ready, he paused at each intersection for a full minute, making sure the riders behind him had fully examined the path behind. He cast an appraising eye down each corridor, alert for anything that might seem out of place in the city that had been his home for so many years.

There should be movement, even at this hour, he thought, remembering back to the days he had worked at the *Maiden*, and the nights he had prowled the streets with Alec and some of the others their age. He would not have missed a fire in the middle of the night for anything, though it might cost him a beating at the hands of his former employer.

"Not a single soul," he whispered, glancing up and down the side streets at the third intersection they passed through.

"Only guard patrols brave the darkness here these days, for what good they are." Alec confirmed. "Sailors stay on their ships, or at inns. It's..." he bit his lip. "An uneasy peace."

The fifth street was the track above the waterfront. It angled from northwest to southeast, curving with the bay to the outskirts of town to the north, to the grand Myrnar embassy that extended into the sea to the east.

"End of the road," Alec announced. "Nothing to do but wait."

The riders behind shifted to spread out evenly, bunching closer together only at the intersections. Bertus and Alec sat side by side twenty yards from the next nearest patrolman.

Bertus.

The Seeker heard his name in a whisper that could have been his own thoughts, but the nudge on his shoulder could not have been his imagination. Scanning the roadway, he noticed a flicker of light to the east.

"Wait here," he told Alec, reining the mare toward the alleyway. He waved off the guardsman's initial protest, and rode around the corner into the darkness.

"Bertus," Kevon whispered, dropping the deepened shadow illusion that he'd used to cover himself and Alanna.

The Seeker's horse shied at their sudden appearance, snorting nervously until Kevon reached out and scratched its muzzle.

"Is all of this your doing?" Bertus whispered, swinging down from the saddle to clasp Kevon's arm in greeting.

"Some," the Warsmith chuckled. "Not all. I had help."

"I see that. Who is...?" His hand froze in mid-greeting.

Alanna's grin widened as recognition crept into the Warrior's face.

"Marelle?"

"Not exactly," Kevon sighed. "There's no time to explain now. The enemy Magi are on the run, we've nearly wiped them out."

"The city guard is helping now," the Seeker commented, gaze still riveted on Alanna's face. "They're sweeping through the streets, trying to drive them toward us."

"I'll have my men move to the rooftops, then," the assassin purred. "We'll close this noose once and for all."

"Your men?" Bertus sputtered, looking over to Kevon. "Who are her...?"

The Adept glanced to where Alanna had been standing. "She does that now," he shrugged.

"You've got to come with me," Bertus declared, climbing back on his mare. "We'll get through this togeth-"

"No." The Warsmith shook his head at the Seeker, and backed further down the alleyway, clutching the staff. "I've got to stay with her, see this through." He formed the runes for Darkness and Illusion in his mind. "I'll see you when this is over." He fed the runes power, and melted into the shadows to begin his search for Alanna.

CHAPTER 45

"What was it?" Alec asked as Bertus rode back to the waiting line of guardsmen.

"I found my friend," he chuckled. "I feel sorry for any of those Magi that get past us. We also shouldn't have to worry about watching the-"

A strangled cry came from above them, and a red-robed figure toppled from the roof to land only feet from where Bertus and Alec waited. A stubby feathered crossbow bolt protruded from the Mage's chest, the fabric of his robes stained a darker crimson radiating from the anchoring projectile.

"The rooftops," Bertus continued, "Are secured by marksmen. Reasonably effective ones, at that." He leaned over to make sure the fallen Mage was dead. "I suggest we hold here, and prepare for the worst."

"Something is happening," Alec whispered to Bertus minutes later, pointing along the waterfront road to where they could just now begin to see the other guard units sweeping toward them.

Cries of fear and anger threaded their way through the dimly lit streets, quick flashes of light illuminating the guardsmen on the road before they charged back to the south.

Alec wheeled his mount around and started to ride toward up the road to where the others had disappeared.

"No!" Bertus called. "We hold here!" He looked down the line of troops to the south. Most of them were having trouble controlling their horses, which were infected with the excitement and confusion of the night's events. *We hold here!*" the

Seeker thundered, causing more than one steed to rear up before it could be brought back under control by its rider. In the span of time it took for Alec to return to Bertus's side, the rest of the guards on their street had settled back to an uneasy watchfulness.

"You've changed more than I would have thought possible these last few years," Alec observed, turning so that he could see the streets running to the south and west before loading his crossbow.

"I've seen some of the faces of war," Bertus shrugged. "Not the ones you hear of in the songs, with lines of men arrayed against each other, fighting for what they have been told to, or what they believe is right. No..." he stared down the street to where the guardsmen had returned and were advancing toward them once more. "I've seen men cultivating weapons they cannot control, growing armies that would be the ruin of us all. Powerful Magi stalking down darkened corridors like thieves in the night, slaughtering innocents." He drew the regal blade from its scabbard at his side, regarded it a few moments before returning it. "If we cannot stand fast against that, we are lost."

Alec said nothing, nodding once, and resuming his watch of the advancing guards and the surrounding area.

I'm not the only one who has changed these last few years, Bertus thought, replaying the scene in the alley with Kevon and Marelle over again in his mind. Everyone thought her dead, but here she is, scarred, capable, elusive... The corners of the Warrior's mouth turned up in the hint of a smile. And she has... men?

The sounds of the oncoming patrols had quieted down to nothing. Lost in thought, Bertus had not followed Alec's gaze to the deepening shadow moving almost unnoticed past them in the street.

"There's no clouds," the guardsman commented, looking up at the unobstructed moon, then back to the wavering miasma that was nearly across to the building between them and the rest of the approaching guards.

"It might be Kev-" the Seeker halted mid-word as he noted the poor quality of the magic. The illusion dissolved and his gaze locked onto the eyes of the black robed figure that resolved before them. Unreasonable fear swept through him, but vanished as he gripped the hilt of the sword at his side. His horse and Alec's both collapsed out from under them with simultaneous sighs. Bertus rolled free, springing to his feet, sword drawn, cringing at the mangled crossbow beneath his fallen steed. He bellowed a fearsome war-cry, but the Mage laughed, glancing to where Alec had fallen, and lay unmoving. Bertus ventured a quick glance at his downed friend, and back up the street to where the rest of the guard waited, oblivious to what was transpiring not a stone's throw from their positions.

"I'm curious, boy," the white-haired wizard chuckled, "As to who you thought I might be, that did not concern you as much as is proper."

"He thought you might have been me," Kevon answered, stepping into view from the corner of the building behind Bertus. "Master."

Confusion clouded Holten's face for a moment as he recognized Kevon, and saw the sword at his side. "No matter," the Master Mage laughed. "I don't know how you survived abandoning the Arts, but it will not be for much longer."

The Warsmith drew his wooden sword, angling the blade to produce the loudest rasp possible as he did so.

"You know as well as I that two blades are no match for my magic," Holten gloated.

"That may be true," Kevon shrugged, and began circling to the right, as Bertus advanced to the left.

The Master Mage began his assault with fireballs, hotter and faster than anything Kevon had witnessed his former Master perform while he studied with him in Laston. Bertus knocked aside the blazing spheres aimed at him with the ancient sword, and Kevon severed the power behind the attacks with spells of his own as they reached his wooden blade.

Holten's attacks intensified as his attention was split between the two attackers and their widening angles of approach. Cobblestones scraped free from their places in the street, and hurtled at the Warriors. Kevon shifted his attention to severing the connections between the stones and Holten, rushing the Mage to further tax his concentration.

Realizing the interference had to come from Kevon, Holten split his focus and drew a whole section of street up between himself and Bertus, each stone supported by its own Movement spell. With an arcane word and a flinging gesture from the Master Mage, the wave of flying stone sped toward the Seeker faster than Kevon could manage to counter.

The Warsmith concentrated on breaking apart as much of the spell-driven flood of rocks as he could, but the illusions he'd been keeping up all evening, and the exertions of the last minute or so had taxed him to the limit. He countered less than a third of the cobblestone projectiles, which slowed only slightly at that.

Bertus leapt and rolled, to the weaker side of the onslaught, but forward, and over many of the flagging projectiles. Several of the cobbles still struck him, and he staggered to his feet, sword knocked free, lost amongst the scattered stones.

"No." Kevon spoke in a commanding voice, stepping forward and pitching the wooden sword end over end in an arc that targeted his former Master.

Panicked, Holten shifted to the side, lurching clumsily at the sudden application of his Movement spell to *himself*.

Kevon used the moment of distraction to his advantage, having decided that Holten was a bit much for himself and the now shaken Bertus to handle alone. He used most of his reserves to end the illusion the Master Mage had been holding to keep the other guards oblivious of the battle. He reached behind his back to grasp the staff, and brought it to bear on Holten, who eyed the alarmed guardsmen who were beginning to ride toward them from down the street.

Flames brighter and hotter than those Holten had just flung at the Warriors spewed from the end of the staff, enveloping the Mage.

He laughed.

The rage that poured from the weapon fueled Kevon's attack, building power until he could feel his fingers blistering at its touch.

Flames wrapped around the Master Mage, spinning like a fiery whirlwind, his long white hair whipping about as if it was nothing more than a dust devil in a freshly plowed field, rather than a raging conflagration that engulfed him.

Holten's arm shot out, directing some of the gathered flame to lance at Bertus, who staggered mostly out of the way, but still collapsed, tunic smoldering.

The night brightened as an increasingly familiar sight rent apart the fabric of reality. The crippled Mage who had given Kevon the staff stepped out, his own weapon pointed at Holten. Flames poured from both staves, but the besieged Mage only laughed louder.

"Here's a trick I learned a few years ago, at the tower," the twisted Mage rasped, and the flames ebbed from his staff, from around Holten.

The Master Mage started screaming.

Whatever it is, it's working, Kevon thought, offering up what little power he had left to his mysterious ally. He felt the runes in the other Mage's mind, Fire, Transformation, and Man. The implications of the spell sickened him, but nothing else seemed to be working. He channeled magic from the staff to strengthen the Fire portion of the spell, and Holten screeched with increasing intensity.

The effects of the spell began to show in a manner not unlike an oil-soaked parchment alighting from the bottom. The flames swirling around Kevon's former master speared inward, beginning at his feet. Boots and clothing charred and flaked away to reveal the change taking place underneath. Holten howled, his voice nearly overshadowed by the wind from the superheated cyclone surrounding him. The transformation crept upward, flesh, and then bone not merely burning, but changing into living fire.

Kevon could feel the crippled Mage holding the portal open, and drawing more power from the opening. He considered trying to do the same, but Holten's change was nearly to the middle of his chest, and it would soon be over. He focused on steadying the magic he was already using.

The Mage at his side began to falter, and it was only then that Kevon saw the lines of power that stretched from Holten back to his attacker, redirecting some of the spell that was killing him. The Warsmith shifted his focus away from supplying more power to the spell, and tried using the scant amount of magic he had left to slice away at the energy flowing back to his mysterious ally. Three feeble attempts, and Kevon's reserves gave out. He threw all the power from the staff that he could stand to draw out into the Mage's spell for precious moments before realizing the power that was being offered back to him.

Borrowed magic swept through Kevon, enough to shape into a counterspell that severed Holten's attack. The deepening of the connection between himself and the other Mage shocked him with the sudden flash of familiarity.

The Master Mage's arms flashed into lashing tendrils of fire, and the screams took on an almost gleeful tone. Holten was no longer attacking Pholos, but he too was now drawing power from the opened portal, beginning to take control of the spell that was almost done changing his entire being into flames.

No longer resisting, Holten's transition to flames was nearly instantaneous. A sudden surge of drawn energy from the portal enabled him to double in size, a disfigured giant of elemental fury. Kevon and Pholos used their staves to deflect the bolts of flame that assailed them, but Holten's size grew steadily, and it seemed only a matter of moments before they were overwhelmed.

"Shoot him!" Kevon screamed above the roar of the inferno that was beginning to engulf buildings on both sides of the street. *One arrow is all it would take,* he realized, to change the monstrosity before him back into a man.

Lances of fire screamed down the street to engulf guardsmen and horses before they could respond. The pained cries of man and beast twined with the crackling of burning buildings to force Kevon to a place he did not want to be, to a time when he had stood with Pholos before, and lost him, he'd thought, forever.

The thing that had once been Kevon's Master turned its attention to the two Magi once again. *"Buuuuurrrrrrrnnnnnn!"* it wheezed, spraying jets of flame that they could barely resist, standing in pockets of free air that were still blistering hot.

"You can burn!" Bertus shouted, peeking over the pile of cobblestones he'd sheltered behind, flinging his recovered sword at the monster.

"Haaaa!" The Holten-flame split, and the sword passed through without effect. It flung a burst of fire toward Bertus, who scrambled back down behind the barrier that had nearly been the death of him moments before.

"Now!" Alanna shouted from the corner of the intersection, stepping out with throwing daggers at the ready.

In response, at least four crossbowmen leaned over different rooftops, bolts trained on the blazing monstrosity filling the street.

Seeing the danger on all sides, the once-Holten flared in anger and rushed toward his only possible avenue of escape. The portal.

Time slowed. Kevon saw where the flaming creature was headed, and that Pholos was in the way. *I won't let you down this time...* he thought, as he lurched toward his friend. Kevon sprang the last few feet, knocking the younger Mage to the ground, flinging his right hand upward to keep it from contacting Pholos, hoping it was high enough to end Holten's fiery rampage.

The howling inferno passed close enough to singe the Warsmith's fingertips, but did not hinder his foe's escape. The last flickers of Holten's new form vanished through the collapsing portal, and the night dimmed a shade, still lit on all sides by burning buildings.

Pholos struggled to sit, and clutched his staff, drawing power from the Enchanted weapon to quench flames rather than start them. He wrestled with the urges his own malice had imbued deep into the ensorcelled wood, and overcame them, mastering both his errant will and the flames.

Guardsmen arrived from all directions. Swords were drawn, crossbows aimed, and accusations leveled. Pholos dropped the staff and lay back, arms outstretched.

"No!" Kevon shouted, climbing to his feet and standing over the fallen Mage. "He saved us!"

One of the guard Commanders leapt from his horse, shoved Kevon back, and drew his sword to hold the tip inches from Pholos's neck. "And who are you, that we should believe?"

"A hero of the Realm," Bertus called, propping himself up on the pile of stones he'd sheltered behind. "Stand down!"

The guard Commander whirled his blade around and resheathed it with a flourish, stepping back and inclining his head toward Kevon before turning to bark orders at those crowding into the intersection after him.

"Are you all right?" the Warsmith asked his fallen comrade, offering Pholos his unadorned hand for support. "Are *we* all right? If Holten could do that much with just the power from the portal, what can he do once he's *there*?"

"*That was Holten?*" Pholos rasped, taking Kevon's hand and climbing to his feet. "No," the Mage answered, leaning on his staff for support. "He's a good as dead in there, after what he's been through," he coughed. "You can't draw power from your surroundings on the other side. If he can't manage to turn himself back quickly, he'll burn out."

I'd rather be certain, but we're in no shape to risk finding out either way. Kevon nodded, and turned to check on Bertus.

"Broken leg," the Novice announced, sitting on the piled stones, face three shades paler than normal.

"We'll get some healing potions in you," Kevon reassured his friend, "You'll be good as new in a few days."

"Those don't always work the way you intend," Pholos cautioned. He coughed raggedly. "Sometimes, things heal *wrong.*"

Unable to think about the implications of the Mage's warning, Kevon turned to check on Alanna. *Who is gone, already, of course.* He shook his head, sweeping his gaze around and past everyone else in the increasingly congested street. *Leave it to her to run off without dealing with-*

Horses shied and reared as a body *crunched* to the cobbles from the rooftops above. Kevon rolled the corpse over with his foot. It was the younger of the two assassins he'd suspected had been one of Alanna's- *of Marelle's-* assailants, throat slit from ear to ear. He glanced upward, but was not surprised when nothing appeared out of place besides the still-smoldering scorch marks on all of the surrounding structures.

Maybe she'll come back to me, after all, the Warsmith thought, unable to stanch the hopeful thoughts that flowed through him in the wake of all the destruction that had just transpired.

"Mirsa!" Kevon nearly shouted at the nearly fainting Seeker. "Is she here? Is she safe?"

"With the Dwarves." Bertus whispered. "You can go fetch them in the morning."

"So touching…" Pholos groaned. "I'll come back when it's over." He swung his staff in a circle, slicing the tip upward, opening another flaming rift that was met with shouts and drawn weapons. "It's a different place!" he rasped, hacking and coughing and stumbling toward it with the staff once again in use as a cane. He stepped into the portal and they both vanished.

"Get a litter!" one of the Guard captains shouted to a nearby subordinate, dismounting to attend to Bertus. He clamped a hand down on Kevon's shoulder. "I think the two of you have some explaining to do."

EPILOGUE

The sun peeked over the placid ocean horizon, its rays glaring into Mirsa's face and waking her slowly. She reached into her pocket and drew out her last mint leaf, began chewing it to quell the nausea.

"No more smoke," Kylgren-Wode commented as he spotted her stirring.

Stretching out and yawning, the Master Mage felt the leather strap of her concealment charm rub on her neck, the wooden pendant dangling against her skin. Out of habit, she removed it and pressed outward, searching for Kevon.

For the first time since they had parted ways, she could sense the Warsmith. He was not in Eastport, he was closer. And he was moving. She replaced the talisman, and looked to her companions.

The ambassador was perched atop the wagon, watching the countryside, axe near at hand. Rhysabeth-Dane was huddled in blankets near the remains of the fire, reading from the book and her notes, whispering softly.

"I thought that book was in Dwarven, not Elven," Mirsa remarked as she moved within earshot.

"It is in..." the librarian began. "Wait..." she scanned down the line on the page of her notes she had been reading. "That is the pattern!" she exclaimed, circling the column of figures, and making a few quick notations. "Ancient Elven is closer to ancient Dwarven, these runes sound much like completely different words, in another language!"

"It's likely the same with the other three, then," Mirsa's

speculated. "We just need to find the right languages for the translation. Brilliant!"

Rhysabeth-Dane beamed with pride for just a moment before turning back to her notes.

I've always wanted to visit the Glimmering Isle, Mirsa thought as she drew her cloak tighter around her shoulders against the morning chill, and sat next to the diligent librarian to wait for Kevon's arrival.

ABOUT THE AUTHOR

Chris lives in a small town in Western Idaho. His interests include hunting, fishing, and camping when time permits, and MTG, Pathfinder, and reading when it does not. He collects various kinds of reproduction weaponry, and enjoys cooking with smoker grills and cast iron. He and his family volunteer in their community, and are strong supporters of libraries and literacy.

Chris is currently working on Volume V of *The Blademage Saga, Archmage Crusader.* He is also working on, among other things, a Sci-Fi/Fantasy hybrid novel, and his first cookbook: *Cooking the Hollaway – Recipes and Philosophies for a Shorter but Happier Life.*

Follow the progress of *The Blademage Saga*, among other things, on Chris's writing blog at sleepingdrake.com.